THE AGENCY

SHAWN OETZEL

THE AGENCY

by

Shawn Oetzel

2nd Edition 2018

1st Edition Trade Paperback 2012

All Rights Reserved

Dark Recesses Press
657 Craigen Road
Newburgh, Ontario
Canada K0K 2S0

Edited by Christine Morgan
Cover design by Bob Freeman

Library & Archives Canada ISBN
978-1-988837-09-3

DEDICATION

For my parents
My mother, Betty Maynor, who always believed in the magic,
and my father, John Oetzel, who has never ceased to be amazed
by the magic.
I love you guys…

ACKNOWLEDGMENTS

A special thanks goes out to friend and fellow writer, Donnie Light, who is always available for some advice or a quick word of encouragement. I look forward to working with you more in the future. Lunch is on me next time.

I would also like to thank David Lee Summers, friend and colleague, for reading several chapters and offering invaluable advice as well as editing tips.

A general word of thanks goes out to Local Authors and the writing community we inhabit. I am proud to find myself among such talented individuals and even prouder to call several of you friends.

Finally and as always, my family of which none of this means anything without your love and support.

TABLE OF CONTENTS

—PROLOGUE

Agent Reggie Blackburn watched through the passenger side window as large flakes of snow fell to the ground. The vehicle he was riding in slowed to a jerking halt in front of a dilapidated brick apartment building. The snow barely covered the ground, but the crisp whiteness gave the surrounding area the false impression of being fresh and new. He knew, however, the blanket of snow was really a lie as this neighborhood had long since sold its soul to decay and corruption.

"You ready to serve and protect?" the driver asked jokingly; the sound of his voice breaking the cone of silence.

Reggie looked over at the young kid. He had to have been fresh out of the academy. The question was meant to be a sign of confidence, but he detected the underlying quiver of fear in the kid's voice. This was probably the rookie's first action since becoming a Secret Service agent.

He did not bother replying to the question, but instead looked in the rearview mirror. He watched with minor annoyance as two other cars pulled in behind where he and the kid had parked.

He knew each one of those vehicles carried another three Secret Service agents, which seemed like overkill, but when suspected terrorists were concerned, you could not be too cautious. With the way things were in the world right now, and paranoia running somewhat rampant, he was surprised the National Guard hadn't been called in to assist as well.

He continued to watch as the Secret Service agents exited their respective vehicles, laughing when he saw all of them were

1

dressed in the requisite dark suits and mirrored sunglasses. They looked like members of some sort of yuppie cult. When he turned to look at the driver of his own car, he realized the kid was dressed in a similar fashion.

"What do they do, hand out those outfits at graduation?" he asked sarcastically. "Might as well hang a sign around your necks with big block letters that say Secret Service."

The young agent, knowing he had been made fun of, took offense. Peeking over the top of his own pair of mirrored sunglasses with disdain, he replied, "Well, we can't all be as sophisticated as you feebies now can we."

Reggie laughed out loud at the scorn the rookie agent had thrown his way. He had almost forgotten he was here under the guise of being an FBI agent when in fact he was here because of a tip the Agency had received from their sister department in Great Britain. He was not all that interested in the possible terrorists hiding in the old apartment building, but what they might have in their possession.

"I like your fire kid," he said as he grabbed the door handle and let himself out. "Now let's go make you a hero."

They left the car, and he and his driver walked over to the other agents huddled around the hood of one of the other vehicles, looking over what he thought were the building schematics. They were all so engrossed in their planning, they did not notice as he approached.

"Well isn't this just a regular meeting of the minds," he said. The looks of utter contempt that were shot his way made having to stand out in the cold air and wet snow almost worth it.

The oldest member of the group of the Secret Service brain trust looked up from the papers and stared directly at Reggie. The smug confidence, the look of self-righteous arrogance, and the almost palpable aura of self-importance which radiated from the elder officer definitely marked him as the agent in charge. This would only complicate matters as Reggie knew the old guy would not take to having his authority questioned, especially in front of his underlings.

"Look, Special Agent Blackburn, this is our show," he began, emphasizing his point by swinging his arm around to encompass the other men standing to his sides. "How you were able to weasel your way into this investigation is beyond me, and I don't really know or care. So why don't you do what you FBI guys do best, and keep your mouth shut and stay out of the way. You might just learn something."

"Yes sir," Reggie said as he snapped off a mock salute.

His ego now satisfied, the team leader turned his attention back to his men. They were all packed around so closely you would have thought the old guy was about to divulge some great secret of the universe. Reggie could only shake his head at the ridiculousness of it.

He knew the Secret Service did not hold the FBI in high regard which was why this it the perfect cover for his own investigation. He worried he would not be able to hold his tongue long enough to see this mission through, however. It was getting harder by the minute to keep his witty sarcasm in check. If these poor fools only knew who he really worked for, and the investigations he had run, they would show a tad bit more respect. He was used to it though. Anonymity was simply a part of the job.

The gruff sound of the veteran leader's voice handing out orders brought Reggie out of his momentary reverie, back to the tense scene. The snow had started coming down even harder, making all of the dark suited Secret Service agents look as if they had the worst case of dandruff on record.

"According to our surveillance and intel, our two targets are holed up in the last apartment on the first floor. As you can see, this is an old tenement housing and there is only the one entrance. I still want two of you to go around back in case these birds decide to fly the coop through a window." He finished this by pointing out the two agents that were to carry out that particular objective. They in turn acknowledged their orders with quick nods of their heads. "The rest of us are going to follow standard operating procedure and apprehend our targets as quickly and quietly as possible."

Reggie listened intently as the elder agent continued to bark out the mission parameters. He could tell the old guy was seriously enjoying himself, and he probably lived for moments such as this when he could feel General Patten-esque while he addressed his troops before a big battle.

"Homeland Security has identified these two pieces of trash as potential threats to national security. They have ties to the IRA, and according to our source, their cell has been activated to carry out terrorist activities against our government. They are to be considered armed and dangerous. Let's try and take them alive, but if they show any signs of resistance we *will* use deadly force," the senior agent said, finishing up his pep talk. By the glint in his eye, Reggie could tell the use of deadly force was exactly what the old guy and his team preferred.

After the agent finished his motivational speech, Reggie watched as the two agents who had been selected earlier trotted off to cover the windows at the rear of the building. Once they were out of sight, the old guy gave a hand signal for everyone else to move out.

Reggie had to hide a chuckle with his hand, pretending he was stifling a cough, as the remaining agents signaled acknowledgement and began heading for the entrance. You would have thought Bin Laden himself was holed up in the rat hole of an apartment the way they were acting. He chuckled again at the thought, bringing a fresh round of contempt from his colleagues.

"Sorry. I think I'm coming down with something," he said as a way of offering up an excuse.

A couple of the agents shook their heads in disgust, while the others chose to ignore him completely, staying focused on their mission at hand. Reggie hung back a bit to regain his own composure before following.

The entrance to the apartment complex was marked by a single metal door which had long ago lost its luster, and was now nothing more than a large piece of rust with a handle. Reggie had a thought that it could be the entrance to hell, and knew for some of the tenants it was indeed just that.

The eerie image caused a shiver to slip down his spine, and he hoped it was not a premonition of things to come. *This should be a relatively easy collar, especially with all the suits around, but you never know what you get when dealing with a criminal element.* Everything could turn against them in a matter of seconds if they weren't careful.

The lock on the door had become a victim of someone with a screw driver. Two agents knelt down to cover the entrance while a third grabbed the door handle and quickly swung the door open, which let out a loud groan of protest. Yet another agent entered the building to clear the hallway of any civilians before waving the others in. The two kneeling agents waited until the others were inside before they entered, Reggie following close behind. He shut the door behind him, and it again let out a low, grinding moan.

Reggie could see four doorways down the hall, with a stairwell at the end. The apartment they were interested in was right across from the stairs. One agent broke away from the others, and stationed himself in front of the stairs in case someone came down. The agents did not want to have any surprises while attempting to apprehend the terrorists.

The inside of the apartment building was no better than the outside. The walls were dingy and the place smelled of trash, old urine, and rat excrement. Reggie wrinkled his nose in disgust; he never ceased to be surprised by the conditions some people would accept to live under. He could only shake his head in frustration as he made his way to the end of the hall.

The hall itself was not overly large so he had to hang back and off to the side as the Secret Service agents positioned themselves. Every one of them had their guns drawn and were ready to shoot to kill if necessary, giving the whole scene a Gunfight at the OK Corral feel to it. He half expected a tumbleweed to come blowing through the hall. He was really starting to worry things were not going to go smoothly.

The lead agent walked over and pounded on the apartment door. The sound of his fist hitting the old wood was louder than expected and caught Reggie off guard, causing him to jump. He looked around quickly to see if anyone had noticed, but the others were too focused on the door. He let out a quiet sigh of relief as it definitely would have been a long ride home if the cocky agents had witnessed his slip.

There was a slight rustling sound from the other side of the door as if people were scurrying around, perhaps trying to tidy up or even more disturbing, trying to hide something. What was even more unnerving was the deathly silence that followed.

Reggie could definitely feel the tension in the air start to thicken. *This is not going to have a happy ending.* He had been in enough situations like this to know when things were going to go sour. He reached under his coat and freed his own firearm. If things started getting hairy, he did not want to be caught with his pants down. All he could do was take a deep breath to help steady his nerves, and watch as the lead agent waited a few more seconds before pounding on the door again.

"Who's there?" a muffled voice with an unmistakable Irish brogue asked from inside the apartment.

"This is the United States Secret Service," the elder agent answered with authority. "We have a warrant to search the premises. Either open this door, or we will knock it down."

There was another wave of silence before Reggie heard the sound of a chain lock being removed. The door opened a crack, and he caught a glimpse of red hair before the agents burst through the door like storm troopers.

He could not quite see what was going on, but could definitely hear the sounds of a struggle. Then, without warning, the thunder crack of a large caliber weapon cut through the immediate area like a hot knife through butter. He heard a grunt of pain, and the sound of someone falling to the floor.

By this time he had made his way to the entrance of the apartment, and had a front row seat to the chaos that followed. He saw one agent down on the floor bleeding from a wound to his right shoulder. The other agents were momentarily stunned, but quickly regained their composure and opened fire. The cacophony of discharging weapons was so loud it caused Reggie's ears to ring. The smell of cordite filled his nostrils, so pungent it made him sick to his stomach.

The terrorist who had shot the agent was hit multiple times by the returning fire. The bullets spun him around several times making him look like some macabre marionette from a kid's puppet show. He was dead before he hit the floor.

"Quinn... *No!*" the red-headed terrorist shouted as he got to his feet.

The sound of the Irish-accented yell caught the agents' attention, and they spun around, weapons ready to fire. The terrorist just stood there, in shock from the horror at having witnessed his compatriot being shredded by gunfire.

"You bastards, you'll pay for this," he stammered as he reached a hand into his pants pocket and removed a cylindrical object.

The agents never gave him a chance. The old agent himself fired two shots in quick succession. They were perfectly aimed as one slammed into the terrorist's chest and the killing shot followed as it hit right between the eyes. The Irishman hit the wall, sliding down to the floor, head resting on his now still chest. Reggie could see what appeared to be a homemade explosive device, still clutched tightly in the terrorist's hand.

"Nice shooting, Tex," Reggie said trying to break the tension.

"That's how we do it in the Secret Service Agent Blackburn," the old guy said with pride.

"Well, while you're busy patting yourself on the back, you might want to get your guy some medical attention," Reggie said pointing to the wounded Agent who was still lying on the floor.

The senior agent scowled back, but accepted the rebuff. He pulled out a cell phone, punched in some numbers, and reported the need for medical assistance along with the address. It wasn't long before sirens could be heard in the distance.

Reggie ignored the agents, and began looking around the small living room; the place was dirty and trash was littered all over the floor. He made one complete pass of the room when something caught his eye. A wrinkled piece of brown paper sticking out from under the bottom of the only piece of furniture, an old green couch.

He casually tried to walk over to get a better view, taking a quick glance at the other agents, but they were preoccupied with their wounded comrade and recounting their own personal heroics. He squatted down and pulled the paper out.

From a distance it had looked like an old paper grocery sack, but in reality it was a centuries old parchment.

Realizing what he had, Reggie quickly rolled the parchment up and slipped it under his coat, into his inside coat pocket. The Secret Service agents stared as he walked by, starting to make his way outside.

"I need to get some air," he offered as he passed through the doorway and into the hall.

"What's the matter, feebie, can't stand the sight of blood?" an agent asked.

He didn't know which one it was, and he didn't really care. There were far more important things going on than these arrogant fools realized. He ignored the jibe as he brushed passed another agent to step back through the groaning outer door, and into the cool air once again. The cold caused a sharp intake of breath that hurt his lungs.

The ambulance arrived along with some of New York City's finest. He flashed his badge as he walked by, and as usual it gave him a free pass. The paramedics from the ambulance ran past with a stretcher in hand, but he barely noticed. Instead he pulled out his cell phone from the clip on his belt, and made his way to the car before entering a telephone number. There was only one ring before it was answered.

"Well?" an anxious voice on the other end asked.

"It's the real deal," Reggie answered. "It's exactly what we feared."

There was a long pause on the other end before the anxious voice replied, "This takes top priority. We are going to have to put an agent on this right away."

Reggie smiled a huge knowing grin. "Don't worry, I think I know the perfect person."

CHAPTER 1

Amy Sommers stood on the front stoop of her apartment building waiting for the car to pick her up. A light snow fell, and she shivered from the cold. That was the only thing she missed from her time with the LAPD; the consistent temperatures. Washington D.C. was nice, and she truly did enjoy the variety of weather conditions, but there was nothing like a warm Los Angeles day. Except for the fact the heat usually brought the crazies out to play, making her job as a homicide detective more difficult and interesting than it already was.

She chuckled to herself as the shiny black sedan pulled up and halted in front of her stoop. She watched as the driver exited, walked to the rear, and opened the back door, signaling her to get in. This was the same scene which had played itself out every weekday for the last three months. Even the driver, a young Latino named Garcia, was the same. It was the one thing she could say about the Agency from her short time here; they had a thing for consistency.

With a last deep breath of the crisp morning air, she went down the steps and entered the sedan, prepared for yet another day of training at the secret government entity known only as the Agency.

She flashed Garcia a smile as she got in the car, and he tipped his black cap in response. Only when he had secured himself with his safety belt, put the car in gear, and pulled out into the morning traffic did he speak to her.

"Good morning, Agent Sommers. I trust you had a good weekend." An unmistakable accent gave evidence of his Central American heritage.

"Oh yeah, it was great," she replied, her voice filled with sarcasm. "Another weekend filled with take-out food and rented movies. I'm really living the good life."

"Don't worry, Agent Sommers; I'm sure things will pick up for you soon." Garcia sounded almost apologetic.

She did not bother replying. Garcia's job was to drive, not offer up pleasantries to make her feel better. Instead, she sank back in her seat and closed her eyes, unable to help reflecting on the last three months, remembering how she found herself here in Washington D.C.

She'd always wanted to be a cop, much to the chagrin of the rest of her family, especially her mother. "Women should get married and make raising their children their career," was Mrs. Sommers's old-school way of thinking. Being fired from the LAPD even after helping stop a serial killer, albeit under rather unusual circumstances, left Amy with a huge gap in her life. Suddenly stripped of the one thing she knew she was good at, solving crimes, she thought she would drown in despair. She'd had no direction to go, nor anyone to turn to for help. Then Reggie Blackburn threw her a life preserver when he offered her a job with the Agency.

She had of course jumped at the unexpected offer. It meant uprooting her life on the West Coast, and starting over new in Washington D.C., but there was nothing left for her in Los Angeles anymore. Without a second thought, she packed her belongings and caught the first flight to her new life.

Between her background and her recent success working with Agent Blackburn, she figured she would hit the ground running with the Agency. She hoped for a juicy case to sink her investigative teeth into and be right back in the thick of things. She had been completely wrong.

That had been three months ago. Instead of working on any cases, her days were spent in classrooms, learning about the mysterious Agency and receiving what they told her was "training". It was almost like being in college again, except with more rules and fewer students. If she could find any other female recruits, she might try and start a sorority. At least that way she might actually have some fun.

The monotonous sound of the wiper blades brushing away the snow was starting to lull her to sleep. She cursed under her breath as she realized she had forgotten to grab her mug of coffee. It was no doubt sitting on her kitchen table, where she'd left it when she grabbed her coat. Definitely an inauspicious beginning to the day.

She looked out the window, watching the snow. It was coming down harder, the visibility next to nothing. All she could make out were the shapes and shadows of pedestrians. The grainy images reminded her of the Agency and the mysterious world in which it dwelled. When all was said and done, she too would be nothing more than a grainy image. To join the Agency, one had to give up most of their personal existence, and take on the role of anonymity.

Early on in her training, she learned the Agency was unofficially founded by Thomas Jefferson in his first term as President. She'd been surprised to learn Lewis and Clark were among the first agents. Though history claimed their expedition was to discover a water route across North America, they'd been in fact investigating rumors of a beast supposedly summoned by Native Americans to stop the white man's further trespass into their sacred lands. Whether Lewis and Clark found the beast, she did not know. The case files were sealed. But, the fate of the Native Americans and their lands seemed like a large piece of highly circumstantial evidence.

The Agency had grown in power and resources into the entity it was today. Even the sitting President of the United States, the only government official who knew of its existence, was not kept completely in the loop of the Agency's activities, in the interest of plausible deniability.

With a limitless budget and the autonomy to act as it deemed necessary, the Agency took on only those cases which involved the side of the world no one else knew about. It was a closely guarded secret that, if ever got out, would change the very fabric of lives. The mysteries and myths the everyday person took for granted were the nightmares of the Agency.

Amy Sommers herself could attest to that notion. A few months ago, she had been on the trail of what she thought was a twisted serial killer who liked to cut out his victim's hearts as keepsakes. It wasn't until Reggie Blackburn and his partner, under the guise of FBI, came along that she'd learned the real truth. Oh, she'd been tracking a serial killer all right, but no mere crazy looking for a way to get his rocks off. The killer was an Elf from another realm, trying to complete an evil ritual that would result in the genocide of his race.

Her whole life changed that day, the day of Detective Hanson's brutal murder. That was when she'd witnessed Reggie's enigmatic companion battle the killer. He, too, turned out to be an Elf, sent by his people's government to stop the ritual. The whole thing was so surreal, she'd been sure she was having some sort of nervous breakdown.

A twinge of hollow pain rippled across the pit of her stomach and settled in her chest, causing a sharp intake of breath. She blew it out in the form of a long sigh. The sound was loud enough to catch Garcia's attention in the front seat. The driver took a quick glance in the rearview mirror, a questioning yet concerned look reflected in his brown eyes. Having no desire to explain her mood, she leaned back and closed her eyes. *This really is turning into a crappy day.*

Her caffeine deprived mind realized she'd been unconsciously fingering the medallion she wore around her neck. *He* had given it to her, Kalen Or'Wain, Reggie's mysterious partner, before returning to his own world. Though their time together had been brief, it was the most loving and passionate relationship she had ever had, a personal connection on a level she had never thought possible,

She had hoped her new career with the Agency would occupy her time, keep her busy, and help her get over the feeling of loss she experienced after Kalen's departure. Instead, she'd been stuck into the Agency's version of mental boot camp, all by herself. She guessed this was in part due to the Agency trying to get her used to the idea of working alone.

It was the Agency's policy. Due to the secretive nature of the cases they handled, the less people involved the better. There were no partnerships except under extraordinary circumstances, and no backup. This meant when agents were out in the field, they were completely alone. A hard pill to swallow for someone like her, used as she was to having a whole department to fall back on. Though she had never really felt a true member of the male-dominated LAPD, she still knew they were there if needed.

She hoped the Agency would be her opportunity to shine. Heck, after helping track down an Elven serial killer, what could they throw at her that would be any worse? She was as ready as she would ever be. The Agency had battered her with psychological tests, history lessons, and investigative procedures. She desperately needed some good old fashioned action, the exhilaration of being in the field, tracking down a lead. She was a law enforcement officer at heart, and it had been far too long since she was able to stretch her investigator's legs.

Reggie kept reassuring her things would change for the better soon, and she needed to keep her patience in check. *Easier said than done.*

He had canceled their dinner plans on Friday and she hadn't heard from him since. That could only mean he was on a case. She probably wouldn't see him again until it was solved, which increased her feelings of loneliness. Reggie was the only real friend she had in Washington. She had come to rely on his presence, and their infrequent dinner outings were major social events for her. This cancellation made for a long boring weekend. She hoped that, wherever Reggie was, and whatever trouble he was undoubtedly mixed up in, he was safe.

The slowing of the sedan for a red traffic light brought her out of her reverie. The snow was still falling, and a couple of inches had accumulated on the ground. The gray sky matched her somber mood. She'd always been the type of person who was sure of what she was doing, confident her decisions were correct; a good detective had to think that way. But doubts had been creeping in the back of her mind. Had she made a mistake coming here? It bothered her more than a little that she was beginning to have second thoughts.

She glanced at her watch. *Almost 9:00am, be there any minute.* Sure enough, Garcia took a right onto Waverly Street, drove to the middle of the block, and turned into an average, nondescript parking garage. Little did the populace know this rather ordinary structure was home to perhaps the most secretive organization known, or more accurately, unknown, to mankind.

Even in Washington D.C., where people were used to secrets and government agencies, she wondered how the Agency and its location went unnoticed. She supposed it simply went with the territory. Amazingly, most people would rather look the other way instead of staring at the unknown right in the eye in hopes of being able to unravel the secrets. Organizations like the Agency counted on just that kind of attitude to help maintain their own secrecy.

Garcia stopped in front of the garage's electric gate. A guard in a blue security uniform, complete with the customary silver badge and flashlight, stepped out of a closet-sized booth. He held a small device which looked similar to a miniature camcorder. He pointed it at the front of the vehicle like he was video taping it, then ran the lens down the length of the entire sedan. Amy had no idea what this device actually did, but she assumed it checked for listening devices or surveillance equipment which might have been hidden somewhere on or within the vehicle.

Once the apparent scan was complete, the guard placed the device back on his Batman-like utility belt. From his booth, he took out what to the layman would appear to be a laptop computer and handed it through the driver's side window to Garcia. All of this was done without anyone uttering a word.

The laptop sprang to life as soon as Garcia opened it and lifted the monitor into position. He stared at the screen without blinking for approximately fifteen seconds before a beep issued from the machine. Once this was done, he gave the laptop to Amy in the backseat.

The first time she had used it, she was worried the thing would fry her brain. Now, however, retina scanners were second nature. She stared at the target in the middle of the screen. Diagnostic information scrolled down the right hand side until she was given clearance by the device with a beep of acceptance.

She handed the laptop back to Garcia who in turn passed it through his window back to the guard. The security officer took the retina scanner and returned to his booth, again without a word.

This was another interesting little tidbit she managed to pick up about the Agency: the employees, at least the ones she had contact with, were not much for small talk. Which was fine with her; most mornings, especially those when she did not get her recommended daily dose of caffeine, like today, she was not in the mood to carry on a conversation either.

Once back in the booth, the guard pushed some unseen button or flipped some lever and the gate blocking their entrance slowly lifted. In this post-911 world, even something like what appeared to be a mundane parking garage and an ordinary, run-of-the-mill-security guard using gadgets like Q from the James Bond movies didn't stir much curiosity.

Garcia drove her to the elevator. "Have a good day Agent Sommers," he said as she got out, the sound of his voice amplified by the emptiness. She replied with a smile and a wave, watching as he pulled away and headed back out to the streets of Washington D.C.

Where Garcia went after he dropped her off every morning, she had no idea. What she did know was that at 5pm when she walked back out of the elevator, he would be right there waiting with the car running, ready to take her home. Though there was a small measure of comfort to be found in this routine, it was starting to grate on her nerves. If she did not get to arrest someone soon, she was going to lose it all together.

When the sound of the departing sedan faded away into nothingness, she dug through her pants pocket and pulled out her ID card. It looked enough like an ordinary credit card of some type that she'd been tempted on more than one occasion to test her theory when shopping. Discretion always got the better of her, however.

On the wall next to the elevator was a keypad with a slot. After running her card, a little green light blinked on, and she punched in her five-digit code to open the doors.

Unlike other elevators, there were no floor buttons to push. Instead, she stared into the lens of an otherwise unseen video camera.

"Agent Sommers reporting for training," she stated, careful to pronounce each word correctly.

Once her voice patterns were recognized by whoever or whatever was on the other end of the camera, the doors slid shut. She held onto the waist-high safety railing as the elevator began to move, knowing from experience it would pick up speed as it descended. When it hit its maximum, she could hear an audible whooshing sound.

Due to the speed, and the lack of lights marking floors, she did not know how far down she actually went. She thought about timing it, but dismissed the notion, deciding it really didn't matter anyway.

The elevator slowed to a gentle rest, and the doors opened for her. She had the usual moment of disorientation as it took her body a few seconds to get its equilibrium back in check. With a deep breath to settle her stomach, she stepped into the Agency.

The room looked like the lobby of any big corporation. The walls were a light, comforting brown; not really a tan, but more like a creamy suede color. The floors were covered in an earth-tones carpet which seemed to absorb any and all footstep-related noises, and which Amy found unnerving.

The secretary stationed behind the large desk was a pleasant woman, young enough to have just stepped off a college campus in anywhere USA, friendly, and pretty in a girl-next-door kind of way. Her light brown hair, which oddly enough matched the lobby color scheme, was cut in a fashion similar to Amy's own. This always made her feel better about her own appearance, as if the trendy young secretary somehow validated her own sense of style.

"Good morning, Agent Sommers," the secretary said politely. "Dr. Waterston is waiting for you in the large conference room."

Great, Amy thought. *More psychological tests.*

"Thanks," she replied, heading down the hall.

Honestly, how many times could she answer those ridiculous questions? What valuable information about her psyche did the Agency expect to glean from them? Yes, she loved her father, and no, not in that way. Yes, the sight of dead puppies bothered her, but wouldn't that bother anybody? And no, she did not think she looked in the toilet before flushing it.

The good doctor was a decent enough man, but how this would help determine if she was mentally fit and competent enough to catch bad guys, even out of the ordinary bad guys like Elven serial killers, was way beyond her.

This day had not started off particularly well, what with her forgetting her coffee. Now, armed with the knowledge she was going to be spending the day with Dr. Waterston and his seemingly never ending list of asinine questions, her mood darkened even further.

"If I don't get to work a case soon, I swear, I might have to shoot somebody on principle alone," she said to the conference room's oak door. It had the common decency to not reply.

She chuckled to herself as she wondered what Dr. Waterston would have to say about that little private conversation. The thought offered her some comfort as she opened the door, and prepared herself for another long day of training at the Agency.

CHAPTER 2

The lush carpet swallowed his footsteps as Reggie Blackburn determinedly marched on to his destination.

What he lacked in height, he more than made up for in girth, which made the carpet's accomplishment of masking his footsteps all the more impressive. He was not an obese man, but neither was he the bodybuilder type. From behind he looked like a square brick wall with a head. His physical strength matched his blocky appearance.

He'd headed straight here from the airport after returning from his excursion to New York. The all-important map from the terrorists' apartment was now safely locked in the metal Halliburton case he clutched in a death grip. This same map had him headed to a meeting with the Agency's higher ups, not a prospect he was looking forward to.

The map itself was a single sheet of centuries-old parchment. It was roughly the size of a legal document, with markings written in a language he did not recognize. Though it looked unremarkable, the secret it potentially held could prove incredibly important to their friends across the pond. Their sister Agency in Great Britain had initially given them the tip in the first place. If the map proved to be the real deal, as Reggie was pretty sure it was, Great Britain's version of the Agency would also send a representative of their own to help in the investigation.

First things first, however, and that meant delivering his report to his supervisors. He really hoped they hadn't made up their minds yet about who would be assigned this case. It had been his job to retrieve the map; now he wanted to make sure Amy

Sommers was the one chosen to follow up on it. She was ready. He just had to persuade the Powers That Be.

It would be a hard sell, especially for something of this potential magnitude. If the map did indeed reveal the location of what they suspected it did, his supervisors might prefer a more seasoned agent to handle the case. Reggie thought this was the perfect opportunity for Agent Sommers to cut her teeth, especially if the Brits sent someone over. She wouldn't have to go it completely alone on her first time out. And, of course, as her sponsor, he'd play a small part as her advisor as well.

Though the Agency was a huge organization with a fairly large employee base, the headquarters was rarely the hub of activity. Most of its employees were field agents, out on assignments all over the world. This place was definitely the nucleus or more appropriately the brain of the Agency's body, but, today, like always, it was quiet as a library.

The meeting room he was headed to was located on the equivalent of the penthouse level, which, in the Agency's case, meant it was the deepest floor underground. Even Reggie, who had been with the Agency for close to eighteen years, did not know exactly how many floors or offices the Agency contained. He did know however, this one was home to the Director's and Deputy Director's offices. As a Senior Agent, this was always where he met his bosses to give his final reports.

He smirked when he realized Sommers was more than likely somewhere above him at this exact moment, being subjected to more of the Agency's special brand of training and no doubt dealing with the frustration of prolonged inactivity in her usual pain in the butt manner. He almost felt sorry for whoever was assigned as her instructor for the day. Hopefully, after this meeting, he would have some good news for her.

Amy Sommers was the first person he had actively recruited. They'd been through a lot together in a short period of time. With the craziness they had dealt with in Los Angeles, Sommers had proven she had the mettle and openness of mind to be a good agent.

Now it was up to him to see she got a shot, and this particular case could quite possibly be the perfect opportunity.

The briefcase brushed against his leg as his long strides carried him down the hall. This brief intrusion into his trip down memory lane served as a reminder to stay focused and remember where he was. Not that he could ever really forget he was several stories underground holding a case that quite possibly contained a secret which could bring one of the world's most prominent countries to its proverbial knees.

In his early years, he would have stood outside and knocked politely on the door while waiting for an invitation to enter. Now, being the grizzled veteran he was, he no longer stood on ceremony. He did not hesitate, but grabbed the polished silver door handle and let himself in. He had done this so many times over the years it had become an automatic response. It was not that he disrespected his superiors, but, after the battles he had been through while on the job, he figured he had earned a measure of respect himself, which left him with an attitude of relaxed indifference.

The meeting room was twelve feet by twelve feet and perfectly square, not overly large nor claustrophobically small. Beautifully realistic landscape portraits on each wall gave the illusion of a room with a view, which helped put people at ease when they had to spend blocks of time in here with the Director.

A large circular table, of glossy and heavily polished English oak, dominated the room. Reggie had to admit this was an appropriate setting for what they would be discussing, the presence of a round table rather ironic. He loved how odd coincidences seemed to follow these types of cases, as if fate felt the need to send reminders of the importance of the work the Agency did. This job was nothing if not unpredictable.

Two men sat comfortably in blue office chairs. Both were in their late forties, with military style crew cuts which were peppered with gray, adding to their looks of quiet authority. Both men looked like they commanded respect by their mere presence, but the one on the right with the most piercing and clear blue eyes imaginable radiated such an aura of command that a lesser agent would be intimidated to the point of shaking at the knees. This man was Director Smith.

Reggie knew Smith was not the Director's real name, but when you are in charge of the most covert organization in the world, what was one more secret? He was obviously a military man, but what branch the man had served with was long since forgotten. It really did not matter anyway, because whoever Director Smith had been out in the world was immaterial. He was the Director of the Agency now.

The other man was Deputy Director James. He was relatively new in his position, having been promoted three years ago. Reggie had known James for close to ten years, and considered him to be an honorable and trustworthy man if a somewhat unimaginative one. James' promotion was a good one and well deserved, and Reggie had no argument with it. The Deputy Director was a better bureaucrat than field agent anyway.

At the moment, Reggie found himself in the line of fire from Director Smith's intense stare. The man definitely knew how to control a room.

"Good morning, Agent Blackburn," the Director said. "I trust your return trip was uneventful."

The Director's voice had a gravelly quality to it, speaking of one who was a lifelong smoker without sounding harsh or demanding. Reggie thought it had a grandfatherly tone. The Director could intimidate if needed, but with Reggie, he was simply the man in charge,

"Yeah, everything went fine," he replied, lifting the Halliburton case and laying it on the table.

"Is that the map?"

This question came from the Deputy Director. Reggie could hear a level of concern in the man's voice.

"It is not so much a map as it is some kind of list, though some locations are clearly marked. The whole thing is written in a language I don't recognize. It looks like a bunch of gibberish, but I think it is the genuine article."

He emphasized his point by popping the clasps on the airplane aluminum case, and removing the ancient parchment. It was sealed in an airtight clear plastic bag which he placed on the table, and gently slid across to the seated Director.

Director Smith put his hand out, and stopped the sliding bag without taking his eyes off Reggie.

"Well, map or not, the Brits have their knickers in a twist over this," the Director said. He pulled the old parchment from its plastic safe haven.

Reggie watched as his boss reached into the breast pocket of his neatly pressed ivory dress shirt, and remove a pair of reading glasses. After settling the designer spectacles on his hawkish nose, the Director briefly scanned the document.

"I don't recognize the writing either, though it could be some sort of old Gaelic hybrid," he commented before handing the document over to the Deputy Director, who looked at the map with silent interest.

"I take it they will probably be sending one of their own to handle the investigation?" Reggie asked.

"Their agent will be on a plane sometime tonight and will be here tomorrow. I am not sure when. This is to be a joint effort between our two Agencies." The Director looked at Reggie before adding, "What do you say, Agent Blackburn; you up for this one?"

"Actually, sir, I had someone else in mind."

That got their attention. Director Smith was already watching him intently, but now Deputy Director James, who had been preoccupied with the intricacies of the map, joined in with his own inquisitive stare.

"Oh?" was the only response the Directors could manage which they offered up in stereo.

"I thought perhaps this might be a good case to break in Agent Sommers."

"Really," Director Smith said questioningly.

"This is potentially a very important and touchy case," Deputy Director James added.

"Begging you pardon sir, and no disrespect intended, but aren't they all?" Reggie said.

"Point taken," Director Smith said, then asked, "What makes you think she is ready?"

"It's been three months. She is as ready as she's going to be. She's passed all the psychologicals with flying colors. We've got to start her in the field some time, and this provides her with the unique opportunity to work with a partner, albeit one from a different Agency. I can stay active on the case too, as a liaison officer. Plus, if I know Sommers, she's chomping at the bit to get started, and if we don't throw her a bone soon, she might stop playing nice with others."

This last part he said halfway jokingly, but knew it held more truth than not.

"Yes, I hear she is giving Dr. Waterston a run for his money this morning," Director Smith said, an amused smile tugging at the corners of his mouth.

"Still, do we really want to hand such a sensitive case off to a rookie?" Deputy Director James asked.

"I think she is ready," Reggie reiterated.

The room grew uncomfortably silent as Director Smith pondered the Agency's options. Reggie knew this was not an easy decision, even though to him it seemed a no-brainer, but he'd meant it when he said Sommers was ready. Heck, with her persistence, she would probably have this whole mess wrapped up by the end of the week.

The silence became oppressive as the Director continued to drag his decision out. Reggie could almost see the wheels turning in the man's head. They had not offered up as much opposition as he had anticipated, and he hoped this was a good omen. He shifted his weight from his right leg to his left, and did the only thing he could: continue to wait.

With a final glance at Deputy Director James, and a quick, oh what the heck, shrug, Director Smith said, "All right, its Sommer's case, but I want you in the background peeking over her shoulder until this is resolved."

Reggie knew a huge grin was spreading across his face, but he did not care. Sommers was going to flip.

"Don't worry Sir. I'll keep an eye on her."

"Well, the first thing she will need to do is get the map over to the translator," Deputy Director James said, sliding the map, resealed in the plastic safety bag, back across the table to Reggie.

"I will take her there myself this afternoon," he said slipping the map back into the Halliburton case and snapping it shut. "It will give me the opportunity to get her up to speed."

"I am sure Dr. Waterston wouldn't mind the interruption," Director Smith said as he got up from the table. He left the room, Deputy Director James close on his heels.

Reggie laughed knowingly.

He figured he better find out which floor she was on so he could give her the good news in person, and save Dr. Waterston from being eaten alive.

CHAPTER 3

A light drizzle caused a mist to rise over Dame Court, and most likely all of Dublin, giving the city the look of what tourists would refer to as old world charm. The sun was setting, and the red light oozed into the rainy mist, causing the Irish capital to be cast in an eerie glow.

Colin O'Connor pulled the collar of his black pea coat up around his neck to protect his exposed skin. His near-platinum blonde hair and fair complexion made him look like a wraith haunting the streets of Dublin. He picked up his pace, wanting to get to The Stag's Head before he was completely drenched. The cold evening air matched his demeanor, and he could not even muster a smile as he saw the yellow lights of the pub just ahead.

The meeting had been originally supposed to be a celebration of sorts, as he'd expected to be bringing confirmation of a successful mission. Instead, it would have to be a strategy session as he and his fellow Patriots reassessed their situation and discussed their options.

He and his fellow *Na Ri` Laoch* members had worked hard to achieve their goal. Unfortunately, when their compatriots in New York missed their last check in, Colin knew something had gone awry. His fears were confirmed a short time ago from his contact within Parliament.

Their friends had not only failed, but been murdered by the American Secret Service. The all-important map had disappeared. It was now his duty to deliver this bad news.

He, Alan Collins and Owen O'Shea had grown up together in the same neighborhood, hearing the stories of Irish Patriots and their constant struggle against the British. When his own father had been unjustly imprisoned after being wrongly accused of participating in an IRA bombing, then died behind bars before getting a fair trial, Colin and his two friends vowed to do anything within their power to bring about the end of Great Britain.

At first, bringing the British to their pompous knees had been simply a childhood fantasy, but as they had grown, their vow took shape. They created the *Na Ri' Laoch*, "The King's Warriors". The group now totaled close to fifty men, all dedicated to the cause.

Years ago, Colin ran across a rumor of a map said to provide the location of a certain artifact that would allow him to bring about the demise of the British government. He had thrown himself into the research. After pooling their resources, the *Na Ri' Laoch* obtained the map. It had come at great expense, but in Colin's mind it was money well spent.

Even with the group's best laid plans temporarily disrupted, he felt a warm sensation settle over his shoulders as he walked through the pillared entrance of The Stag's Head. It was like the feeling of returning home after being away for a long period of time. Warmth washed over him anew as he opened the door, and was welcomed by the comforting sounds of a busy pub.

The place was packed, mostly by college students due to its proximity to Trinity College. It was kind of out of the way, but that was one reason Colin liked it. Most tourists could not find it, and he loathed tourists, especially Americans with their ridiculous preconceived notions about the Irish. With their stupid ideas that all Irishmen were red heads who loved to sing 'Danny Boy' while crying in their beers and gorging themselves on corned beef and cabbage, Americans were second only to the Brits in his hate. Though, with the recent killing of his fellow *Na Ri' Loach* members, the Americans could easily find themselves number one, at least for the time being.

He pushed his way through the crowd of students and off work businessmen, pausing long enough to stop at the marble topped bar. The Stag's Head was famous for its pints of Guinness, but he decided to forego his usual order for the calming effect of good Irish malt whiskey and ordered a snifter of Bushmill's. After his walk through the cold rain, he needed a way to help get warm.

When the bartender, an older gentleman rumored to have once been a captain with the IRA, slid the glass across the bar, Colin took a quick sip, letting the golden liquid fire work its magic through his body. He turned and raised his glass in salute to "Natch", the large stuffed stag's head which kept watch over the place.

The crowd thinned as he made his way to the stairs and climbed to the third floor, which provided a level of privacy they would need. He and his partners would have to come up with a way to get their plans back on track, since the Americans had seen fit to derail them.

Along with the unsavory news of his colleagues' untimely deaths, his contact had also been able to give him some information on a certain person who might be able to help the *Na Ri` Laoch*. This particular individual's help would not come cheaply, but in reality they may not have another choice.

As he cleared the last step, he spotted his friends right off, sitting at their customary table near the back of the room. The Americans considered them to be a terrorist group. They considered themselves to be Patriots, fighting for the betterment of Ireland and her people.

In his own mind, the best way to improve the lives of his Irish brethren was to wipe out Great Britain and rid the world of its tyranny. He knew this was an unrealistic goal, but he and the *Na Ri` Laoch* were attempting the next best thing: complete control of the British government, and the subjugation of its citizens. The map was the compass leading them down the path to the means of achieving their lofty yet righteous goal.

He took another sip of his Bushmill's before sitting down with his co-conspirators. The potent whiskey helped to strengthen his resolve so he could share the fate of their mission.

"So what's the word?" Alan Collins asked as soon as Colin had gotten settled and comfortable.

"Yeah, have you heard from our cell in the States?" Owen O'Shea followed up.

"Not exactly." Colin watched as the looks on his two friends' faces changed from optimistic hope to deep concern.

Alan ran his hand through his jet black hair before taking a long pull off his pint of Guinness. Owen sat statue still, staring at him intently.

They had worked so hard and sacrificed so much to get this far. These two men had stood by his side, and believed unconditionally. It nearly crushed his spirit to now have to tell them of the setback the *Na Ri` Laoch* had suffered.

"Tell us what happened," Owen O'Shea said, a definite edge to his voice speaking as to how deeply the disappointment went. It touched Colin to know his friends were so emotionally invested in the cause born out of his own father's death.

"They're dead." He shot back the rest of his whiskey. It burned all the way down as if to emphasize the gravity of the news he had shared, but it was nothing compared to the inferno blazing deep down in his gut marking his desire for vengeance.

"How...how could this happen?" Alan finally managed to stammer.

"According to our contact, the Americans' Homeland Security was somehow tipped off. They sent in the Secret Service to investigate, and when they found our cell, they gunned them down in cold blood."

A stunned silence followed his explanation. He could see it in their eyes, the disgust and then the hatred. All of their preparations and careful planning had seemingly been for naught. They'd thought every base had been covered.

With the Americans paranoid about terrorism in their own country, the *Na Ri` Laoch* knew it would be a difficult task getting their men into place, but they'd hoped a couple of Irish tourists would go unnoticed. Unfortunately, they had guessed wrong, and their mission was in desperate jeopardy.

"What about the map?"

The question from Alan snapped Colin out of his concentration. He took a minute to gather himself before answering. "Thanks to our contact, I have been able to examine copies of the official reports. There was no mention of a map. However, I was able to discover that a Special Agent for the FBI was also at the scene. I thought it was strange the FBI would only have one agent on hand. When our contact tried to get access to a FBI report of the incident, even stranger, he couldn't find one."

"So?" Owen asked. "What does this have to do with the map?"

"It is our contact's belief as well as my own that this agent was not FBI at all, but possibly a member of a more top secret security force. I believe this man, Reggie Blackburn, has the map."

"Well, if it is some secret security force, that will definitely complicate matters," Alan said in frustration.

Owen nodded his head. "This has the potential to be a disaster for us. It's turning into a nightmare which could blow up in our faces."

"Maybe not," Alan said. "Just because the Americans may have the map, security force or not, it doesn't mean they know the full value of it. You know how overconfident those fools are. I'm sure the map is locked up in some evidence locker. All we need to do is retrieve it."

"Are you suggesting we somehow breach a top security agency?" Owen asked, with a hint of sarcasm mixed in his tone.

"Not the *Na Ri` Laoch*, but there are certain individuals who specialize in these sort of operations. We could try someone of that nature," Alan said.

Colin, who had remained silent during the brief exchange, smiled. This would make broaching the subject of hiring the mercenary a little smoother. He hated having to rely on the Brits for anything, but desperate times called for desperate measures, and as far as he was concerned, the *Na Ri` Laoch* were desperate. Besides, the contact had never steered him wrong. In fact, it was the contact who had led then to the map in the first place.

"The sword is of the utmost importance," Owen said. "Without the map, we have no way of finding it. I think we should do whatever it takes to get it back from the Americans."

"If we don't want to bring an outsider in, we could always train a new cell, but that will take time," Alan said.

"We don't have that kind of time, and frankly I don't think any of our men would even be capable of a mission of such a sensitive nature," Colin said. "I think we need a professional. We need to get the map back before the Americans figure out the real importance of it and piece together what we are doing. The map needs to be recovered and the sword must be found and brought to us at all costs, and I think I might have someone who can do both."

Alan finished off his Guinness, and motioned a nearby waitress for a new pint before asking, "What's your plan?"

"I know of a certain individual who provides services of the nature we require," Colin said. "If, and this is a big if, we are able to find this person, we can not only hire him to get the map, but also locate the sword and bring it home to Ireland. He will not come cheap though."

"Price is not an option," Owen said. "Who is it?"

Colin stared intently into each of the eyes of his friends to measure their resolve. When he was satisfied that both were committed to taking this extremely dangerous and costly next step, he leaned over the table, and motioned for the others to follow his lead. Then, in a hushed whisper, he uttered the last name his fellow Patriots and *Na Ri` Laoch* leaders expected to hear.

"The Ghost."

—CHAPTER 4

The screen flashed a bright, nearly blinding white before being replaced by yet another crime scene style photo. This one was different from the previous few, in that it was not in color.

It showed several men who had obviously been gunned down execution style. The victims were dressed in '20s or '30s style suits, and it did not take Amy Sommers long to realize this was an old gangland murder. The image was vaguely familiar, and after looking for a few seconds at the bodies shown on screen, she recognized it as a police photo from the St. Valentine's Day Massacre in Chicago.

As a former homicide detective, she had seen far worse. From drive-by shootings to decomposing homeless, along with overdosed prostitutes and domestic battery incidents so severe the victims were unrecognizable, it never ceased to amaze her what one person was capable of doing to another. Murders, such as the ones depicted in the photo, had been part of her daily routine for several years. She had grown accustomed to the brutality humankind had to offer. Unfortunately, this was an attitude that simply went with the job.

Why the Agency felt the need to bombard her with these often graphic images was beyond her comprehension. They called it psychological testing, but she was starting to wonder if they were really trying to see if she would crack under the pressure. The crime scene photos did not bother her per se, but the sheer boredom might drive her right over the proverbial edge.

She did her best to sit still and at least pretend she was paying attention, though she felt her already beat up nerves begin to fray.

Whatever the point Dr. Waterston was trying to make with this round of testing had long since slipped her mind.

She chanced a look at the psychiatrist as he sat stoically at the head of the table, his ever present laptop propped open in front of him. He had a yellow legal pad next to the computer, and every now and then would scribble some note onto it. She would have given anything to get a peek at those notes. What sort of fascinating tidbits and pieces of information was he getting about her by watching her reactions?

She caught the subtle hint of movement as Waterston pushed an unseen button on his computer. Knowing what this meant, she shifted her gaze back to the screen. A new image popped up, showing what looked like three uniformed soldiers of Middle Eastern descent laying facedown in pools of their own blood. The blood shone a garish red, and she felt her last nerve finally snap.

"Oh, for crying out loud!" she exclaimed in exasperation, leaning over and smacking her forehead onto the finely polished mahogany conference table.

"Is there a problem, Agent Sommers?" Waterston asked in his monotone voice.

She did not immediately answer. Instead, she kept her head on the table and shook it back and forth. Her usually tight grip on her anger started to lessen. If the good doctor did not watch his step and tread softly, he might get a first hand experience of what it was like to see her explode.

Waterston was obviously not as perceptive as he thought, because instead of picking up on the warning signs of her impending outburst, he pushed forward with another of his asinine comments.

"You know, Agent Sommers, these tests work so much better if you pay attention and actually look at the screen."

"Does it?" she asked letting her pent up ire of the last few months slip free. "Because I am so tired of paying attention to your stupid pictures, I might actually throw up. I have no idea what you're getting out of watching me look at those pictures. I'm a cop, damn it! I should be out there catching weirdos and locking them up, not sitting here watching your version of America's Grossest Videos!"

"The Agency needs to know if you can handle the stresses of the job. These tests will help to show that."

"Well, if you are worried on whether or not I am going to flip out, I can tell you with complete honesty that if you put one more crime scene photo on that wall depicting some poor bastard's untimely demise, you are going to see what a psychotic episode is like up close and personal. So help me God, if you push a button on your computer, I am going to feed it to you."

The stunned and shocked look on the doctor's face was priceless. If this was the end of her budding career with the Agency, so be it. She would take the mental image of the prim and proper Dr. Waterston with his mouth hanging wide open with her for the rest of her days. Rendering him speechless was almost worth what would surely result in her immediate termination.

At that moment, the door of the conference opened, and Reggie Blackburn came in, out of breath and with tears in his eyes from laughing so hard. "Oh, Sommers, man have I missed you," Agent Blackburn said, in between chuckles.

"Reggie?" Amy asked, caught completely off guard.

"I love it when that temper of yours gets the best of you. I wish the doctor would push the button, because I would pay top dollar to see you force feed it to him."

The frustration she had felt moments before began to drift away in the presence of her friend. Her anger was quickly replaced by feelings of relief, and then joy. "Is there something I can help you with, Agent Blackburn?" Waterston asked, breaking the spell.

"Actually, Doctor, you can," Agent Blackburn answered. "You can start by taking your View-Master from Hell there, and giving Agent Sommers and myself a little privacy."

Amy watched, confused over the sudden turn of events, as Dr. Waterston closed his laptop, causing the images of the dead soldiers to vanish. He picked up his notepad along with the laptop and exited the conference room.

"I didn't think he would ever leave," Agent Blackburn said sarcastically as he settled his large frame into one of the empty chairs.

"Don't get me wrong, Reggie, I'm grateful for the reprieve from Dr. Kevorkian and his little computer of horrors, but what is this all about?"

"I just thought you could use a break since you've obviously been working so hard. And, after listening to your mini meltdown while I was out in the hall, I would say I was correct."

He sat like he did not have a care in the world, but she could tell by the smirk working at the corners of his mouth and the mischievous glint shining in his eyes that he was holding something back. He was definitely up to something, and knowing him like she did, he would not make it easy for her to find out.

"All right Blackburn, I know that look. Fess up."

She folded her arms across her chest and did her best to stare him down. To his credit, he was able to withstand her best LAPD interrogation room glare, which had reduced more than one grown man to tears, and had resulted in numerous confessions. Unfortunately, Agent Blackburn was made of sterner stuff. Her impatience finally got the better of her.

"That's it, Blackburn. Either tell me what's going on or I am going to knock that smug look off your face with a sharp crack from my backhand," she jokingly threatened.

"You know, I'd almost like that, Sommers."

"That's the only thing holding me back," she said, winking at him to emphasize her point.

He snorted out a chuckle in appreciation of her wit, then he surprised her anew with a quick switch of his demeanor to a more serious mood.

"A little over a week ago, the Agency got a tip from friends in Great Britain that an Irish terrorist organization calling themselves *Na Ri` Laoch* had slipped a cell into the U.S."

"*Na Ri` Laoch*?" she interrupted confused.

"Yeah, it roughly translates to The King's Warriors," Agent Blackburn said. "Normally, this wouldn't be a case for us to take an interest in, but according to the information Britain provided, this Irish terrorist group had in their possession a certain map which may contain the location of a certain artifact."

"I take it this is not your ordinary run of the mill artifact, but something of an extraordinary nature," she said.

"You would be correct in your assumption. Anyway, I was asked to do some checking, and sure enough, I discovered the *Na Ri` Laoch* had entered the country in New York of all places. These guys were not on any terrorist watch lists as they are pretty small time, so there was no reason to think they were anything other than tourists. The Agency contacted Homeland Security, who in turn brought in the Secret Service. Under the guise of being with the FBI, I was allowed to join in the attempted apprehension of the terrorists. I say attempted because the Secret Service agent in charge thought he was Wyatt Earp and blasted the *Na Ri` Laoch* to pieces before I could talk to them. My real objective was to get my hands the map."

"I am guessing you were successful in your endeavor or you wouldn't be here."

"Again, you are right on the money." Agent Blackburn set a Halliburton case on the table.

"So what does this have to do with me?" she asked, desperately trying not to get her hopes up.

"I thought you might ask that. It seems the British are more than a little concerned the artifact this map may or may not lead to might fall into the wrong hands. They have asked the Agency to find the artifact, if possible, and return it."

She waited for him to finish, holding her breath in anticipation, and gripping the edge of the table so hard her knuckles turned white.

"After some deliberation," Agent Blackburn continued, "It has been decided that you, Agent Sommers, will handle this case."

"Yes!" She jumped to her feet so fast she knocked her chair over. "I swear, Blackburn, if this is one of your lame ideas for a joke, you're a dead man."

This brought a fresh round of laughter from the big man.

"Sommers, you do not disappoint. This is no trick. The case is yours."

To prove his point, Agent Blackburn slid the metal case across the table where it came to rest right in front of her. She wanted to reach down, snatch it up, and run out before the Agency had a chance to somehow change their collective mind. It took every ounce of self-restraint she could muster to stop herself from doing just that.

"Now, before you get too excited, I must warn you that the British don't completely trust us to handle this job. They are going to send their own agent to be a part of the investigation. You will be working closely with their representative."

This bit of new information did let the air out of her sails a little. She had never been one who liked working with a partner. She was a loner when it came to investigative work, and she was at her best when she was unencumbered and not shackled to someone who would only slow her down anyway. Still, if it meant she would finally be working an active case, she would gladly bite the bullet, and do her best to play nice.

"If I have to, then I have to," she said, not the least discouraged. "When can I expect this lovely new partner?"

"Honestly, I'm not sure. With as much importance the Brits are putting on this, it wouldn't surprise me any if someone wasn't already on their way."

"I'm not gonna sit around and wait for some guy to finish eating his fish and chips. The sooner I can get started the better. In any investigation, every second counts. You know that, Reg."

"I figured you'd say as much. So, if you've got nothing better to do, let's get going."

"You mean right now?" she asked, surprised.

"Sure thing; grab the Halliburton, Agent Sommers, and let's get moving."

She liked the way he emphasized the word "Agent." This was Blackburn's way of saying she was ready; that she finally had made it and he was proud of her. She knew he had stuck his neck out for her, and she had no intention of letting him down.

She reached down and grabbed the Halliburton case. The handle felt cool against her palm. The case was heavier than she anticipated, and when she pulled it off the table, the unexpected weight caused a painful tug on her shoulder and arm.

"Maybe you need to hit the gym a little more, instead of the take-out food you're so fond of," Agent Blackburn teased.

"Screw you, Blackburn," she replied with friendly sarcasm. "If I hadn't been holed up in here with Dr. Boredom the last three months, you wouldn't be talking. Besides, with that spare tire you call a gut? I don't think you should be commenting on how out of shape anyone is."

"Yeah, Sommers, I definitely missed you.".

They shared a laugh before heading out of the large conference room, and making their way down the hall.

"So what's my first step?" she asked.

"The map is written in some kind of ancient Gaelic, so the first thing we need to do is get it translated. You and I are going to pay a visit to a language specialist who works for the Agency. After that, you will be on your own, more or less."

By this time, they were at the elevator waiting for the doors to glide open allowing them entrance.

"Do you know why this map is so important to the British, other than it might lead to an artifact?"

"Yeah, I think so." Agent Blackburn sounded somewhat cryptic.

"It has to do with whatever it leads to, doesn't it?"

He nodded. The elevator doors opened, and they both stepped into the small confines without any hesitation.

"What does it lead to, Reggie?" she asked, her voice taking on a serious tone.

"If all the reports are correct, and the information given to us by the British Agency is accurate, then the map you are carrying in that Halliburton case leads to the hidden resting place of none other than King Arthur's sword, Excalibur," Agent Blackburn answered as the doors to the elevator slid shut.

CHAPTER 5

Loud techno music thumped out its rhythmic beat as young men and women writhed and intertwined with each other on the mirrored dance floor of Club Shadow. They moved seemingly unconscious of their surroundings, with blank expressions on their faces like they were in a trance or under a spell. Better yet, they looked like puppets, or members of some ridiculous cult worshipping the even more ridiculous music.

That was the way he liked to think of them; as mindless wretches he could control at his whim.

He watched them through the tinted glass windows of the office, which overlooked the entire club. He took a long sip from his glass containing the most pleasurable of concoctions: Jack Daniels and Coke-Cola. It was his favorite drink. In fact, anymore, it was all he cared to drink. It fueled the fire burning deep in his gut, the same fire that had helped make him the most successful, highest paid, and most sought after assassin in the world.

He had many names and identities he used worldwide, but to his prospective customers he was simply known as the Ghost. This simple name, when uttered, could bring spine-tingling fear to government officials and high ranking crime syndicate bosses all around the world. He had earned the nickname for his uncanny ability to slip into the most secure of places, kill his intended mark, and then slip out again completely undetected.

He ventured a glance at the gold and jade bracelet clasped to his right wrist, the same bracelet which had quite literally changed his life. A knowing smile worked its way across his handsome face and an evil glint seemed to sparkle in eyes so brown they could easily be mistaken for black.

He stared at the dancing fools a few minutes more before turning and walking to the large, antique, oak desk which dominated most of his office with its presence. Once there, he flipped an unseen switch, and heavy wooden panels came sliding out of the walls, covering the windows and muffling the loud music to a more tolerable level. The pounding of the music was causing an equal pounding inside his skull.

The noise was a small annoyance, however. This nightclub, his club, was his base of operations. It provided him with the cover he needed to help maintain his identity and to mask his true business. Though he had not been particularly active in recent months, he was still on just about every security force's Most Wanted list.

That is what happens when you have killed such high profile targets, he thought, bringing another evil grin of glee to his otherwise serene face.

Two years of semi-retirement left him feeling that he had been inactive far too long. He'd nearly been caught, and decided discretion was the better part of valor. Now, though, he'd grown increasingly bored.

He had made an obscene amount of money in a relatively short period of time. It was amazing what individuals would pay to have him off some rival. He had more money than he could ever hope to spend in his life time, though since his near capture he'd had all kinds of fun trying.

Like many other times in his charmed life, fate had decided to intervene.

A while ago, while enjoying the company of several naïve college girls at a slightly out of the way Irish pub, he had met those idiots calling themselves *Na Ri` Laoch*. Over an evening of shared drunkenness, he had learned their entire pathetic story, and had decided right there on the spot that he could have some fun exploiting their poor excuse for a political terrorist group.

Little did those morons know, but he was actually their supposed high ranking contact in the British Government. They never even bothered to check his story, not that it would have mattered. He covered his tracks well enough. He manipulated them just as easily as he did the patrons who piled into his club every night.

The *Na Ri` Laoch* provided him the in he needed to become active again. After he had put the bug in their ears about the sword, it became increasingly easier to steer them to the paths he wanted them to choose. He was the one who actually tipped off the British government who then, true to form, contacted the Agency in the States. His plan moved along so smoothly, it could not have been scripted any better.

Once the Agency got their hands on the map, it was easy to convince the *Na Ri Laoch's* fool of a leader that they needed to bring in a professional to get the map and retrieve the sword for them. He knew the idiotic brain trust of the *Na Ri` Laoch* were probably discussing whether or not they should hire someone as dangerous as "the Ghost."

He chuckled to himself, thinking about those three jackasses having their idea of a team meeting. The whole situation was comical.

He knew they would choose to acquire his services. They really did not have any other choice, at least none he left them. He made sure to dangle the carrot of success in front of their faces, driving them into a near frenzy thinking about what they could accomplish if they managed to get their hands on the sword. It was only a matter of time before he was contacted and given the go ahead to proceed. He would charge them an enormous sum for his services, but truth be told, this had very little to do with money.

He had grown bored and stagnant this past year. More than that however, it was time he eliminated the only loose end he had allowed to go unchecked. This was his opportunity to settle a score with Agent Reggie Blackburn.

Oh, he would get the map and find the sword. If he was feeling generous, he might even give it to those fools in Ireland, though he would probably take them out as well and keep the mysterious blade for himself. But that was secondary. What he really wanted to do was stare into Blackburn's eyes, and watch with measured intensity as the life drained out of them.

Many nights, he had lain awake plotting out Agent Blackburn's painful demise. He had visualized hundreds if not thousands of scenarios in which Blackburn suffered an excruciating death; each more horrible than the last. The fat agent was the only person he truly hated. In his business there was no such thing as freebies, but in Blackburn's case he would make an exception. Getting to Blackburn would be collateral damage on his way to the sword. Thanks to the *Na Ri` Laoch* and their lofty dreams, he would have his chance to settle a score once for all.

A loud knock at the office drew him out of his murderous fantasies.

"Enter," he said, loud enough so whoever was standing on the other side of the door could hear him over the pulsating music.

The door slowly opened. His beautiful and young assistant stood sheepishly in the entrance. She was a gorgeous little thing with an exemplary body he had spent several enjoyable occasions exploring. That body was the sole reason he had hired her to manage his club. With his charm she had been so easy to seduce, and as a result he knew she was now completely in love with him; a situation he exploited to his advantage whenever he so desired.

When the young woman made no move to enter the office, he waved her in with annoyance. He hated it when she tried to play coy. He was a busy man and had no time or patience for her little girl games.

"I said enter, Gretchen."

"Yes, Mr. Clauson," the pretty club manager said, lowering her head in submission.

Clauson was the name he had chosen for his identity here in London. James Clauson was a successful business man with many influential friends in high places. He had similar personas in various high profile cities throughout the world.

He stared at her like a hungry wolf ready to take down its unsuspecting prey. Depending on how things went this evening, he might have to sample a taste of her delicacy once again. By the mischievous look in her eyes, he could tell she was of a like mind.

"What can I help you with?"

"The bartender would like permission to open up a new case of Cristal."

He heard a subtle hint of luridness in her soft-spoken voice, inviting him to come out and play. He got up from his plush leather office chair, planning to grab her and take her right here and now. He knew she would not resist, and would give herself up totally to his carnal whims.

Before he could get around the desk to satisfy his lust, the cell phone sitting on the same desk began vibrating. He paused in mid-stride, his sexual desires forgotten. Normally he would ignore an intrusion like this. But that particular cell phone was meant for only one caller, the *Na Ri` Laoch*. They must have come to a decision, and though this was a most inopportune time, this was a call he wanted to take.

"Excuse me, my dear, but I need to answer this," he said, reaching for the vibrating phone. He could see the disappointment in her eyes. He would take care of that soon enough. "You may tell the bartenders they have my permission. And, please check back in with me in about twenty minutes."

The disappointment in his manager's eyes turned to anticipation. This caused his own excitement to grow. He waited until she left the room; watching the sway of her hips before answering the phone.

"I take it you have come to a decision," he said into the receiver.

An Irish-accented voice said, "We were given this number through a mutual contact."

"I am well aware of the arrangement."

"So you know what we would like you to do." This was a statement of fact and not a question.

"Standard retrieval of a certain old world artifact. My regular fee for a job like this is 5 million dollars. I will get you the account number where the money will be deposited. This will be the last time we communicate. I will contact you when I have completed the job. If complications should occur, it's my decision on whether to abort or not. Whatever heat may come your way is up to you to handle. Either way, I keep the money. These are my terms and they are nonnegotiable. I need to know your decision right now."

"We're in," the *Na Ri` Laoch* leader answered without hesitation.

"Good. I will forward the bank account information shortly, and begin as soon as the money is transferred."

He hung up and smiled with satisfaction. This had been almost too easy. Anyone else might have thought it was some kind of elaborate set up, but he knew this was legit. The *Na Ri` Laoch* were too stupid to be Interpol or any other international police force. They were simply foolish idealists willing to do whatever it took for their cause, which only made them easier pickings for him. As the puppet master pulling all the strings, he was in complete control of this operation.

He went to the laptop sitting on his desk and forwarded the information the *Na Ri` Laoch* would need to make the money transfer. When that task was finished, he removed a Cuban cigar from the hand polished humidor he also kept on his desk. After striking a match and lighting the long, dark cigar, he took in a long puff, filling his mouth with the rich flavor. The evening continued to get better and better.

With the music still thumping away he felt good enough to dance himself. He was finally going to be able to take steps towards getting his sweet revenge against the Agency, and especially Agent Reggie Blackburn. This was cause for a celebration. He decided to enjoy one of those bottles of Cristal his bartenders were opening. In fact, sipping some Cristal out of Gretchen's belly button would hit the spot.

As if on cue, the door to his office opened and the leggy club manager stepped in.

"Are you ready for me now Mr. Clauson?" she asked teasingly.

A chime from his laptop caught his attention. He looked over, and noticed the $5 million had been successfully transferred to his account.

"I am now, my lovely," he said, his excitement building. "I'm going to call down and get us something to drink. I have a rather specific thirst this fine evening."

CHAPTER 6

The drive over to see the Agency's official translator was uneventful, though with the couple of inches of snow which had fallen earlier in the day, it seemed traffic was moving at a snail's pace.

Amy was so anxious to get started that the slow and cautious drivers in the other vehicles ahead of them caused her frustration to heat up. She was always of the attitude that time was of the essence no matter the case, and having to wait to begin her investigation due to something as trivial as winter weather induced driving was a hard pill for her to swallow.

The initial shock of Blackburn telling her she had been green-lighted for her own case had started to wane, but knowing she was going to be looking for the fabled sword Excalibur was still blowing her mind. When Blackburn dropped that particular bombshell on her, she had nearly tripped and fallen on her face. She was lucky enough to have caught herself and righted her balance. If she had given in to gravity and taken a spill, she would have never heard the end of it; Blackburn would have teased her mercilessly.

She was still having a hard time putting her mind around the fact that the Halliburton case sitting on the backseat of Blackburn's blue sedan contained a document which might lead to King Arthur's sword.

Excalibur! Who would have ever thought the possibility of its actual existence was even a viable option?

She always considered herself to be a rather open minded person, and she'd learned a few months back when she had helped track down an Elven serial killer that this world held way more secrets than she could have ever imagined, but still, Excalibur?

She ventured a look into the backseat to reassure herself the whole thing was real, and not some elaborate daydream. She had a moment of pure terror at the horrifying thought that she was still at the Agency, lulled to sleep by Dr. Waterston and his streaming video of death, and this was some boredom-induced hallucination. The momentary panic passed quickly at the sight of the silver aluminum case gleaming in the afternoon sunlight was pouring through the driver's side rear window. It put her mind at ease.

She and Reggie had barely spoken once they had gotten into the car and on their way. She had a million questions to ask concerning the investigation, but decided to wait until after they met with the translator in hopes of having some of her queries answered then. Besides, from what little Blackburn had told her, it was apparent he really did not have much information to share with her on the subject anyways.

The traffic finally began to pick up, and it was not long before Reggie parked the car in front of an unimposing gray stone building. The sign painted on the large front picture window named the facility as Capital Translation Services. Directly under the business name was a hand drawn facsimile of the iconic Capitol Building. The whole set up was unimpressive on first glance, but Amy had quickly learned from her short time with the Agency things were often much more than they appeared to be. If this translator they were going to meet with worked for the Agency, she was sure there would be more to him than met the eye as well.

Reggie had explained to her the Agency kept certain individuals with specific talents on the payroll. Steven Jackson was such a person. He had a knack, or better yet, a talent for deciphering languages, even those long forgotten by time. If the map was written in a form of ancient Gaelic or some hybrid of the language, it was their hope this Mr. Jackson could translate the descriptions which could point to Excalibur's hidden resting spot. She just hoped the guy was as good as his reputation.

When she pushed the door to the translator business open, it hit a bell hanging over the entrance way, causing it to jingle. She supposed this effect was to remind patrons who entered of a simpler time, and add a quaint charm to the atmosphere of the place. The effect was lost on her; she found it more of an annoyance. She rolled her eyes and spared a look over at Blackburn, who only shrugged his shoulders in indifference.

A phone rang loudly as they entered, mixing with the tinkling of the bell and only adding to her annoyance. After three rings the phone was answered by a heavyset forty-something woman.

"Capital Translation Services, how may I direct your call?" Amy heard the receptionist ask.

The lobby, if you could even call it that, was basically a small room with a door off to the right, which she guessed led to offices where the different translators worked their magic, so to speak.

The receptionist and several file cabinets were situated behind a half wall counter which ran the length of the lobby. The floor was covered in a dingy and worn light brown carpet. Faux wood paneling covered the walls. The whole place gave Amy the impression this was the office time forgot. The musty smell filling her nostrils only added to this feeling.

There were no chairs, so she and Reggie stood waiting for the receptionist to finish her phone conversation.

Amy glanced at her watch and was surprised to see it was closing in on 1pm. The day was starting to slip away from her, and she had yet to really accomplish anything important concerning this investigation. If things did not pick up soon, she might fall asleep standing up. She wanted to hit the ground running with this case so she could prove her worth to the Agency, but so far she had been stuck playing the waiting game.

"I have you down for Thursday the 11th at 2pm. Go ahead and bring all your materials at that time…Sure thing, Mr. Williams, and thank you for thinking of us." Once the phone was hung up back on its receiver, the middle aged secretary put on her best welcoming smile of greeting, and turned her attention to Amy and Reggie.

"May I help you?"

Finally, Amy thought, as Reggie stepped up to the counter.

"I'm Agent Blackburn and this is Agent Sommers. We have an appointment with Mr. Jackson."

"Let me call back and see if he is ready for you." When she again hung up the phone, the receptionist smiled and said, "Mr. Jackson will be right up to take you back."

"Thank you," Amy and Reggie said at the exact same time, then looked at each other with goofy smiles upon hearing their stereo reply. Amy was tempted to yell out "jinx," but thought the humor would be lost on Blackburn.

After roughly two minutes passed, the door to their right opened, and out stepped a short elderly man. At first glance, Amy thought she was looking at the real life version of Mr. Burns from *The Simpsons* animated television series.

The senior translator was dressed in khaki pants, a brown button down shirt, and a brown tweed jacket. It seemed to her that brown and its many shades was the official color scheme at Capital Translation Services.

She watched as the dour expression on the translator's face morphed into a friendly grin when he caught sight of Agent Blackburn. That put her at ease. If Blackburn trusted this man, then she had absolutely no objections at all of using his services or his involvement in this investigation.

"Agent Blackburn, it's good to see you again."

"Hey, Steven. I see you still haven't got around to updating the décor."

"Well, you know how it is, you have to stick with what works," the translator said. "Who is this you have with you?"

"This is Agent Amy Sommers. You will be working with her from here on out. I am just along for the ride this time."

"Nice to meet you, Agent Sommers. Why don't you and Agent Blackburn join me in my office?"

Knowing she could not pass up the opportunity, she turned to Blackburn, steepled her fingers, and with her best Mr. Burns imitation said, "Excellent."

Reggie bellowed out a loud guffaw. If the old guy heard or even noticed the laughter, he never let on or acknowledged it. He simply continued on his merry way down the short hallway, which was also covered in the same dingy brown carpet as the lobby. They were accompanied by the same musty aroma as well.

The translator's office was larger than the lobby and definitely more modern. Every wall was covered floor to ceiling with bookshelves, filled to capacity. Jackson's desk was a glossy black lacquer, featuring a liquid crystal computer monitor on the left, and a plasma screen television on the right. From the looks of it, Steven Jackson had his own personal media center from which he could complete his translation projects.

Amy and Reggie each took a seat without waiting to be invited, ready to get down to business.

"Well, let's have a look at it," the translator said once everyone was seated.

Amy gently laid the Halliburton on the desk. After releasing the catches, she lifted the lid, and spun the metal case around and nudged it across the desk.

Jackson gently removed the plastic-sealed document. With the care the old guy was using, it looked to her as if he was handling a delicate piece of priceless china. Jackson briefly gazed at the map as if trying to get a feel for it, before putting on a pair of bifocal glasses. A look of determined interest was clearly marked on the old guy's face.

"What do you think?" she asked. "Do you recognize the language?"

"Yes and no," Jackson said. "I am pretty sure this is some form of Gaelic, which I am sure the Agency had already surmised, but it is no form that I have ever seen. It's almost as if this was written in some kind of Gaelic code."

"Can you decipher it?" Reggie asked.

Jackson thought it over, his curiosity obviously piqued. "It's going to take some time," he finally said.

"This is kind of a rush job, Steven," Reggie said.

"Yeah," Amy said, wanting her opinion to be heard as well. "This investigation has already been stalled long enough. I can't really proceed until I know what the map says, and I can't afford to sit back and wait for very long."

"I'm not so sure it is a map, even though there are some kinds of areas marked," Jackson said.

"If it's not a map, then what is it?" she asked.

"I don't know yet," Jackson said, emphasizing the word *yet*. "Give me twenty-four hours, and I should be able to get some results and tell you more."

Amy looked at Reggie, who nodded. She was not happy about having to wait, but as things stood, she did not have much choice. Besides, she had already waited somewhere in the neighborhood of three months to finally get working on a case again; what was one more day?

Even if the next twenty-four hours will feel like an eternity, she thought.

"Okay then, Steven," Reggie said, interrupting her private one-woman pity party. "One of us will be in touch with you tomorrow morning."

They exited the Capital Translation Services, and stepped back into the cool crisp Washington D.C. air. She could see her breath roll out of her mouth in small puffs of wispy mist, which quickly vanished.

"You wanna go grab a bite?" Reggie asked, fishing through his pockets looking for the car keys.

"Throw in a beer and you got yourself a deal."

"Finally, a woman after my own heart."

"Slow down there, big fella. I may be cheap, but I'm not easy."

"Yeah, Sommers, I know, but I'm too hungry to care," Reggie said. He unlocked the car and they both got in.

Amy's stomach rumbled loudly as they pulled into traffic. "Better hurry, Reggie, the beast is growling," she said.

Across the street from the Capital Translation Services at a family diner, sipping coffee, sat the Ghost. He watched through the large front window as the two agents drove away.

The internationally-feared assassin took special note of the fact that the silver case the cute female agent had carried upon her arrival was not with her upon exiting.

So, the translator has the map. It was exactly what he had hoped for. *Once again, all going perfectly according to plan.*

The Agency was incredibly predictable in their methods for those who paid attention, especially to one who knew them so well. It was really a no-brainer for him to come to Capital Translation Services almost as soon as he'd arrived in the country. Steven Jackson was among the best; the Ghost had once used the vaunted translator's services himself, in what now seemed a lifetime ago.

His vigilance in staking the place out paid off almost immediately. Much better, in fact, than attempting to scope out the Agency headquarters. And who had shown up, with his pretty little sidekick? None other than Agent Reggie Blackburn in the flesh.

Seeing Blackburn in person after all the time which had passed was a shock to his system. Part of him wanted to walk out of the restaurant, draw the silver-plated .45 resting comfortably in his shoulder holster, and blow away his fat nemesis in cold blood right there on the street for the whole world to see.

He could do it too, then easily blend in with the surroundings, casually slipping away unnoticed. But he needed Blackburn alive for a little while longer, to lead him to the sword as a fall back plan if all else failed. Once the heralded blade was in his hands though, Blackburn's life would be forfeit. That was going to be a special moment indeed; one he looked forward to with eager anticipation akin to a child waiting for Christmas morning.

He was a patient man, however. In his business, one had to have patience in abundance, and be able to wait for the ideal moment to strike. If frustration somehow found its way into his psyche and took hold, it could prove extremely costly. As the

Ghost, he knew this, and so Blackburn would be allowed to live...
for now, at least.

His objective now was the retrieval of the map. If the Agency
was bringing the translator into their investigation, it must be
more troublesome and cryptic than first imagined.

He took another sip of the greasy spoon's wretched excuse
for coffee, thinking he should do a service to the community and
dispose of the cook who brewed such garbage out of principle.
And the fools had the audacity to advertise they served the best
cup of coffee in Washington D.C.? The brownish liquid was little
more than dirty lukewarm water with a few grounds floating
around in it. Even the most warped sense of propriety said he
would be justified in executing whoever had come up with the
fabricated boast.

His gold Rolex watch informed him it was getting late.
Motion from across the street caught his attention. An old man
carrying a sliver Halliburton metal case exited the building of
Capital Translation Services, and began walking up the street. The
sight of him brought a feral grin to the Ghost's face.

He removed a couple of bills from his money clip and
nonchalantly tossed then onto the table. He slipped his long
black coat on over his shoulders, and walked out into the winter.
afternoon.

The eerie feral grin stayed etched on his face. As the Ghost,
he had a knack for putting people in a position where they could
not tell him no, and felt compelled to offer up any information he
required.

It was time to pay a visit to an old acquaintance, and enlist
Jackson's services whether the old man wished to provide them or
not.

CHAPTER 7

The lunch with Blackburn ended up being more like an early dinner, as it took them longer than expected to come to an agreement on a place to eat. Once they settled on grabbing a steak at Jimmy's, a local bar and grill, they then spent the majority of the meal discussing some of the stranger nuances of the investigation.

Amy also forced Blackburn to sit through more than a fair share of complaints. She figured he deserved it, and having to listen to her was his penance for her suffering the Agency's idea of training for as long as she did.

By the time they finished eating, and drinking more beer than she initially intended, the sun was going down, dropping the outside temperature from barely tolerable to downright cold. Winter was not yet in full swing, but with the snow already on the ground, and the near freezing chill, one would have never known.

The evening traffic was not as bad compared to the gridlock at lunchtime. With Reggie driving, they made pretty good time, and before long, they were pulling up in front of her apartment building. The sun had completely set, and despite the street lights, her block was encased in darkness and the street deserted, as if her neighbors and any late stragglers had settled down comfortably in their warm homes.

A pang of loneliness settled in the pit of her stomach. Excited though she was about finally having an investigation of her own, it was disheartening knowing she did not have anyone waiting at home to share her good news with. It was a situation she would have to get used to, however. Being in the employ of the Agency did not leave much time for a personal life.

She glanced over at Reggie, momentarily considering asking him up for another beer so she would at least have someone to talk to. She quickly dismissed the notion as selfish. It had been a long and busy day for Reggie as well, and she was sure he wanted nothing more than to go home and relax himself.

"So, what's on the agenda for tomorrow?" she asked.

"I will get hold of Jackson early tomorrow to see if he has made any headway. I'll call you after that, and we'll just have to go from there," Reggie said.

"Sounds like a plan. Talk to you in the morning then."

"Have a good night, Sommers."

"You too," she said as she opened the car door.

The cold wind hit her directly in the face. She was not prepared for the blast of frigid air, and it stole her breath. After finally sucking in a lung full of cold air, she readjusted the collar of her coat. Then, with a final wave at Blackburn, she turned and marched up the steps.

She looked over her shoulder at the sedan's red tail lights disappear onto the cross street. Once again, she felt the sting of being alone.

She fished her keys out of her coat pocket, a harder task than she thought due to her fingers having gone numb. With her head still buzzing from the multiple beers she and Reggie drank, she was looking forward to kicking back in her apartment, and let herself into the building.

The building's interior was tastefully decorated in an elegant Victorian style, and even more importantly in her estimation, it was warm. The Agency had helped set her up in this place. She often wondered how many other agents might be sharing this complex with her. So far she had not recognized any of the neighbors, but then, met very few employees at the actual Agency as well. No doubt, discouraging employees in general from having much contact with each other helped the Agency maintain its vaunted secrecy.

She walked past the two Victorian sitting chairs in the lobby without a second glance. The only chair she was interested in at this point was the soft, well worn, broken-in recliner waiting for her upstairs. It might be a little on the ancient side, but she loved it. Heck, it was almost as comfortable as her bed. She'd spent many a night curled up in the chair's welcoming arms rather than sleeping in her room.

Exhaustion finally took hold of her as she exited the elevator on the third floor. It had been an emotional roller coaster ride of a day, from the low of having to suffer through another session of absurd training, to the high of finding out she was being given an investigation, then back to a more minor low of having the investigation stall until the translator could work on the map, she had experienced a week's worth of emotion since morning. She was definitely ready to unwind.

She was so tired; the keys looked like one big blurry metal blob. After a couple of tries, she managed to find the correct one. Without any more delays, she slipped the key into the door knob, and let herself in to 310.

A small stream of yellowish light slipping through the blinds in her living room from a streetlight down below, and bathed the interior in an eerie, almost ghoulish, glow. She moved to turn on an end table lamp when her police instincts kicked in and she paused. Something was not quite right. She could not put her finger on what it was, but something definitely felt out of place. In her tired state, she had nearly missed it, but now her senses were on full alert.

An unusual thickness in the air made her breathing labored and sluggish. As she continued moving more slowly towards the lamp, she inched her hand to unzip her coat, thinking to free her sidearm from the shoulder holster located under her blazer.

The hair on the back of her neck stood. The deathly silence only added to the oppressive weight in her chest. It was like the air was turning into water, and she was drowning in it. If she did not get her labored breathing under control, she was in danger of hyperventilating.

It was not that she was afraid; as a cop she had been in similar situations before. But what was going on in her apartment was causing a negative reaction within her body.

She knew she was not alone.

She managed to get her coat unzipped, hoping it appeared casual. She took a quick glance around but everything seemed in order.

Still, the premonition or sixth sense or whatever sent up warning flares one after another. Someone was here, watching her. She could feel it all the way down into her bones as sure as she could feel her gun against her ribs.

She hesitated before turning on the lamp, wanting to make sure she had a solid grip on her gun first. Brightness flooded the living room. Her vision dropped to nil as yellow spots danced in front of her eyes, but she drew the weapon, dropped to one knee and aimed in the vicinity of the still-darkened kitchen.

"Bravo, Agent Sommers," an English accented voice said from the darkness. "But I do not think you will be needing your weapon."

The blurry image of a tall form gradually came into focus. She kept her gun leveled on the intruder despite his comment to the contrary.

"I don't know who the hell you are or how you got in here, but if you take one more step, I'm going to pull this trigger, spray some serious lead, and definitely lose my security deposit," she said.

"I promise you, I will be good. I do not believe you will be needing to spray anything."

Her eyes adjusted enough to give her a better look at the stranger.

He did not look like much of a burglar, or any other type of criminal for that matter. He was tall, lean though not skinny, in good shape. The way he carried himself spoke of an underlying strength and definite confidence. She did not sense any immediate threat coming from him. In fact, he seemed as comfortable as if he were a regularly invited guest, making himself at home. This annoyed her, tempting her to shoot him even more, if for no other reason than to knock the smug look off his face. That he used her name like an associate was another reason for her instant dislike.

He had short hair, combed forward in much the same style George Clooney had made so popular a few years back. It was sprinkled with gray, as were his mustache and goatee giving them a salt and pepper look. If pressed, she would have put him in his late forties or early fifties.

He was dressed in a well tailored and obviously expensive suit. It was navy blue in color, and truth be told, he wore it well. His crisp white shirt and blood red tie stood out. His eyes, black like a shark's eyes, were the most striking thing about him. His gaze was piercing and unnerving, as if he could look through her all the way down to the pit of her soul. They were old eyes as well, like he had seen far more years than his age let on. A shiver actually ran up and down her spine.

He was smiling at her, revealing perfect white teeth. His demeanor seemed friendly enough, like the amicable British gentleman sort, but there was an aura of dangerous power emanating from him. What she did not know at the moment was whether or not he was a danger to her.

If he'd been there to rob her, he could have picked the place clean and been gone before she ever arrived. He did not look like he was hurting for money, and she had little worth stealing anyway. She also did not get the vibe he was there to attack her in any sort of physical manner.

She lowered her sidearm, letting it rest against her leg, but kept her finger on the trigger however in case the guy decided to do something stupid. This whole thing was starting to take on a surreal feel. .

"Well, I guess that is a start," the stranger said.

"All right, I'll play along, but don't think for a minute I won't put a few holes in that nice suit of yours if I decide it's necessary," she said, trying to sound confidant. "Now tell me who you are, and what you're doing in my apartment before I get an itchy trigger finger."

He grinned at her in amusement. It was nice to know she was providing him with some entertainment. Under different circumstances, she would have punched him square in the jaw. His obvious comfort with the whole situation was grating on her nerves as it was.

"Yes, of course. Where are my manners? I am Emrys Myrddin Ambrosious, and I am at your service."

"Wow, that's quite a mouthful." she said. "And I don't remember ever having asked for your service."

"It's mostly Welsh."

"Yeah, whatever," she said sarcastically. "So Mr. Ambrosious, just what the hell are you doing in my home?"

"Didn't they tell you I was coming?"

She stared at him, not sure how to respond. She felt like she was in the middle of one of those stupid reality shows where people play tricks on one another. She half expected to see Ashton Kutcher come running out at any minute.

"I am sorry if my being here startled you," he continued, "but I am to be your partner in the investigation of the sword Excalibur."

Upon hearing this, everything fell into place. She let out a long breath half in frustration and half in relief as she slipped her sidearm back into its holster.

"You're the representative from the Agency in Great Britain," she said.

"That I am, Agent Sommers."

"It's nice to meet you, Mr. Ambrosious, but that doesn't explain all this cloak and dagger crap, and why you felt the need to break into my apartment."

"I beg your pardon. I am truly sorry if I frightened you in any way. It was not my intention. I do admit I have a bit of flair for the dramatic. I like to test the people I am going to be working a case with, especially those I have never met before. I wanted to see how you would react to the unexpected. I thought a fellow agent would appreciate the gesture."

"Well, you thought wrong, and I don't," she said. "Besides, the last time I checked, I wasn't in high school anymore and so the need for tests has long since passed. The very fact I am an agent should be proof enough for you that I know how to handle myself. If it isn't, then maybe you should hop back on your plane and zip back across the pond and find someone else's home to break into."

She was caught off guard as he once again smiled at her. This time it seemed genuine, and apologetic. She did not believe he truly meant to insult her, and if she was not mistaken he was somewhat embarrassed by the reaction his behavior had caused.

"I am deeply sorry for my affront, and I offer my humblest apologies."

"Cool," she said, not really knowing how else to respond, and then added, "Now that we're all chummy, let me be honest. I don't like working with a partner. I think it's a waste of time, and if I had my way, you would be on the first plane back to England, in time for tea. Oh, and another thing, the next time you feel the need to let yourself into my home uninvited, don't."

"It is nice to know where I stand with you, Agent Sommers. I understand your reservations about me, but I promise you, if you let me tag along, I will not be a hindrance or get in the way. As a matter of fact, if you allow me, I will prove to be extremely valuable. I want this case solved as badly as you do. Maybe even more, dare I say."

She stared at the British agent, still sizing him up. If first impressions counted, then this partnership was going to be trouble. Still, he definitely had a presence. There was something about him. He was different in a way she could not place. His eyes were serious as if they had seen centuries instead of decades. A new chill sent more shivers down her spine.

"I can see I have overstayed my welcome. Thank you for not shooting me, Agent Sommers."

"No problem, Agent Ambrosious. We'll chalk it up to American hospitality. I hope you managed to get a hotel because there is no way you are staying here."

"I figured as much. You will be happy to know I was able to procure lodging for myself. You see, I am an agent as well, and equally capable of taking care of myself."

She took the jibe in stride. She guessed she had that one coming for insulting his intelligence. Still, it felt good to know she could get under his skin.

"Yeah, I'm jumping for joy," she said. "Look, since we're going to be working together, why don't you meet me here around 8am tomorrow morning? We are going to visit a translator who's working on the map."

At her mention of the map, his body stiffened up and looked taut, like he was ready to pounce. She took a cautious step backwards. He quickly caught himself, once again shifting to the British gentleman comfortable in any situation. These sudden attitude changes hinged on the brink of the bizarre.

"Thank you, Agent Sommers, until tomorrow then," he said politely.

"Tomorrow, when you get here, one thing," she said. "Make sure you knock first."

She was surprised when he laughed at her comment. It was a deep, genuine laugh which broke the tension.

"Why don't I give you my card instead, and you can call me in the morning when you are ready?" he reached to an inside pocket and produced a small business card, which she took without looking at. "This is going to be quite interesting working with you isn't it Agent Sommers?"

"How *did* you get in here?" she asked, curiosity getting the better of her as he walked to the door.

He paused, and without turning around to look at her, said, "For the time being, I think some secrets are better left untold."

With that, he left, quietly closing the door behind him. She stared at it for a long time, trying to figure out what his last comment meant. Finally deciding it was merely another attempt at having some fun at her expense, she let the matter drop.

The excitement now over, her exhaustion returned in force. She was surprised by how tired she was. Events had definitely taken an odd turn, and now all she wanted was a cold beer and a hot bath.

Shaking her head to clear the last bit of tension Agent Ambrosious' unexpected visit had caused, she went to the kitchen.

—Chapter 8

The Ghost followed Steven Jackson for nearly six blocks. The translator moved at a frustratingly slow pace as he meandered his way through the afternoon throng of pedestrians going about their daily business. He was completely unaware the Ghost was on his heels.

With the weather the way it was, there were more people out on the streets than the Ghost would have thought. It worked in his favor, making blending in with the crowd much easier. If he played his cards right, he might not even need to draw on the magic of the bracelet for help.

Most of the people lining the sidewalk did not pay him much attention, as they were too busy trying to stay warm. Many of them had their winter hats pulled down low on their heads. Some had hoods drawn so tight over their faces they looked like the sort of creature you might see in a John Carpenter horror film.

He knew he stuck out with his long black coat, a stark contrast against the pure white of the snow. He tried to act casual, and hoped if anyone did notice him, they would think of him as nothing more than a happy go-lucky tourist visiting the Nation's Capitol. The determined look on his face might have been a dead giveaway, however, that he was not interested in merely sightseeing.

Jackson continued on his merry way toward his destination, oblivious of the danger following close behind. The Ghost never took his eyes off the metal case gleaming in what little sun was shining through the gray clouds.

It would take some time even for someone with as much experience as Jackson to decipher the map's strange Gaelic-like language, the Ghost knew. He had seen the map for himself, and it would be no easy chore.

Those fools of the *Na Ri` Laoch* had sent operatives to the United States without even knowing what the map said. How they were going to locate the sword was beyond him. If it had not been his tip to the Secret Service, those idiots would still be bumbling around New York. But, thanks to the quick trigger fingers of the Secret Service, it was quite literally a dead issue. The three *Na Ri` Laoch* soldiers were deceased, the map had found its way into the hands of the Agency, and he had been hired to retrieve it; all just as he had planned.

The wind was beginning to pick up in ferocity, bringing with it an increased chill. His feet were getting cold, and he lamented that his expensive Italian Leather shoes would probably be ruined from the wet snow. He hoped the old guy did not live too much farther away.

"Why couldn't you drive a car like a normal person?" he mumbled under his breath.

The temperature was cold enough he actually wished he had brought a cup of the awful coffee from the diner. The taste was disgusting, but the warmth of the steaming liquid would be a welcome relief. He was definitely going to make Jackson pay for this trudge along the dirty and freezing sidewalks of Washington D.C. Jackson would know the meaning of pain before he died. The thought of torturing the translator actually helped warm him up, brining the feral grin to his face once more.

Jackson crossed and came to a halt in front of an old red brick building.

The Ghost watched as his prey looked around, as if some sixth sense finally decided to kick in and warn him about being followed. At one point the translator's gaze fell directly on him, and for a brief second, he thought he had been made. Then Jackson turned his head to scan the other direction, and the deadly tension building up in the Ghost's muscles began to subside. When the time was right, he would most definitely act in an extremely deadly manner, but he made a silent promise to himself that it would not be quick.

Steven Jackson entered the building, attempting to quiet the warning bells going off in the back of his skull. He had done plenty of covert work for the Agency, and understood a certain level of a risk went along with the job. He had never felt such a strong ominous sense of impending danger, however.

He glanced at the case clutched tightly in his aged fist. Whatever was out there stalking him was likely tied to the case's contents. There was no other logical explanation. Whatever information Blackburn wanted him to translate was more dangerous than the agent had let on.

He had not spotted anything out of the ordinary on the street or sidewalk. The local shops and stores all seemed in order as well. But there was someone, or worse, something out there watching him. He could feel it all the way down deep in his elderly bones as sure as he'd felt the cold wind slapping his face and chapping his skin.

With the safety of his loft apartment so close and beckoning him, he took one more quick glance around before he walked straight to the heavy wooden door marked STAIRS in black letters. He rarely used the elevator, figuring at his age a little exercise was more important than a few minutes of convenience. His loft was on the top floor, but seeing as how the building only had four, it was not too terrible of a climb.

As the door to the stairwell closed behind him, he thought he heard the whoosh of cold air being sucked into the building as someone else entered. A chill worked its way up and down his spine. He paused, trying to catch any other sounds, but was met with silence.

He gave thought to going back to the lobby in hopes of proving his mind was only playing a trick on him, but decided peace of mind would only be attained once he was home. He began his ascent with an extra push of adrenaline. It was amazing how fear was such a motivator.

When he had seen the old man pause and look around before going inside, the Ghost picked up his own pace.

His eyes gleamed with intensity as he let himself into the building. The lobby was deserted, and from the thin layer of dust covering everything, it looked like this was the norm. Still, he did not want to take any chances. If one of the other tenants happened along and saw him, it could be problematic. With that in mind, he decided to utilize the gift which earned him his nickname.

The gold and jade bracelet clasped to his left wrist, a seemingly simple little trinket, had changed his life. He owed everything he had to the ornate piece of jewelry. It was his most prized possession, and other than himself, it was the only thing he truly cared about. The gold band with its jade inlay was the most beautiful thing in the world, and he would die before giving it up.

The true value of the bracelet was not the gold or precious gems it contained, though they were one of a kind, but the magic it possessed. The bracelet gave whoever was wearing it the ability to blend in with any surrounding; making the owner virtually invisible and undetectable. This was why he had become so successful of a professional killer, and this was why he was known as the "Ghost".

He focused his gaze on the greenish piece of jade, which contained the caricature of a jaguar intricately carved into the stone. The image seemed to sear itself into his brain. He closed his eyes, and concentrated on this mental image. Within seconds, a warm sensation washed over his entire body. He felt a slight tingling in his fingers and toes. It was not unpleasant, akin to what happens when a part of the body falls asleep, the same needle type feeling.

When the initial sensation played itself out, he opened his eyes. Everything appeared the same as before, but he knew from experience if anyone would have been watching, he would have seemed to have vanished. He was now camouflaged, and could move about freely, unencumbered from prying eyes.

According to the nameplates on the mail boxes in the lobby, Steven Jackson lived on the fourth floor. The Ghost did not hesitate in moving into the same stairwell Jackson himself had used minutes before. He quickly climbed the stairs, hoping to catch the translator before the old man could enter his apartment.

CHAPTER 9

As Jackson mounted the last couple of stairs, and stepped onto the landing, he again had the eerie feeling he was being watched. He turned to give the stairway one last look, but everything appeared normal. He could have sworn a couple of times on his ascent he had heard footsteps yet every time he paused, no one ever appeared.

He knew there was some unknown presence about. He was almost sure of it.

Deciding it would not be a good idea to let his paranoia get the better of him so close to his front door, he pulled out the key to his apartment to be ready to let himself in. He really did not want to be alone in the hall any longer than necessary. The metal case was already starting to get heavy, and if it was as important as he suspected, would become even more of a burden with each passing minute.

He would be glad when his translation of the parchment was complete and he could return it to Agent Blackburn. He was beginning to be sorry for even taking on the job, but his insatiable curiosity had gotten the better of him, as it always seemed to do. He could not resist a good puzzle, and, whatever else this Halliburton case contained, it certainly had presented him with an irresistible quandary.

The climb had left him a little winded, but the excitement of being able to delve into the world of ancient languages and mysteries spurred him on. Once his door was open, he felt a very slight breeze brush against his wrinkled cheek, and froze in his tracks. He thought he caught a whiff of expensive aftershave as if a visitor had brushed past him. He surveyed the interior of his home, wondering what was causing his nerves to be on such high alert. Everything appeared to be exactly how he'd left it when he went to work earlier in the day.

The slamming bang of the door as it shut made him jump in spite of himself.

"Geez, Jackson, get a grip on yourself, old man."

He put on a pot of coffee. It was probably going to be a long and busy night trying to decipher the parchment, and he would need the extra boost of caffeine to help him see it through. The normal task had a calming effect on him as well, the comfort of routine a cool balm placed on the irritation of his frayed nerves.

Once the coffee was ready, he filled his favorite mug. It was white with the phrase "translators do it better because they can talk dirty in any language" written in large red block letters across it. He took a cautious sip, careful to not burn himself. The warmth of the black liquid was a welcome relief after his stroll through the cold and snow.

His earlier edginess began to waft away, much like the steam drifting out of his coffee mug. He was finally starting to feel relaxed, and was even able to convince himself it had been his overactive imagination getting him so worked up.

The metal case sat shining in the fluorescent overhead light like a beacon, calling out to him to come and solve its wondrous mysteries. He thought briefly of the old Greek tales of the Sirens calling sailors to their deaths, but dismissed it as quickly as it had come, in favor of excitement at the prospect of discovering some ancient secret in Agent Blackburn's document.

It was time to work his own brand of magic and do what he did best.

His home office was almost a mirror image of his working environment at Capital Translation Services, containing all the resources he needed to successfully pry every ounce of vital information from the Halliburton case's contents.

He set the case on his desk, and settled himself into his comfortable leather office chair, confident with his ability. The document would be translated in a matter of hours.

As he opened the case, the uncanny sensation of being watched overcame him again, but he chalked it up to nervous energy. The browned and aged document was the center of his universe now, and the sole focus of his attention.

He stared at it for several long moments, trying to get a better feel for the language, which was some sort of Gaelic, but nothing like he had ever seen before. Agent Blackburn seemed sure it was a map, but he was not as certain. Whatever it was, it posed a puzzling question he was going to enjoy unraveling.

He scanned it into his computer, and let the software go to work, looking for similarities of words and sentence structures, comparing all known languages.

As far as he was concerned, this was where the fun began.

The Ghost watched as the old man worked. He did not know how long the process would take, but he did not really care. One way or another, the translator would provide him with the information he required.

This was not the first time he'd had to wait and bide his time before taking out his intended target. He could be an extremely patient man if the situation called for it. On the other hand, he could be an equally explosive and dangerous man if need be.

So, he would wait, all night if necessary.

The end result would be the same. The map's secrets would be his, and the translator, Steven Jackson, would no longer be among the living.

Six hours, several trials-and-errors and a multitude of failures later, Jackson found the key he was looking for. The document relinquished its cherished contents much like a maiden on her wedding night.

He had been correct in his assumption that the language was a form of Gaelic, but it was far older than he would have ever thought. He would have to describe it as archaic, quite possibly a language that had not been used in close to a thousand years.

"How does this ancient Gaelic tongue end up on a two hundred year old parchment?" he wondered aloud, but that was not a mystery for him to worry about. His job had been to decipher the language, and pass it on. He had fulfilled his end of the bargain. It would be up to Agent Blackburn to fill in the rest of the blanks.

He had also been correct in his guess the parchment was not a map, not entirely, though it did seem to be indicating the location of an object. He found several mentions of "The King's Sword," which apparently was hidden right here in the States.

Jackson saw that it was nearing midnight. With the excitement of solving the riddle now subsiding, he was amazed at how tired he felt. A long, drawn-out yawn only emphasized the point.

Writing out a full report for Agent Blackburn could wait until the morning, giving him time to catch a couple hours of sleep.

He stood and stretched his arms and back, trying to work out the kinks in muscles that had grown stiff and sore from sitting in one position for so long.

Then he felt the slightest brush of air against his face, followed by a stinging pressure on his throat, right next to his Adam 's apple.

He froze, and sucked in a deep breath of surprise. He felt the slow trickle of blood as it worked its way down his neck. Afraid to move any other part of his body, he lowered his eyes.

To his complete astonishment, he saw a hand and arm materialize out of thin air.

"No sudden moves, old man, or I'll slit your throat," a voice said from directly behind him, speaking with a calmness that convinced Jackson the intruder would make good on his threat.

"Tell me what the document Blackburn gave you says, or I'm going to start slicing off body parts."

Jackson was too frightened to speak. If Blackburn needed that information, then it was of the utmost importance. He did not want to die for the agent, but he had no intention of telling some psycho with a knife to his throat anything vital.

"I don't know what you're talking about," he said, trying to sound sincere.

"Wrong answer," the intruder said.

In one swift motion, his attacker shoved him back into his office chair, grabbed his hand, slammed it onto the desk so all his fingers were splayed out, and sliced off his pinky finger.

It happened so fast that the pain did not immediately register. When it did kick in, Jackson was unable to make any kind of sound except for a childlike whimper. He balled his now ruined hand into a fist and grabbed it with the other, watching in shocked terror as blood oozed its way through his clenched fingers like lava from a tiny volcano.

His heart pounded in his chest, thundering against his ribcage. He was having a hard time catching his breath. He felt on the verge of having a major heart attack.

The intruder spun the chair around so they could stare at each other face to face.

"You," Jackson whispered, his voice trailing off in shock as he recognized his attacker.

"Do not be mistaken, Mr. Jackson. I want this to be perfectly clear. You are going to die tonight. So, the only two things you should be concerned about at this point are how quickly will it happen and how much pain you will experience before the end does come. Do you understand?"

He could only nod in response. A sharp pain was working its way down his left arm.

His attacker was right, he was going to die, but it would be on his terms and not those of a deranged, knife-wielding killer.

"Good," the Ghost said. "I am going to ask you again, and if you don't tell me what I want to hear, I am going to jab this knife into your right eye." He emphasized his point by holding up the blade. "Where is the sword?"

Feeling like his heart was about to explode, knowing he did not have much time left, Jackson blurted the first thing that came to his mind.

"New York City."

As soon as the words tumbled out of his mouth, a jolt of electricity seemed to strike his chest. He clutched at his sweat-soaked shirt with his still bleeding hand, and slipped from the chair as his body seized. There was a sharp pain, and then he blissfully slipped into unconsciousness.

The Ghost watched, stunned, as the old man fell to the floor. He nudged the still body with his foot, and when the translator showed no sign of coming to, bent down and felt for a pulse. When he could only find a hesitant beat, he realized what had happened.

In a burst of anger, he stood up and kicked Jackson in the ribs. Once the first kick landed, he lost control and lashed out repeatedly with his foot, kicking the defenseless body again and again. The crack of splintering bone was a satisfying sound and had a calming effect. He took a deep breath to get his anger fully under control. When his breathing had steadied once again, he looked around and snatched up the document on the desk.

His plan had not gone smoothly, but he had the map and the name of the city. With a final contemptuous look at the crumpled body of Steven Jackson, he fell back into the magic of his bracelet, and exited the building.

As he slipped in and out of consciousness, Jackson knew he was done for. The pain was excruciating and it was getting harder and harder to breathe, let alone concentrate. Yellow dots sparkled in front of his eyes. He came to the understanding that the next time he slipped into unconsciousness, he would never wake up again. He reached up with his good hand, using the blood from his severed pinky finger, and scribbled what he hoped was a legible message for Agent Blackburn to find.

—CHAPTER 10

The alarm kicked on, the clock radio blaring an Aerosmith tune. Amy reached over to the bedside table. Though she desperately wanted to hit the snooze button, and enjoy another ten minutes of blissful slumber, she switched the alarm off, forcing herself to sit up. Knowing Blackburn would be punctual in picking her up to meet the translator, she could not afford to play the snooze game.

The roller coaster ride of emotions the previous day had left her exhausted. As soon as Agent Ambrosius had left after his impromptu visit, she had gone straight to bed. She had fallen into a deep sleep more akin to a coma, and had not wakened for any reason until Steven Tyler's voice singing *Dream On* pulled her back to consciousness.

She was nowhere near being a morning person. It usually took her several attempts to drag herself out of bed.

Today was a different story. There was a tingle of excitement about the day, and she found herself actually looking forward to getting up and getting ready because the quicker she did, the quicker she could begin the investigation.

Sure, she would have Ambrosius tagging along, but so what? If it meant being able to work an actual case instead of sitting through another day of mind numbing training at the Agency, she would have gladly allowed the entire British Navy to come along for the ride.

Amy was surprised to find herself smiling as she kicked off the blankets and climbed out of bed. She was able to shower, get dressed, and do her hair and make-up all within a half an hour, while the coffee was brewing. The welcoming aroma had an instantaneous effect, as whatever lingering weariness she was experiencing was suddenly vaporized by the glorious caffeine-laden liquid

She was normally a low maintenance kind of woman anyway, but this was near record breaking readiness even by her standards. She was starting to feel like a real cop again. After being fired from the LAPD, it was like a part of her had died. Now, thanks to Blackburn and the Agency, she was on the verge of taking her first step into a much larger world of law enforcement.

She was enjoying her second cup of coffee when her cell phone began playing the theme from the movie *Halloween*. The caller ID confirmed Blackburn's number. "Morning Reggie. It's about time you called."

"Well, don't you sound all bright-eyed and bushy-tailed this fine morning," he answered.

"Hey, just you never mind my tail," she said. "That's what happens when you have actual casework to do. Maybe someone should explain that to the Agency."

"Be my guest, Sommers, but I gotta warn ya, from my own personal experience, the Agency does not take to kindly to being told what to do, especially by rookies."

"Well, at least we have that in common," she said. "Where you at anyway? It's almost 8am."

"I'm on my way. I tried to call Jackson earlier this morning but no one answered. Why don't we go by his apartment and see if we can save ourselves a trip to that dusty office of his."

"I'm ready as soon as you get here. Oh, by the way, I met my new partner last night."

"Really?" Blackburn asked. "What was he like?"

"Let's see, for starters he broke into my apartment, and scared the hell out of me after you dropped me off," she said, still a little angry about the scene from the previous evening, and the emotion could be heard in her voice.

"Oh, Christ, Sommers, you didn't shoot him did you?" Blackburn asked, only halfway joking.

"No I didn't. But if I had, it would have served him right. I still have to call him about meeting with the translator. I think I'll tell him to just meet us there."

"Sounds like a plan. I'll be at your place in about fifteen minutes, so tell him to meet us at 8:30. Oh, and Sommers, please try to play nice."

"You know me, Reggie. I'm a regular Miss Congeniality," she said. She could hear him groan on the other end of the line before hanging up. This caused her to chuckle quietly. She loved giving him a hard time. Having already gotten Blackburn flustered only added to her good mood.

She barely had time to enjoy the moment when her cell phone rang again. This time, she did not recognize the number right away.

"Hello?"

"Good morning, Agent Sommers. I hope this morning finds you well."

The British accent was a dead giveaway. "Good morning to you too, Agent Ambrosius. It's funny you called just now. I was on the verge of giving you a ring myself to fill you in on this morning's agenda."

"Well, you know what they say about great minds, don't you Agent Sommers?"

"Whoa, let's not get ahead of ourselves. Just because I didn't shoot you last night doesn't mean we are of a like mind and going to be swapping spit in the shower anytime soon," she said, a little more defensively than she intended to.

"I would never dream of being so presumptuous with you, Agent Sommers."

"Good, we got that settled at least." At this point she was still not sure if she was going to like Agent Ambrosius, but she did not want to come across as a jerk either. She was starting to feel comfortable speaking with the British Agent when a sudden realization came over her. "Wait a minute, how did you know my number? I thought I was supposed to call you."

"I got tired of waiting, and honestly, Agent Sommers, if I could get into your apartment undetected do you really think something as trivial as a phone number could stop me?"

She did not know how to respond. On the one hand, he had a point, but on the other he was overstepping her boundaries again. She decided to let the matter drop in light of the more important issue of getting started.

"If you say so," she said after a long pause, and then switched topics. "I just spoke with Agent Blackburn. He is going to be picking me up in a few minutes. We both thought it would be best if you meet us at the translator's place around 8:30. Does that work for you?"

"It does," he said. She gave him directions, and before she could say goodbye, she heard him say, "Thank you Agent Sommers. I look forward to seeing you."

She hated how his politeness always somehow put her in her place. It was like his presence here somehow validated the importance of this case. It could be her imagination or she could be reading more into it because of some left over anger from the previous evening, she supposed. Either way, she was determined not to let the *über* important Agent Ambrosius dampen her spirits .

A car horn from the street below drew her to the window. Seeing Reggie's blue sedan idling in front of her building, she grabbed her coat and headed out to begin her day.

The frigid wind hitting her in the face was a harsh reminder she was no longer in Los Angeles. This was her first winter in Washington, and if it was already this cold, she knew she was not as prepared for the elements as she thought she was.

She leaped down the final two steps in her hurry to gain the warmth of Reggie's waiting car. True to form, when she got to the passenger side door, it was locked. She lifted the handle several times, then peeked through the window, and could see Reggie laughing at her predicament.

"If you don't open this door, I swear I will start shooting," she said, her voice rising to be heard over the blowing wind.

The "ka-thunk" of the lock let her know Blackburn had received her message loud and clear. She glared at him as she opened the door and let herself in. The warm air blasting from the vent in the dashboard helped put her back at ease.

"Easy, Sommers. Man, am I glad looks really don't kill," Blackburn said.

"Good thing for you, because you would have been pushing up daisies," she said, the beginnings of a smile working its way to her face.

"Yeah, no kidding," Blackburn said. "Were you able to get hold of your partner? What was his name again?"

"Agent Ambrosius, and yeah, I talked to him. He's going to meet us there."

"Ambrosius huh? Sounds like a pansy to me."

"Wait 'til you meet him," she said "He's …something, all right."

She could feel Blackburn staring at her as he tried to figure out exactly what her last statement meant. After a few seconds, he shook his head in exasperation, and refocused on the road ahead.

Luckily, they did not have to go far. Amy was so geared up as to what Jackson might have discovered that she tapped her fingers against the car's armrest. Blackburn, to his credit, did not seem to notice or if he did, chose not to mention it. Wise on his part. As anxious as she was to get moving, she would have made him pay dearly for any sarcastic comment.

The snow from the day before had given way to the cold breeze and as a result there was no further accumulation. The city's snowplows had done their job well as all roads were clear.

"That's it," Blackburn said, pointing in the direction of a four story brick building. "That's the one."

"Well, pull over, and let's go see what Jackson has for us," she said, her excitement mounting.

"Geez, Sommers, rein it in a bit will you? I gotta find somewhere to park first."

Her impatience grew as Blackburn circled the block twice before finally finding a spot to park, half a block away. It meant another walk in the cold, but at this point she was so ready to get the information that she would have dog-sledded across Antarctica.

"Earth to Sommers, anybody home?"

"What?" she asked startled, so focused on getting to the apartment building she hadn't realized Blackburn was speaking. "I'm sorry Reggie; I didn't hear what you said."

He chuckled. "I said, I tried calling Jackson again while I was waiting on you, but still no answer. I called his office too, on the off chance he decided to go into work early, but he was a no show there as well."

They stopped in front of the old brick building. Sommers asked, "That's a little odd isn't it?"

"Yeah, I guess, but Jackson himself is a little odd, so, go figure."

She shrugged and stepped through as Blackburn held the door for her, then followed right behind her.

Agent Ambrosius stood in front of what appeared to be the tenants' mail slots. His expensive overcoat was a stark contrast against the severely outdated lobby, which looked like it had been decorated in the 1970's, and had not seen an updating since.

She was annoyed by how casual Ambrosius appeared to be. Here they were on the cusp of possibly cracking this case wide open, and the British agent looked like he had just returned from a Sunday stroll. He must have picked up on her feelings or read the frown clearly showing on her face because he cracked a knowing grin when she glanced at him.

"Ah, Agent Sommers, we meet again," Ambrosius said.

"Yeah, this is starting to become a regular habit," she said, then turned her head so only Reggie could hear, "a regular bad habit."

She winced as Blackburn elbowed her in the side before offering his hand.

"You must be Agent Ambrosius. Agent Sommers told me you two had the chance to get acquainted last night. I'm Special Agent Reggie Blackburn."

The British agent clasped the offered hand and said, "Nice to meet you, Agent Blackburn. And yes, Agent Sommers and I did get acquainted, if you can call it that."

"I hate to break up the love fest, but we do have more pressing matters to attend to," Sommers said, having had enough of the display of male bonding.

"Have you worked with this Mr. Jackson before?" Ambrosius asked as the three of them headed for the elevator.

"Yeah, I have used his services a couple of times and I know a few other agents have as well," Blackburn answered. "Trust me, if anyone can figure out what the document says, it's this guy."

"I trust your judgment Agent Blackburn. I also understand the document in question is very old."

"We think is at least 150 years old; maybe as much as 200," Sommers said.

"I have been instructed by my Agency to bring the document back to London for safe keeping, if at all possible," Ambrosius said.

The elevator arrived, and they all piled in. Reggie reached over to the control panel and pushed the button for the fourth floor. "After we are through translating it, and finding whatever it is those IRA terrorists were after, you are more than welcome to it."

Sommers thought she detected a hint of annoyance in the large agent's voice. She liked how he subtly explained the case came first and then Ambrosius could make whatever requests his heart desired. It seemed the British agent was starting to rub Reggie the wrong way as well. There was just something odd about the guy, something more to the guy than he was letting on. He gave off a strange vibe which set off her investigative early warning system. The fourth floor was as quiet as a church. They had not seen any other tenants. It was almost as if the place was deserted.

Her law enforcement honed senses picked up on something else, something was not quite right. Her instincts were telling her to proceed with care.

To her surprise, Agent Ambrosius seemed to be picking up on the feeling as well. The British agent seemed to be sniffing the air. She was still watching this curious behavior when Reggie's voice caught her off guard.

"The door is open," he said.

She took a look for herself, and sure enough, the door to Jackson's apartment was slightly ajar, as if someone had left in a hurry, and had not bothered to make sure it latched behind them.

This immediately put her on alert, and after sharing a knowing look with Reggie, a look only veteran law enforcement officers understood, she reached under her jacket and removed her gun.

"Do you think there has been some sort of foul play?" Agent Ambrosius asked quietly.

"I'm not sure," Blackburn responded. "But I'm not taking any chances."

"Are you armed?" Amy asked Ambrosius.

"No, I'm not carrying a firearm."

"Then you might want to stay behind us." She looked at Reggie, who also had his gun drawn and ready. She nodded.

Blackburn knocked on the door, and when there was no immediate response, he pushed it open all the way.

"Mr. Jackson?" Blackburn called loudly from the hallway. "It's Agent Blackburn and Agent Sommers. Are you at home?"

Again there was no response. Sommers had been at countless crime scenes in her time as a LAPD homicide detective, and the apartment she now found herself standing in had the same feel. Something bad had happened here, she was sure of it.

"You check the kitchen, I'm going to take a look in the back," Blackburn said, his voice barely over a whisper. "Ambrosius, stick close to Sommers."

The British agent nodded, and moved to stand right next to her. She could smell the man's cologne, which must have been something expensive as she did not recognize the scent. She was impressed by how calm he seemed. The guy was used to seeing action. This immediately increased her opinion of him. At least she would not be working with a wet behind the ears paper pusher.

"Come on," she said. Agent Ambrosius followed.

The kitchen was empty. She heard Blackburn calling from the other end of the apartment.

"Dammit! Sommers, back here, quick!"

She and Ambrosius found Blackburn squatting by a pair of legs sticking out from behind a desk.

There, lying facedown on the floor, was Steven Jackson. He was dead, and by the looks of it, had been that way for at least several hours. His body was bruised and battered, appearing as though he had been trampled, his chest sunken, giving the body an eerie appearance.

She lowered her gun, and dropped her head to her chest, feeling like she had been punched in the gut.

She re-holstered her weapon as Blackburn stood back up and did the same. They looked at each other, not really knowing what to say. It was Agent Ambrosius who finally broke the silence.

"Is this the man you hired to look at the document, Agent Blackburn?"

"Yeah, that's him." Blackburn sighed. "But I have no idea who would do this."

"What is that up by his head?" Ambrosius asked.

"I think it's blood," Blackburn said.

Sommers took a careful step around the crime scene to get a better look. The man's pinky finger had been severed. There was blood on the desk and floor. At first she thought the dark red lines by Jackson's head were simply more splatter. As she took another step, she realized she was looking at a message.

"Hey Reggie," she said. "I think he tried to write something."

"What's it say?" asked Blackburn and Ambrosius at the same time as they also moved in for a closer look.

"I'm not sure I can make it out," she said before leaning in. "I think it says sword, Boston…and ghost."

She looked at Blackburn to see if he knew what the cryptic message might mean, and was startled when she saw the look on his face. All the color had drained out of it, leaving him looking as pale as the corpse lying at their feet.

"What is it Reggie?" Do you know what he was trying to tell us?" she asked.

It took Blackburn several deep breaths before he could answer. She found it a strange and extremely unpleasant feeling seeing the usually rock steady agent so unnerved.

Blackburn cleared his throat. "I think the first part means the item we're looking for must be in Boston. The Ghost is a warning, and our killer."

"I'm not sure I follow," Ambrosius said. "Yeah, Reggie," she said. "What does all this mean?"

He tossed her the car keys. "It means you and Ambrosius get back to the Agency. I'll call the authorities and handle this scene."

"Look Reggie, if you know something..." Sommers began, but was cut off.

"Sommers I will tell you everything as soon as I can. I promise. But for right now, you are just going to have to trust me. Get back to the Agency. Ask for Director Smith. Tell them it's a Priority Red, and explain to the Director what happened. I will get in touch with you soon."

"All right." She turned to Ambrosius, who appeared just as confused as she was. "Let's go."

As she walked out of the room, she took one last look at Blackburn. The stricken look on his face left her chilled.

Whatever was going on, it was not good. Her first case had all of a sudden taken a bad turn, and it left her with an uneasy feeling in the pit of her stomach.

—Chapter 11

As she pulled into the darkened garage, Amy was unsure where to park or what proper Agency protocol was. She did not want to waste valuable time dwelling on such a minor dilemma, and so she pulled into an empty space close to the elevator. Agent Ambrosius sat silent as a statue in the passenger's seat. He had not uttered a word since they left the crime scene at the translator's apartment.

She had sped through the busy downtown streets of Washington D.C., so many questions running through her head that her mind raced as fast as the sedan's engine. Here she thought her first case might be a simple lost and found, but with the murder of Jackson, it was getting more complicated than she would have imagined. Nothing like having an unexpected homicide thrown into the mix to really make things difficult. Her time in Los Angeles had taught her that.

Beside her, the British agent seemed lost in his own thoughts. He had flashed some sort of identification at the guard as they were going through the security checkpoint, but other than that, had barely moved.

She could not help dwelling on Reggie's reaction to Jackson's bloody message. The look on his face left her cold inside. Blackburn had been her anchor over the last few months. To see him shaken was downright frightening. Reggie scared, that was something she never thought she would see.

Now she was supposed to go talk to Director Smith, when she had no idea who Director Smith was. She'd never met the man.

What she did know was that she did not want to look like a rank amateur in front of Ambrosius. She did her best to put on a confidant demeanor. "Come on, we've got work to do."

They crossed to the elevator. Ambrosius still didn't say anything, which she found strange. He didn't strike her as someone to be at a loss for words. If anything, she'd gotten the impression he was the type who liked the sound of his own voice.

As she slid her ID card, she pushed her hair back from her face. She'd let it grow out to shoulder length, a far cry from the tomboy cut she'd worn in California.

She noticed Ambrosius staring at her as if he was studying her.

"What's on your mind?" she asked bluntly. Politeness could be damned. A man was dead, Reggie was on edge, and she had to meet with the mysterious Director Smith. The time for manners was long past.

"I was wondering if you had picked up on how frightened Agent Blackburn had been back there," Ambrosius said.

"Yeah, I noticed."

"I take it that is rather out of character for him."

"You got that right," she said, not about to stand here and listen to the snob of an Agent put Reggie down. "Agent Blackburn is probably the bravest and best Agent you will ever meet."

She'd been set to debate the virtues of Reggie's ballsiness to the death if necessary, but Ambrosius nodded, conceding the point.

"If Agent Blackburn is as brave as you say, and I have no doubt he is, what could be so potentially hazardous as to have him so worried?"

"I don't know." She exhaled a deep breath wondering the very same thing. "Honestly, I have never seen him like that before."

She punched in her code and they stepped into the elevator. She turned to the camera lens, and without really knowing what to say, repeated the instructions Reggie had given her.

"Special Agent Amy Sommers, I have a Priority Red situation, and need to see Director Smith immediately."

Once the words were out of her mouth, she felt weak in the knees. They had sounded so official, bringing home how serious her case had become.

"You might want to hang on," she said when she noticed Ambrosius standing casually. "This thing picks up speed pretty fast." Following her own advice, she grasped the handrail. As if on cue, the elevator really picked up speed. She laughed at Ambrosius' expression. His eyes looked like they might pop right out of their sockets.

"Told ya," she said after she stopped chuckling.

Her laughter faded as the elevator showed no signs of stopping for almost a full minute. They had to be incredibly deep underground. She had a momentary image of the doors opening onto downtown Hong Kong. She could not decide if the thought was funny or terrifying.

Finally, the elevator slowed. When the doors opened, instead of seeing China, she was looking at reception area identical to the one she saw when she came in for her training, except for the receptionist sitting behind the desk.

What if it was one big hoax? Maybe the Agency was actually only a couple of floors and they used the elevator to throw people off, like some kind of elaborate hi-tech carnival ride. It seemed like a lot of trouble to go through, but with the Agency anything was possible.

This receptionist was in her mid to late fifties, with gray hair pulled back in to a tight bun. It gave her a stern look, reminding Amy of the Hollywood version of an old schoolmarm.

Before she could even introduce herself, the receptionist spoke up.

"Agent Sommers, Director Smith is expecting you. He asked if you and Agent Ambrosius would wait for him in the conference room. "Despite the woman's stern visage, her voice held a gentle grandmotherly quality. Since the floor had the same layout, she already knew which door belonged to the conference room, and probably could have found it with her eyes closed. It gave her a weird kind of déjà vu. The last twenty-four hours had brought her full circle. She had started the previous day in training within a conference room, and now here she was again a day later heading to a similar room, except this time she would be briefing Director Smith on a dangerous problem.

"I bet you didn't think you would be caught in the middle of a homicide investigation when your bosses handed you this case," she said as she and Ambrosius took seats on the far side of the table from the door. "I know I sure didn't."

"I have learned over the years to expect every case to take a wild turn at some point," Ambrosius answered. "Then again, it is the unexpected which gives you and I our jobs."

"Good point," she said. She was getting ready to ask him about his previous experiences working for his own country's version of the Agency when the sound of the door opening stalled her.

A man in a charcoal gray suit entered. Presumably, the Director. He had a salt and pepper crew cut and sideburns, neatly trimmed. He stood approximately 6'0 and was a lean 185 pounds, in exceptional shape for his age, which she guessed was in his sixties, though to the untrained eye he would appear much younger.

Everything about him screamed ex-military. He had a dominant presence which demanded your attention, a man used to giving orders and having them followed. Just seeing him gave her the overwhelming urge to stand and salute.

When he closed the door and focused his full attention on her and Agent Ambrosius, she did stand. Ambrosius also rose to his feet, either imitating her behavior or as if he too felt the need to show the respect Director Smith's presence seemed to command.

She looked into the Director's eyes to try and get a read on him, and was shocked by their intensity. They were the deepest blue she had ever seen, as piercing as if he had the ability to look into the deepest recesses of a person's soul and judge their character by what he found there. His gaze fell upon her and she had to momentarily look at the glossy surface of the table to gather her thoughts again before she could look back up.

"You must be the Agent Sommers I have been hearing about," the Director said, after pausing to look her over. "Agent Blackburn speaks very highly of you."

He had a deep, almost baritone, voice. It was a voice used to commanding. Even a whisper coming from the Director would be like a drill sergeant barking out orders. Everything about him, from the way he moved, dressed, and spoke, oozed control. Here was a man used to being in charge.

She did not know what to say to the unexpected compliment. The Director's presence had sucked some of her own self confidence away like a black hole. This was the first time in her adult and professional life she truly felt intimidated by the mere presence of another person. It left her more than a little flabbergasted.

"Uh...thank you sir," she said, finally remembering she could speak. "This is Agent Ambrosius from the British Agency."

"Yes, Agent Ambrosius, I spoke with your Director yesterday. It is a pleasure to have you aboard. I have the feeling we are going to need all the help we can get on this particular case."

"Thank you sir," Ambrosius said. "I hope I can be of service."

He sounded comfortable, completely at ease, as if he was simply talking to a comrade instead of someone so intimidating. This only reinforced her belief there was more to Agent Ambrosius than met the eye.

She felt the Director's powerful gaze fall on her again once he was seated. "Agent Sommers, I understand you called a Priority Red."

"Yes sir, I did," she said, feeling like a school girl addressing a principal. "I was following Agent Blackburn's instructions. He asked me to come and speak to you and to say we had a Priority Red situation. To be completely honest, sir, I'm not sure what Priority Red means."

"Needless to say, it's a serious situation which requires urgent and immediate attention," the Director said. "If Agent Blackburn deemed it necessary, then I am sure he had good reason. Why don't you tell me everything that happened, so I can see how best to respond."

"Excuse me sir, but does this mean there has been no contact from Agent Blackburn?" she asked.

"Not as of yet."

She nodded. She hadn't expected Reggie to have called in just yet, but she was hoping he might have been able to clear things up quicker than expected. Some friendly support would have been nice.

She proceeded to tell the Director everything she knew, starting from the point where Reggie first told her she had the case. When she got to the events leading up to this meeting, Agent Ambrosius also spoke up, providing additional information, and giving his own point of view. Together, she felt the two of them did a respectable job of giving the Director the whole story.

If she'd expected some sort of an emotional display in his reaction, she would have been disappointed. The Director remained calm, cool, and collected as he leaned back in his chair and steepled the fingers of both hands in front of his face.

After a few seconds of mulling over all they had told him, he spoke. "Are you absolutely certain that what you saw was the word 'ghost'?"

"Yes sir, I am one hundred percent positive," she said. Why was this so disconcerting to everyone?

At this point, Ambrosius surprised her by asking, "Exactly who or what is this 'Ghost,' Director Smith?"

"That is the million dollar question," the Director said. He leaned forward, resting his arms on the table. A frown furrowed his brow. "For starters, the Ghost is perhaps the most dangerous individual in the world. He is the top international assassin money can buy." He paused, and Sommers knew he was about to divulge some information that would be the most troubling of all. "And, he is a former agent."

Her eyes widened and her mouth dropped open as if she was saying "ah" at a doctor's office. Ambrosius looked startled as well.

A former agent? No wonder Reggie was so upset! she thought

The Director waited for the importance of his revealing words to sink in before continuing. "His real name, though you will not find this information anywhere, is Thomas Granderson. He joined the Agency around the same time as Agent Blackburn. The two were rather close, as I recall."

She began to understand Reggie's reaction back at the crime scene. This Ghost was obviously a part of his past, and sometimes having to unexpectedly face your past could throw anyone off their game. She continued to listen intently as Director Smith continued his explanation.

"Agent Blackburn and Granderson completed their training together, and early on even worked a couple of cases together. As you know, Agent Sommers, agents generally handle cases alone, but there are always exceptions."

"Yes, I know," she said. "My exception is sitting right next to me."

She meant her statement as a joke and was glad to see Ambrosius smile. So, the man had a sense of humor after all. She had been worried he was going to be a stick in the mud, but at least now she knew he could take a joke. The Director, on the other hand, seemed a little perturbed.

"Sorry sir," she said.

"Yes, well, a little levity never hurts, I guess," the Director said. "I do believe, however, there is a time and place for everything, and we have more important business to discuss here. Wouldn't you agree, Agent Sommers?"

"Yes sir," she said, mentally kicking herself for letting her mouth get her in trouble. Here she was with a Director of the Agency, and she was making wise cracks.

"As I was saying, the Ghost, Granderson, worked successfully with the Agency for the better part of a decade. There were no outward signs of his intentions during that time. One day, he was assigned a case, and he never returned." The Director paused as if deciding how much more he should say.

"What kind of case was it?" Ambrosius surprised her by asking.

In her opinion, if it was pertinent, then she and Ambrosius needed to know everything, but she also knew this was not how the Agency operated. It was built on secrets, and those who were the keepers of those secrets, like Director Smith, would not have an easy time giving anything away. He must have decided in their favor, because he went on.

"The actual case was not as major as many of the cases we handle. Granderson was assigned to go to Mexico and inspect an archaeological site which had recently been unearthed. There were some rumors circling about a few of the artifacts. His job was to inspect the objects, and if any turned out to be anything other than what they were supposed to be, he was to bring them back to the Agency for research and safe storage. Like I mentioned earlier, he never returned."

"What about the artifacts?" Sommers asked. "What happened with them?"

She felt her face get warm and knew her cheeks were turning red when the Director smiled and nodded his approval. Being accepted by Director Smith was important to her. The man simply radiated an aura, and she could not help but be swept up in its wake.

"The artifacts turned out to be quite normal. Except for one, which, coincidently, also disappeared. It is this item, a gold bracelet, which we believe allows Granderson to do the things he has done."

"You said this Granderson is probably the most dangerous man in the world. Why is that?" Ambrosius asked. "Does it have something to do with this bracelet?"

"Yeah, and what is this about him being an assassin?" Sommers asked.

"According to an Aztec text also found at the site, the bracelet was a gift from Mixcoatl, a god of the hunt. It supposedly gives the wearer the ability to blend into any environment, making them virtually invisible. Within six months of Granderson's disappearance, there were a couple of high profile assassinations pulled off. One was a Russian mafia leader in Moscow and the other was a Saudi oil tycoon. Both of these men were murdered right under the noses of some of the best security money could buy. There was no evidence of the killer. It was as if he was able to walk through walls; hence the nickname the Ghost."

"So let me get this straight," she said, trying to put all the pieces together. "This Granderson steals a magic Aztec bracelet, disappears from the Agency, and then opens up his own little murder for hire business?"

"That about sums it up pretty succinctly, Agent Sommers," the Director said.

"So what did the Agency do about all this?" she asked, but before Director Smith could answer, the door to the conference room opened

"They sent me to find and bring Granderson in," said Reggie Blackburn.

"Reggie!" She was about to barrage him with questions, but he held up his hand to stop her before she could get started.

"I was able to handle everything with the local authorities," Blackburn said, but she knew it was more for the Director than for her or Ambrosius. "We won't have an official cause of death for another twenty-four hours, but from the look of it, Jackson had some kind of heart failure. The old guy took a pretty good beating before he died, though. If I had to guess, I would say he was tortured. There was no sign of the document either. Whoever killed Jackson took it with them."

"I think we both know who killed Mr. Jackson," the Director said, a grave tone in his voice. All of a sudden, it felt like the air had been sucked out of the room. The tension level rose by the second, and if it continued to increase, they would need the proverbial knife to cut their way free.

"So what happened when you went after the Ghost, Reggie?" she asked, trying to bring the stress down to a more manageable level. Unfortunately, her question had the opposite effect, especially on Reggie.

"I chased after him across the globe for the better part of a year," he said. "The killings continued every couple of months. I almost had him in Singapore, but that was as close as I ever got. After that, he dropped off the map. The killings stopped, and he seemingly vanished. I figured with the money he made, he probably retired somewhere secluded. Granderson always did have a thing for money."

"It would seem he has decided to become active again," the Director said.

"So, what does this all mean?" Sommers asked no one in particular, but it was Director Smith who answered.

"It means you and Agent Ambrosius will be on the next flight to Boston. It means we have to find that sword."

She shared a look with Ambrosius, and saw fierce determination etched across his face. This got her own blood pumping. She felt re-energized, like a bloodhound with a fresh scent. She glanced at Reggie, but the look of concern he was leveling her way only fueled her desire to get moving even more.

She slammed her palms down onto the shiny table top, and pushed herself to a standing position. After looking into the eyes of each of the others, she knew what she had to do.

This was her case, but by solving it, she just might be able to lay to rest a personal demon from Reggie's past. It was the least she could do after everything he had done for her. She was not about to let him down.

"All right," she said. "Let's get to work."

CHAPTER 12

Once the meeting with Director Smith concluded, things began moving very quickly.

Sommers and Ambrosius were assigned drivers to take them to their respective places to pack a few items, then deliver them to an airport, where a private Agency plane would fly them to Boston.

It all happened at such a whirlwind's pace, Amy did not have time to speak to Reggie. She wanted to grill him about this Ghost character. Instead, she had to watch helplessly as Director Smith whisked him away.

"What just happened?" she asked no one in particular, left in the lobby with Ambrosius, still trying to get her head around the craziness this case had become.

"Apparently we are going to Boston," Ambrosius said.

"Gee, thanks for enlightening me," she said sarcastically. "I'm sure glad you're here to fill in those all important blanks."

She could not help but smile when he leaned his head back and laughed. With all that had happened, it seemed the perfect response to sum up how she felt. She joined in, and soon both were giggling like junior high school girls talking on the phone.

The receptionist's voice pulled them out of their moment of mirth. "Your cars are ready."

Not only did the elevator begin moving without her telling it where to go, the ride back up did not take as long as their earlier descent. It only strengthened her theory that the whole contraption was a well orchestrated ruse to keep agents from becoming too familiar with the inner workings of the Agency.

Two black sedans were waiting for them in the parking garage. As she and Ambrosius exited the elevator, the driver of each car got out of their respective vehicle, and opened the rear driver's side door for their passengers. Their movements were so synchronized, they might have spent countless hours practicing the routine.

"Agent Sommers," Ambrosius said. "I will see you in a couple of hours."

"Sure thing," she said. As he started walking to his ride, she called out, "Agent Ambrosius, don't forget to bring your gun this time."

She smiled as he turned and fired off a salute in her general direction. The guy did seem to be loosening up. It would have been nice if Reggie could accompany her, but if he was going to be wrapped up handling the details from this end, then at least she would have someone. Ambrosius may have not been her first choice, but he appeared to be as dedicated to solving this case as she was, and that was all she could ask for.

Thomas Granderson, the Ghost, sat comfortably in his window seat, waiting for take off. The document he had taken from Steven Jackson was secured in a leather attaché case resting on his lap. It was still a good fifteen minutes until departure, which would put him in New York some time in the early evening.

He took a sip of the Jack Daniels whiskey the pretty flight attendant had brought. She had been receptive to his flattery, and he knew if he continued to lay on the charm, he would have a pleasant diversion before they landed.

Even though everything was going according to his plan, there was a nagging feeling in the back of his mind, a tugging sensation trying to tell him something was not as it should be. Like a good hunter, he always listened to his instincts; they had never steered him wrong.

Things had gone too smoothly. The death of the translator was the only blemish on this otherwise spotless mission. He had intended for the man to die, just not factored in the possibility of a heart attack doing his work for him. Perhaps that was the cause of this annoying sensation

Had Jackson given up the city's name entirely too easily?

He finished off his whiskey in one final gulp. The potent drink helped clear his head. He leaned back and closed his eyes to mentally replay everything. Checking off every detail as he remembered them, he kept coming back to Jackson offering up New York City as the hidden location of the sword.

Torture could be an effective tool when conducting an interrogation, but was often a long, drawn-out process. He had barely begun when Jackson blurted out the information. The man had started showing signs of a coronary within minutes of having his pinky finger removed. Was he so weak, or was he far craftier than the Ghost had given him credit for?

The nagging in his head intensified, and then it hit him.

Jackson had known he was dying. He knew what was happening to him, so why help his tormentor in his last few minutes of life? In a last act of defiance, the translator had tried to throw him off the correct path.

Jackson spoon fed him false information, and in his own haste to beat Blackburn to the punch, he had eaten it up like a rich dessert. How could he have been such a fool?

When the pretty flight attendant returned to ask if he wanted another drink, he was gathering his things.

"Sorry, honey, maybe some other time," he said, before exiting the plane.

Amy wasted no time in packing her bags for the trip.

She had no idea how long her stay in Boston would be. If fortune was favoring her, she could wrap things up and be back by tomorrow. She knew better than to be too optimistic, however, and so she packed accordingly.

The time slipped by quicker than she anticipated. She was zipping up her carry on when the *Halloween* theme began chiming. "Your chariot awaits," Blackburn said when she answered.

"Did you get demoted?" she asked. "Or was Director Smith so impressed with my powers of observation that he recognized true investigative talent and decided only a senior agent was an acceptable choice to be my driver?"

"Cut me some slack, Sommers. Are you ready to go or what?"

"Yeah, I'm ready. I'm on my way down right now," she said, feeling better now that she would have the opportunity to talk to Reggie.

She grabbed her bags and hurried out. When she saw Reggie standing at the rear of the car, she had an overwhelming urge to hug him. She was so happy to see him; she did not even notice the chill in the air which had been following her all day.

"You ready?" Blackburn asked.

"Let's do it," she said, tossing her bags in the trunk and slamming it shut.

"What can you tell me about this Granderson?" she asked, once they were on the way to the airport.

Blackburn tensed up at the mere mention of the name. "He's dangerous. And when I say dangerous, I mean the worst possible kind."

The seriousness in his tone left no doubt. She got the distinct impression he was actually scared for her, and this simple fact frightened her even more.

"What's the whole story here, Reggie?"

"First of all, there has been no confirmation this is even Granderson we are dealing with. All we have are the scrawling of a dying man to go by. For all we know, Jackson could have been referring to something completely unrelated. I mean, jeez, the guy was in the throes of a major heart attack."

"You don't really believe that though." It was a statement of fact not a question. She noticed how he was gripping the steering wheel so tight his knuckles were powder white. After a long pause, Blackburn confirmed her suspicion.

"No, I don't. This has Granderson's stink all over it."

She could see the private airport up ahead, and knew their time for discussion was running out.

"Look Reggie, whatever info you can offer here would be helpful," she said.

"Everything Director Smith and I have told you is true," Blackburn said. "Granderson is a killer. Why he would be interested in something like this, I can't say. But since he is obviously tied in with this case, it raises the bar. You watch your back in Boston, Sommers. Granderson won't hesitate to kill you or anyone else to get what he wants. What happened to Jackson is only a small taste of what he is capable of."

She stared out the window blankly. She'd wanted to glean some valuable insight into who Granderson really was, but all she had gotten was a few dire warnings. Their conversation had left her feeling more frustrated than anything else.

A large hangar came into view. It looked like a long white warehouse with a small office attached and a tower standing off behind. Sitting out in front was a strange looking little plane. She assumed this was to be her and Ambrosius' ride.

The plane was white with red striping, had a long yet stubby body with a pointed nose, and two sets of wings: a small set jutting off either side of the nose, and the more traditional pair sticking out from the sides. It was this larger set of wings which carried the twin engines. The whole thing had a very foreign look to it.

"It's a Piaggio P180 Avanti II twin-engine turboprop," Blackburn said, like she was some sort of private plane aficionado and understood everything he had just said.

"I guess this is the part where I am supposed to be impressed," she said, smiling at the look that Blackburn leveled at her. "As long as it gets me to Boston in one piece, I really don't care about the particulars."

Reggie did not respond. Usually he liked to play along, matching her sarcastic comment for sarcastic comment. When he did finally speak, the sound of the apologetic inflection in his voice caught her attention.

"I have to be honest with you, Sommers. I tried to get you taken off this case. I did everything in my power to persuade Director Smith to hand it over to me."

She could not believe what she was hearing. She was so shocked she found she could not speak, which, for her, was a first. She never in a million years thought Reggie would betray her like this.

"I can see by the look on your face you're mad as hell at me," Blackburn said. "You probably have a right to be. It's not that I don't think you can't handle this. It's just that Granderson is a mess the Agency should have cleaned up a long time ago. A mess I should have cleaned up. I don't feel right having you get caught in the middle."

Hearing his words took some of the sting out of his confession, but only a little.

"You're just going to have to trust me, Reggie," she said, feeling a bit like a child who just found out there was no such thing as the Easter Bunny.

He removed a folded sheet of paper from his coat pocket and handed it to her.

"This is the name and number of a college professor. I did some research, and this guy is supposed to be one of the foremost authorities on the Arthurian Legend. Maybe he can point you in the right direction once you get there."

She took the offered note, and put it in her own pocket without looking at it. She was still angry, and did not want him to see how appreciative she was of his gesture. He was still her best friend, and in all honesty, her only true friend at this stage of her life, but his betrayal had hurt her and she was not going to be quick in forgiving him. Another black sedan pulled into the parking lot next to theirs. Ambrosius got out, retrieved his bags from the trunk of his vehicle, and shot a questioning glance in her direction as if to ask if she was ready. He then began making his way to the awaiting plane.

She was on the verge of following Ambrosius' example when Reggie surprised her even further by reaching out and softly grabbing her hand. It looked so small compared to his massive paw.

"I know you're pissed, Sommers, but don't let your anger cloud your judgment. If things take a bad turn in Boston, or just plain get crazy, don't hesitate to call. If you need me, I'll be there. Agency protocol can be damned."

Still upset, she was genuinely touched by his sentiment. She had never seen Reggie act like this.

"Thanks, Reggie," she said. Then, without another word, she exited the vehicle.

She stood out in the crisp air and tried to get a handle on her emotions. She knew Blackburn was only trying to look out for her, but still, he had no right to go behind her back, to try and get her taken off the case especially knowing how hard she had worked.

She grabbed her bags slinging them over her shoulder and slamming the trunk with more force than was necessary. It was her way of letting Reggie know things were still not right between them. A childish display, she knew, but she could not help herself. Without waiting to see if Reggie had even noticed, she headed towards the plane. "Are you all right?" Ambroisus asked as she drew closer.

"I'm fine," she answered. "Let's just get this show on the road."

They boarded the plane together without any further ado.

The image of Reggie sitting in the sedan holding her hand like a doting father was still burned into her head, and she feared it would haunt her for the remainder of the case. She had been so excited and grateful when he had told her she had been given the investigation, but all that excitement was gone. In its place, a strong sense of resentment was growing. She could only hope that seedling of harsh emotion would not take root and grow into something worse.

An Agency aide welcomed them aboard, took their bags, and led them to the back of the plane where a living area was set up. Though smaller, the Piaggio was nicer and definitely cleaner than Amy's own apartment.

The aide was a young man in a tailored navy blue suit, who might have looked like an anchorman for the evening news if he'd been a little older. As it was, he had the look of fussy perfection.

When he spoke, his voice was pleasant, and his spiel was well rehearsed.

"We will be taking off soon, so I do ask that you take a seat and buckle in. Once we are in the air, feel free to move around. If you get hungry or thirsty, there is a well stocked refrigerator across from the baggage storage. If you need anything else while we are in transit, push the call button on the wall next to the table, and I will be happy to assist. By the time we land, I will have arranged transportation and lodging for you. Do you have any questions at this time?"

"Nope, I think you got it covered," she said, impressed with his efficiency.

With a respectful tilt of his head, the aide did an about face, and walked to the front of the plane, disappearing from their view.

"Ten to one says that guy was an Eagle Scout," she said.

"I think that would be a fool's wager," Ambrosius said dryly.

There was a crackle of electricity from a speaker located somewhere in the ceiling before the recognizable voice of the aide announced, "We will be taking off in five minutes. If you have not done so already, please take a seat and strap yourselves in now. Thank you."

"At least he's polite," she said, sitting in the closest chair and fastening the seat buckle tightly around her waist. Ambrosius nodded indifferently as he chose the chair directly across from her and buckled his own safety harness.

With a low hum, the Piaggio's twin engines began to warm up. Slowly, the plane began moving and the hum turned into a high pitched whine as the pilot throttled the engines. They picked up speed until the landscape outside the windows became a colorful blur. With a slight lurch, the landing gear left the runway, and Amy's stomach bottomed out like it always did when she drove over a hill too fast, and she knew they were airborne. To confirm this, she peeked out the window again, and watched as the private hangar got smaller and smaller.

They reached the desired altitude. The pilot leveled the plane out, and the ride became so smooth she could barely tell they were moving at all. She had one last flash of disappointment concerning Reggie's reaction before the intercom crackled again.

"You may now feel free to roam about. We will be landing in Boston in roughly an hour and a half's time. Enjoy your flight."

She did not move right away, but Ambrosius quickly unbuckled his seatbelt and stood up.

"I am going to raid that well stocked refrigerator. Care to join me, Agent Sommers?"

"No thanks," she said. "I think I'm going to get some rest. I get the feeling we may not have another chance once we hit Boston running. Do me a favor, though, and wake me before we land."

"Certainly," Ambrosius said.

She unbuckled her own safety restraint, and leaned into her chair, surprised by how comfortable it was. She rested her head against the cushion and closed her eyes. This day had left her exhausted both emotionally and physically. She hoped things would get better once they touched down in Boston. Within seconds after closing her eyes, she was fast asleep.

CHAPTER 13

She felt as if her eyes had only been closed for a few seconds when the distant sound of someone calling her name intruded into her slumber. In a half sleep and half awake state, she could not be sure if it was real or part of a dream. The force of someone physically pushing her shoulder, however, brought her fully back to consciousness.

She opened her eyes and the blurry image of Agent Ambrosius materialized. It took a moment to remember where she was, but the soft hum of the Piaggio's twin engines brought it flooding back to her.

"I take it we are almost there," she said, between yawns.

"The pilot just announced we would be starting the final approach shortly, and asked that we get buckled in," Ambrosius said as he took the seat directly across from her.

She glanced out the window and noticed the light was starting to fade. Ironically, this would match her mood, as it too was growing steadily darker.

She wanted to stand up and stretch out her tight muscles. Dozing off in the plane's chair had left her feeling stiff and sore. But, since they were so close to landing, she re-buckled her safety belt. She could deal with the uncomfortable feeling for a little while longer.

"You know, I could really use a drink," she said. "What do you say, when we touch down, you and I go find a bar or maybe even a restaurant?"

"I think you just read my mind, Agent Sommers."

She smiled, about to elaborate on exactly what she was going to order and how much she was going to drink when the pilot's voice came over the intercom.

"We have the airport in sight, and will be landing in a few minutes. If you have not done so already, please buckle yourselves in. Thank you and I hope you enjoyed your flight."

She could tell by the barely perceptible butterflies beginning to flutter away in her stomach that they were starting their descent. Within a few minutes they would be back on the ground. It could not come fast enough as far as she was concerned. She found herself gripping the armrests of her chair so tightly her hands began to cramp. At the sight of Ambrosius sitting calmly like he did not have a care in the world, even giving her a little smile when he noticed she was looking his way, made her let go of the armrests and fold her arms across her chest, hoping she was giving a similar appearance of unflappable nonchalance.

The Piaggio rocked a few more times and rolled to a stop. The whine of the twin engines lessened as the pilot switched them off. She let out a long slow breath. It was not that she was afraid of flying, but she always felt better once she was back on solid ground like God intended.

Their personal flight attendant returned, as fresh and fashionable as ever.

Is it some male gender trait? she wondered. *Let them look great, while I feel like something the cat just hocked up?*

"I hope your flight was satisfactory," the attendant said.

"Oh, it was just peachy," Sommers said, finally able to stretch out some of the kinks in her tired muscles. The attendant either did not hear her or he simply chose to ignore her sarcasm all together.

"Once you retrieve your baggage, I would ask that you meet me outside. An Agency car has been prepared for us. I will take you to your hotel so you can get checked in. I will leave the car with you, and take a cab back here. Once you have completed your business here in Boston, contact the Agency and I will make the necessary preparations for your return trip. Do you have any questions for me?"

When they didn't, the perfectly coiffed attendant turned crisply on his heel, and went to open the doors for them

"Helpful little toady isn't he?" she said.

"Quite." Ambrosius got their bags from the baggage compartment. "Now, how about we go see about that drink."

"You know, Ambrosius," she said taking the offered bags and slinging them over her right shoulder. "I am really beginning to like the way you think."

They made their way to the front of the little plane; where a chill wind blew in through the open doors. Sommers stood in the doorway at the top of the steps with her head held high, letting the cold air wash over her face and clear some of the leftover fuzziness from her abbreviated nap out of her mind. She felt immediately better despite the daunting task ahead.

The private airport looked identical to the one they had departed from back in Washington D.C. For all she knew, they had flown in a circle and landed in the same place. It reminded her of the elevator rides of varying lengths back at the Agency.

"Agent Sommers, if you are ready?"

She looked over at the flight attendant, now turned chauffeur, by another familiar Agency black sedan. Even with the brisk breeze blowing, the man's hair was still perfect, without a strand out of place. She would have bet a tropical storm would not have fazed the guy's 'do.

How much gel does he have to use to achieve that level of hair perfection? she wondered, knowing only that it had to be an enormous amount.

Ambrosius had already seated himself in the rear of the sedan, waiting for her. She handed the perfect-haired assistant her bags, and got in. It was time to take this traveling freak show on the road.

She leaned back into the backseat and tried to relax. All she wanted to do was get checked in, grab something to eat, and get some serious rest. Neither the driver nor Ambrosius had much to say, but Sommers did not mind. Right now, she gladly welcomed the silence.

She hadn't thought to grab a pair of gloves, as a result, her hands were freezing. She slipped them into the pockets of her overcoat. It was then she felt paper and remembered the note Reggie had given her.

She removed the note from her pocket. It was a small piece of paper torn from the notebook she had often seen Reggie use, folded in half, hiding whatever was written upon it. She stared at the paper for several long moments, thinking about how they had parted ways.

Seeing his handwriting only reinforced that. For such a large and burly man, he had near perfect penmanship. It was such an odd contrast to his often gruff personality. The note read: Professor Jack Foshay, English Literature Department, Boston University. Underneath this was a phone number, presumably to his office.

It was closing in on 6pm and she figured the Professor would probably already be gone for the evening, but, with nothing really to lose, she took out her cell phone and dialed the number.

Her movement caught Ambrosius' attention and he asked, "Who are you calling?"

"I'm following up on possibly our only lead," she said

An answering service picked up on the other end of the phone after three rings. "You have reached the office of Jack Foshay, Professor of English Literature. I am currently away from my desk, but please feel free to leave a message. I will do my best to get back to you as soon as I can. Thank you."

There was a brief silent pause followed by an annoying drawn out beep.

"Professor Foshay, this is Special Agent Amy Sommers of the FBI. My partner and I are in Boston following a lead in an ongoing investigation. We were hoping we could meet with you at your earliest convenience, and that you might be able to provide us with some background information which could prove valuable to our case," she said, also giving her own cell phone number so the professor could return her call.

She was surprised by how young the professor's voice had sounded. When she thought of English Literature teachers, the stereotypical image of an ancient stuffy bookworm came to mind. This guy, on the other hand, sounded more like he should be a student. It really did not matter either way as long as he could help them in some manner.

She felt Ambrosius staring at her, and when she looked over at the British agent, she smiled when she saw the questioning look on his face.

"Agent Blackburn slipped me this professor's name and number before we left Washington. He is supposed to be some kind of King Arthur expert. If the sword is in Boston, this guy might be able to help."

"An expert," Ambrosius said. "I hope so." There was an odd skeptical tone in Ambrosius' voice as he made his comment, and a look of righteous indignation on his face. For the life of her, she could not figure out why.

They drove through Boston and stopped in front of the Hilton The driver let the car idle as they stepped out. The wind was not as strong as it had been, but the temperature was still icy cold. She was shivering by the time she and Ambrosius moved to the rear of the vehicle to retrieve their bags.

"Agents, if you would follow me, please," the driver said. Mr. Perfect Hair handed over the keys to a parking valet, and then waved them toward the entrance.

"Shall we?" she asked Ambrosius.

"I believe we shall," the British agent said, motioning for her to take the lead.

The lobby of the Hilton Hotel was huge, and tastefully decorated in a 1920's art deco style. Their Agency assigned attendant, aide, driver, or whatever his title happened to be, was at the front desk, already checking them in. He was helpful, Amy had to admit, but she was getting the distinct impression she and Ambrosius were being handled. The sooner he, his placating pleasantries and his styling gelled head were gone, the better.

"Agent Sommers and Agent Ambrosius, you will be staying in rooms 305 and 307," he said, handing each of them their room keys. "When your case is completed or if you need to return to

Washington or travel to anywhere else, contact me through the Agency and I will make the arrangements for you." At this point, the aide handed her a business card. It was plain white with only a phone number printed on it. He also handed her the valet ticket for the sedan. "If you do not have need of anything else, my cab will be arriving shortly."

With that, he turned sharply and walked back out into the early Boston evening. She stood a little taken aback by the abruptness of his departure, though she could not say she was sorry to see him go.

"Gee, I didn't even get the chance to say goodbye," she said. Out of the corner of her eye, she saw Ambrosius smile at her joke. "What do you say to dumping our bags in our rooms, and finding out if this place has a decent restaurant? And, more importantly, a bar?"

"I would have to say that is the best plan I have heard yet," Ambrosius said.

CHAPTER 14

The hotel's restaurant had filled to near capacity in the short time it had taken them to drop off their bags and return to the lobby. The rumblings coming from her empty stomach reminded Amy it had been awhile since she had last eaten. This day had been so chaotic there had not been time to sit and enjoy a meal. It started to catch up to her as what little strength she was doing her best to maintain waned. The incredibly appetizing aromas did not help either, making her head spin.

One look at Ambrosius, and she could tell he was experiencing the same dizzying effect.

"I don't know about you, but if we are made to wait, I might have to shoot the maitre d'," she said.

"If you do, I don't know how they could call it anything other than a justifiable homicide," Ambrosius said.

"Good, as long as we are in agreement then," she said before walking to the restaurant. She did not bother to see if Ambrosius was following. At this point, it was all she could do to keep from sprinting like a school aged kid running to get to the front of the line on pizza day in the cafeteria.

The restaurant was called Caliterra Bar & Grille. According to a sign in the front window, it specialized in California and Tuscan cuisine. She planned on putting that claim to the test. As a former resident of the Golden State, she was pretty familiar with the food it had to offer. To be honest, though, she was so hungry they could serve her an old boot smothered in gravy and she would have devoured it and probably asked for seconds.

The maitre d' did not know how close to death he came when he paused while looking for a table for her and Ambrosius. She was sure they were going to be told there was a wait, but as luck would have it the restaurant was not completely full. They were led to a table large enough to seat four towards the rear of the place. The noisy clatter of the restaurant's other patrons enjoying their own meals followed them.

The warm lighting only added to the comfortable ambiance. Under different circumstances, she would have considered Caliterra's atmosphere to be romantic, but she had no intention of being prim and proper. Her plan was to scarf down a steak and guzzle back a couple of drinks in a very unladylike manner.

Their waiter, young enough to be in college and good-looking enough to be a magazine underwear model, approached before she had to resort to eating her napkin.

"May I start either of you off with a drink?" he asked. He wore the customary black slacks, white dress shirt, black vest and black bow tie, with a white apron tied around his waist which included a pocket for his order pad. He had wavy brown hair with matching eyes. She also caught the glint of a diamond stud earring in his left ear.

"Yes, I'll have a scotch neat," Ambrosius said.

She could not help but chuckle at the sound of near desperation in her partner's voice. She felt for him, though. It had been a long day, and a drink would definitely hit the spot.

"And I will have a rum and Coke with lots of ice," she said, foregoing her usual cold beer. She was in the mood for something a little more potent.

"Very good. I will be back with your drinks and take your food order," the waiter said, before doing an about face.

"So, Agent Sommers," Ambrosius said, catching her off guard as she looked over the menu. "What do you know about this expert you called earlier?"

She thought for a few seconds before responding. "Not much really, other than the fact he is a professor at Boston University.

All Agent Blackburn said was the guy is supposed to be one of the foremost experts on the Arthurian legend."

Ambrosius had been doing his own perusing of the menu, but peeked over the top with the same look of skepticism that he had shown in the car. She was about to question exactly what his problem was, but the waiter returned with their drinks and her only thought returned to the basic necessity of food. She ordered a 12oz. New York strip steak, medium rare, with a baked potato and a side salad. Ambrosius decided on the pan roasted Atlantic salmon and a bowl of clam chowder. No matter what else transpired with this investigation, they were at least going to eat like royalty this evening.

She had just taken her first glorious sip of her rum and coke when her phone vibrated on her hip. She did not immediately recognize the number.

"Hello?" she said, some annoyance in her voice.

There was a pause on the other end. She was on the verge of saying "hello" again, this time a little more forcibly, when a familiar-sounding voice finally answered.

"Uh…yeah, I am looking for Special Agent Amy Sommers."

She had a sarcastic comment on the tip of her tongue about being interrupted during her dinner when it dawned on her where she had heard the caller's voice before. It was Professor Jack Foshay.

She cleared her throat in an attempt to cover up the attitude she had already thrown his way, and did her best to sound as professional as possible.

"This is Agent Sommers speaking."

"Oh, hello, Agent Sommers, this is Jack Foshay from Boston University. You left a message for me to contact you."

She could hear his uncertainty. It was not every day a college professor was contacted by the FBI, or in her case a Special Agent working for an ultra secretive Government agency posing as a FBI agent, so he was probably a little nervous.

"Yes Professor, as I mentioned earlier when I called, I was hoping you might be able to help us. My partner and I are here in

Boston working an investigation with some literary connections. We were told you might be able to offer some insight."

"Well, of course I will do whatever I can, but I'm not sure how much help I will actually be."

"You might be surprised, Professor," she said, trying to sound encouraging. "It might be some small piece of information you provide which will blow this case wide open. When could we meet?"

She thought she could hear pages being flipped and guessed the Professor was looking over his calendar. She hoped he did not expect them to make some kind of an appointment for next week. She and Ambrosius needed to speak with him as soon as possible if they were going to have any hope of finding the sword before the Ghost did. "I just finished with my last class for this evening. I know it is a little late, but if you and your partner are available, we could meet in roughly an hour."

"That would be perfect," she said trying to keep herself from sounding like an excited teen who had just been asked to the senior prom by the captain of the football team. "We are staying at the Hilton on Broad Street. Why don't you meet us in the bar?"

"I will see you then, but again, I must reiterate, I don't know how much help I can be."

"Why don't we just wait until we can speak face to face," she said.

"Okay, Agent Sommers. I will see you in an hour," the professor said before hanging up.

She clipped her phone back to her belt, and took a long sip from her drink. The ice had melted somewhat, but she barely noticed. The weariness of a few minutes ago was gone, replaced by a renewed energy. Maybe this impromptu meeting was a portent of things to come with this investigation. Foshay's willingness to meet with them so soon was the first positive thing that had happened since she had first been told she had been given this assignment.

The male model/waiter returned with their side dishes. She knew Ambrosius wanted to ask about her phone conversation, but the lure of his steaming bowl of clam chowder was too much. Instead of giving her the third degree, he began spooning the soup into his mouth like it was going out of style. To her own credit, she was spearing her salad with her fork as if it might try to escape from her plate.

A short time later, the waiter returned again, this time bringing their entrees. She stared at her beautiful steak as if it was the Holy Grail and not simply a piece of meat, then smiled at the irony of the thought. Ambrosius was equally as enthralled with his own food. She watched with humor as he laid into the Atlantic salmon with as much vigor as a drowning person desperately trying to grab hold of a lifeline.

"I can see you are taking your time to savor the moment," she said, mocking Ambrosius for his haste. "But, you might want to eat faster, if that is even possible. We have a meeting with Professor Foshay in less than an hour."

Ambrosius paused in his chewing long enough to stare at her like he was trying to decide if she was joking or not. She watched as he swallowed the bite in his mouth, and then laughed as he tried to stifle a very ungentlemanly like burp without much success.

"Well, I guess there is no time like the present," Ambrosius said, resuming his unfettered attack on a now mutilated salmon.

"My thought exactly," she said, starting her own little private war on the steak.

Things were starting to pick up, and the investigative itch was tugging at her once again. She could feel it, the tides of this case were about to turn.

The same time Amy and Ambrosius were ordering their respective drinks, Reggie was at the bar of his favorite tavern enjoying his own adult beverage of choice, an ice cold bottle of Bud Lite. He had driven straight to the Pug, a little boxing themed tavern he often frequented when he needed to get away, after dropping Sommers off at the airport to catch her flight to Boston. He had been so disappointed with himself, and for how their last meeting went, he decided the only cure would be a steady stream of alcohol.

He knew he had let Sommers down by trying to get her taken off the case. He still felt like he had done the right thing, but that did little to massage away the guilt settling on his already overburdened shoulders. Sometimes he really hated this job, and especially hated the decisions it forced you to make in regards to the people you cared about.

"Screw it," he mumbled, as he took one last long pull from his beer, finishing it off. He slammed the bottle back down on top of the well-worn and scarred bar to get the bartender's attention. When she looked up, he motioned for her to bring him another.

The bartender, who may have been attractive in her day, but now looked beaten down by a hard life and had nothing left to show for it except accelerated ageing and feeling constantly tired, nodded in understanding.

"You don't look like a very happy camper," she said, placing another bottle on a fresh coaster.

"That's a very astute observation," he said, taking a drink. "They teach you stuff like that at bartender's college?"

Her already wrinkled brow furrowed even more as a deep frown settled on her worn face.

"Look guy, I get paid to serve drinks, not to care about your crap, so if you want me to serve you any more beers, I suggest you lose the attitude." She moved to the other end of the bar, where apparently the other patrons were more friendly.

"Well, I guess I'm just pissing off everyone today," he said, more to himself.

He nursed his beer without speaking to anyone else, uncomfortable, his large frame not meant for something as scrawny and unsteady as a barstool. He had to shift his weight periodically to keep his back from cramping, which only added to his annoyance, and soured his mood even more.

He thought about giving Sommers a call, but dismissed the notion. If he knew her, she would still be angry and in no mood to speak with him anyways. At this point, he figured she would see it as meddling or that he was checking up on her, and that would only serve to anger her even further.

He tried to get the whole mess out of his head, but even after several beers, he could not stop dwelling on it. This case stunk from the ground up. He had pushed to get Sommers on it, and now she was running around Boston completely blind, with a stranger for a partner. To top it all off, she was being hunted by a killer he himself should have stopped a long time ago.

He was not a man who normally felt guilt. He usually did his job and then walked away, letting the consequences fall where they may. This time he could not simply let it go. Sommers was his friend, and he had practically thrown her to the wolves; walking away from this one was not an option he could live with.

This was now completely Sommers's case, so, according to Agency policy, he could not interfere. But that did not stop him from trying to dig up more information which might prove beneficial.

Even with his brain somewhat muddied by the effect of the alcohol, he knew with pristine clarity what he had to do. The only place where he might find some answers would be to return to the proverbial scene of the crime. He would go back to Jackson's apartment and do some snooping around.

He paid his tab and left a generous tip for the bartender for having to put up with his downward spiral into depression and poor manners. The near freezing temperature outside helped sober him up. That and his sense of duty and loyalty to his friend were leading him back to where this God awful day had begun.

He crossed the street toward his car with a single minded determination. He was going to find something to help Sommers, even if it took him all night.

CHAPTER 15

From the glances thrown their way by the restaurant's other patrons, Sommers knew she and Ambrosius must have caused quite a comical scene, tearing into their dinners like they had just been rescued from a deserted island and this was the first real food they had eaten in years. With all the chomping, slurping, and belching, they probably were closer to resembling a couple of gremlins eating than a couple of respectable government agents. She could not bring herself to care however. This meal was the first good thing she had experienced in awhile.

Their bill, in her opinion, looked more like the gross national product of a small country than the tab for a couple of dinners, but she had to admit, the food was well worth the cost. Their waiter pointed them toward the bar, through a set of double doors to the left of the restaurant's entrance.

As they walked through the dining area, she noticed the other customers were still staring. She nodded and smiled in mock politeness at as many as she could, not really in apology for her or Ambrosius' poor manners while eating, but more to acknowledge that she knew she had been rude, but those who were staring were being equally as rude in their own behavior.

The Caliterra's bar resembled more of an upscale New York City gentlemen's club than it did an actual pub. It was decent sized, about half full, and they made their way around a haphazard layout of tables to an empty booth. If there had been a faint odor of cheese on the air, she could have almost believed she was the rat caught in some alcoholic's version of a maze.

When they finally reached their destination, she slid into the booth without waiting. Ambrosius remained standing, looking over in the direction of the bartender.

"I'm going to go to the bar and order us a couple of drinks," he said. "Would you like the same as you had with your dinner?"

"Yeah, you know what they say, if it isn't broke, don't fix it," she said.

She stole a look at her watch. It was nearing 7:30pm, which meant the professor should be here any minute.

Even though she had an unobstructed view of the bar's entrance, she wondered if a table would have not have been a better choice for their meeting. The booth would offer a little more privacy for them to speak with Professor Foshay, but it was not overly large. Things could get cozy real quick depending on how large of a person the professor was. She was considering switching to one of the closer tables when Ambrosius returned, carrying a glass in each hand.

"Any sign of this professor?" Ambrosius asked, placing her drink on the table and sliding into the seat across from her. "I did tell the man behind the bar we were expecting someone so he could send them our way when he arrives."

"Not yet," she said sipping at her second rum and Coke of the evening. "It hasn't quite been an hour yet, though."

As if on cue, the bar's double doors opened, and then closed. Even though she had never met the man before, she knew right away the bar's newest patron was Professor Foshay.

She fell back on her LAPD homicide detective training as she quickly sized him up. Early thirties, short dark brown hair. Black-framed glasses caught the bright lights behind the bar, obstructing her view of his eyes. He was of medium build, perhaps 190 to 200 lbs., and stood roughly 5'10.

He was dressed in what she considered to be the standard uniform for college professors these days: blue jeans, black pullover shirt, brown loafers, tan corduroy sports jacket with the requisite patches on the elbows. Even having never seen him before, she was pretty sure she could have picked Professor Foshay out of a crowd.

She was trying to get some kind of read on his behavior so she might better know what to expect in the way of cooperation, when he turned and looked her square in the eyes. His gaze was friendly but intense. It made her uncomfortable, and also guilty, like she had been caught staring at someone with a disability. She averted her eyes quickly before realizing she had not done anything wrong. It made her wonder how the professor's students felt, having the man direct his focused attention on them on a regular basis. She did not envy them if he carried that intensity with him into class, that was for sure.

"I think that's our guy," she said as the man walked over to the bartender, who motioned in her and Ambrosius' direction.

"I believe you're right," Ambrosius said, having witnessed the same exchange.

Sommers and Ambrosius stood as he approached their booth.

"Professor Foshay?" she asked.

"Yes, that's me," the Professor said forcing a nervous smile onto his face.

"I am Special Agent Amy Sommers," she said, flipping open her ID. "And this is my partner, Special Agent Ambrosius."

She could not help but notice his curious glance when she introduced the British agent. "Ambrosius? That is a rather interesting name," the professor said, after shaking hands.

"Thank you," Ambrosius said dryly.

"May I ask, is it Welsh?"

Sommers decided to try and head things off before Ambrosius became even surlier.

"Why don't we all have a seat," she said, motioning for the professor to sit down.

He sat where Ambrosius had been sitting minutes before. She moved back a step so the British agent could take her spot on the opposite side of Professor Foshay, and she took a seat right next to him so that they could both look at the professor while they talked.

"Yes, it is Welsh," Ambrosius said, surprising her by answering the question.

Foshay nodded as if confirming to himself that his guess had been correct.

"May we get you a drink?" Sommers knew from experience that people were more forthcoming with information in a friendly environment than they were in a confrontational atmosphere.

"No thank you," he said. "Maybe I will have one in a minute, but honestly, I am curious as to why the FBI would need my help."

"We have it on good authority that you are an expert on Arthurian legend," she said, watching closely so she could gauge his reaction.

At first, he looked somewhat confused. Then, to her amusement, he tried to downplay his expertise.

"I don't know if I would describe myself as an expert. I have studied the literature, and written several papers on different aspects of the tales. I also teach a literature class which focuses on Arthurian legend as you put it, but so do several other literary professors."

"Well, that is more than I have done. So, in my book that makes you an expert," she said.

"Speak for yourself," Ambrosius muttered under his breath. He did not acknowledge her reprimanding look. Instead, he paid more attention to his drink.

To his credit, the professor did not take Ambrosius' bait. "Who gave you my name?"

She decided the truth was the best approach, but she would need to put some spin on it to match their FBI cover story.

"When we realized the case we are working on was going to bring us to Boston, our research department discovered you might be someone who would have information which could prove helpful."

"I don't know if I should be flattered or worried that the FBI deemed me a person of interest," he said jokingly, but she could tell by the slight waver in his voice that it was less of a joke than he wanted her to believe.

"You're not suspected of any wrongdoing, Professor, we just need some information."

She wanted to instill a level of confidence so he would be more apt to open up. She did feel for the guy, however. Had she been unexpectedly asked to meet with a couple of FBI agents, real or otherwise, she would have been on the defensive as well.

Her statement seemed to have the desired effect. She could see the professor relax a little. He shifted his weight so he could get more comfortable, and leaned forward, folding his hands and sitting them atop the booth's table.

"Okay, Agent Sommers, how can I help you?"

"For starters, what can you tell us about the sword Excalibur?'

He leveled his intense stare at her once again, his handsome face turning into a confused scowl. He looked around the bar like he was expecting some kind of hidden camera crew to pop out and yell "surprise". She knew this whole conversation was going to seem surreal to the Professor, but her patience would only stretch so far.

"Let me get this straight," he said. "The FBI wants to know about Excalibur, King Arthur's sword?"

"That's correct, Professor," she said sternly. "Now can you help us or not?"

"I guess so. What is it exactly you want to know?"

She looked over at Ambrosius to see if he had anything to add, but apparently his scotch had become the focal point of his universe.

"I'm not that familiar with the stories. Maybe you could start with a brief overview," she said.

His intense look seemed to gain more power with every passing second. Now that he was sitting a few mere feet away from her, she got a pretty good look at the man's eyes. They were the darkest brown she had ever seen. They were so dark in fact, they were almost black. Under different circumstances. she would have found them to be compelling and attractive. The lenses of his glasses only seemed to focus their intensity even more. She was so caught up in their stark beauty she almost missed the beginning of the professor's explanation.

"Well, obviously Excalibur was the sword of King Arthur," he began. "But, it was not the Sword in the Stone like most people believe."

This comment seemed to pique Ambrosius' interest. He shifted his gaze from his now empty glass to the professor. She was glad he was at least partly paying attention now, without her having to give him a swift kick in the shin.

"I thought Arthur pulled Excalibur from the stone, thus becoming king. Hasn't that always been the legend?" By his tone, Ambrosius seemed to be testing the professor rather than simply asking a question.

"That is the Hollywood version, Agent Ambrosius, but according to most of the literature, especially the post-vulgate stories, the sword Arthur pulled free from the stone was broken in a fight with King Pellinore. Arthur was then given Excalibur by Merlin the Magician and the Lady of the Lake as a replacement. Supposedly, Excalibur, or Caliburn as it was called by Geoffrey of Monmouth, was forged in Avalon, or Otherworld as it is sometimes translated. As with many supposedly magical swords of that era, Excalibur was created by Wayland, who was the blacksmith to the Gods, similar to Vulcan in Greek mythology. The Irish refer to the sword as Caladbolg. The Welsh, as Agent Ambrosius may know, call it Caladvwlch. Both of these roughly translate as hard lightning."

Ambrosius smiled, looking at the professor with a new found respect. It would seem his knowledge had won the British agent over. She had to admit she was equally as impressed. Reggie was right; this guy just might be able to help them after all.

She noticed Forshay begin to visibly relax, his whole demeanor changing after giving his brief explanation. He seemed no longer on edge, as if sitting here and discussing a topic he obviously knew a lot about had made his comfort level rise. The way he spoke about the sword gave her a better understanding of his passion for the subject. At first he had been hesitant, but once he got going, she witnessed his enthusiasm growing. He was not just giving them information by spewing facts at them, but was trying to teach them at the same time. She got the distinct impression he was actually enjoying himself.

"According to the stories, what happened to Excalibur?" she asked.

"Well, most of the legends tend to agree that one of Arthur's knights, a Sir Bedivere, was given the task of returning the sword to the Lady of the Lake," the professor said.

"Why him?" she asked. "Why not one of the more famous knights you always hear about that are associated with King Arthur?"

"This was after the Battle of Camlann when Arthur defeated Mordred. Arthur himself was gravely wounded. Sir Bedivere found him on the battlefield as he lay dying. Arthur then gave Bedivere Excalibur and told him to throw it in a lake, and then return and tell him what Bedivere witnessed. Bedivere, who was naturally reluctant, takes the sword, but could not bring himself to throw such a valuable weapon away. He returned to Arthur's side and initially lied about throwing Excalibur into the water."

"Why does he lie?" she asked interrupting. She was completely caught up in the tale at this point.

"He didn't want Arthur to die, and he knew the power both symbolic and literal Excalibur held. By keeping the sword, Bedivere thought he could save both king and kingdom."

"So the legends say this Bedivere keeps Excalibur?" she asked, wondering how this related to the piece of information about the fabled sword now residing in Boston.

"At first," the professor said. "Supposedly, after returning to Arthur's side two times, and begging Arthur to reconsider and keep the sword, on the third attempt he finally throws Excalibur into the lake where it is caught in midair by the Lady of the Lake before disappearing back into legend under the surface of the water. There is an interesting debate among Arthurian scholars as to what lake it might have been. The leading candidates are Dozmary Pool on Bedwyn Moor and the lake at Pomparles Bridge near Glastonbury."

"And what side of the argument would you choose, Professor Foshay?" Ambrosius asked.

The two men stared at each other like a couple of prize fighters sizing each other up at the weigh in. At first she thought Ambrosius' attitude was merely male ego, but now she was not so sure. He acted like he was on the defensive about something, his every question seeming to be leading in some way, or trying to give Forshay enough rope to hang himself with.

But, so far, the professor had managed to keep his neck out of the noose. Whatever the dynamic building between the two was, it struck her as more than the proverbial male pissing contest.

"I guess if I had to choose, I would go with Pomparles Bridge since it is so near Glastonbury," the professor said.

"What is so special about Glastonbury?" she asked, and was surprised when it was Ambrosius and not Professor Foshay who answered.

"Glastonbury is home to Glastonbury Abbey, which is where the grave of King Arthur is located."

She looked at him. It would appear he knew more about the subject matter at hand than he had let on. She was just about to call him out on it when the professor chimed in with his own new found admiration for the British Agent.

"That's right, Agent Ambrosius. King Henry II supposedly unearthed Arthur's tomb. Many of the historical papers I have seen seem to agree that the grave is indeed of a local chieftain who went by the name of Arturius. I have even seen reports which say that this Arturius may have been close to seven feet tall, which would have been almost unheard of during that time period. Many believe this is where the legend of King Arthur sprouted from. I actually have plans to visit the site next summer."

Sommers sat back in the booth, trying to take all the information in. She took two long sips of her drink, welcoming the calming effect the alcohol had on her. She mulled over the new details the professor had given them. It was all very interesting, but really had no bearing on their case. She needed to know how

Excalibur got to Boston and more importantly if it was here, where it was hidden.

She did not know if it was a side effect of her rum and Coke as well, but the more she listened to the professor speak, the more she liked him. He was clearly an intelligent man, but in a modest way. She also liked the way his exceedingly dark eyes seemed to sparkle when he was discussing a topic he was passionate about. Her mind drifted enough to wonder what those eyes might look like in a more personal setting.

Catching herself she shook her head and put the glass containing her drink back on the table, vowing not to take another sip.

"That is all very interesting, Professor," she said, getting herself back under control. "But could you tell me why an IRA terrorist cell would be interested in Excalibur, and maybe even more importantly why they would be looking for it here in the U.S.?"

Her question left him dumbfounded. A wide range of expressions played across his face. Ambrosius was equally as interested in the professor's potential response, waiting and watching Foshay closely.

"I...uh...," he stammered. "Wait a minute. Is this what this meeting is really all about?"

"Yes," she said. "Several days ago a three man IRA terrorist team was apprehended. In their possession was a document which just so happened to mention the location of Excalibur. This document was then stolen by who we believe to be someone in the employ of the same IRA group."

"But the sword isn't real, Agent Sommers. It's only a myth, a fantasy legend," he said, though she thought she picked up on the slightest trace of what she could only describe as hope.

"Look, it doesn't matter if you don't think the sword is real or not, Professor Foshay. The IRA terrorists who came to this country did, and the man they hired to find Excalibur has already murdered one person. That, I can tell you is very real."

She could see the Professor did not know how to respond to this strange turn. One minute he had been in his element, giving them a history lesson on Arthurian legend, and now he was smack in the middle of a murder investigation. She knew from first hand experience how unsettling the situation could be.

"I'm sorry, Agent Sommers, but this seems a little out of my league. I mean terrorists? I'm just a college professor. I'm not sure what you want from me."

"Look, Professor," she said, "We are not asking you to strap on a gun and badge and join a posse. We just need information. So far, you have been very helpful. Now could you give us any idea why the IRA would be willing to go through all the trouble and expense of trying to find a sword, which, as you say, is only a legend?"

She could not tell if he was trying to come up with an answer or trying to decide if this was some kind of sick joke. She thought she had made her point perfectly clear that this situation was serious, deadly serious. He must have been able to pick up on the grave tone of the moment because he finally answered her question.

"The only thing I can come up with at this time is also the most obvious answer," the professor said.

"And what exactly would that be?" she asked, steadily losing her already strained patience.

"Well you see, Agent Sommers, according to legend, whoever is able to possess Excalibur is the rightful king of Britain."

This last statement seemed to suck the air out of the room. All the background noises vanished, and the only sound she was still aware of was the raspiness of her own breathing. She felt rather than saw Ambrosius' attention switch from the professor and land on her. She turned to look at the British agent, who nodded in affirmation.

Things seemed to fall into place, even though it was unresolved, this case began to make at least a little sense. Why else would the IRA, even if it was some fanatical offshoot of the once powerful organization, be so intrigued in a legendary weapon? They were going to use Excalibur as the focal point for some strange kind of coup-de-tat.

"I guess we at least know why they are so desperate to get their hands on the sword," she said, breaking the silence that had settled over the booth like a blanket. "But we still do not know why they are looking here."

"Where exactly were these terrorists looking?" Foshay asked with a renewed interest.

"The IRA cell was apprehended in New York City, but we have reason to believe the search for Excalibur has shifted to Boston," she said.

"Are you serious?" He almost choked on his excitement.

The sparkle had returned to his mesmerizing eyes, and she once again found herself caught up in their powerful wake. With eyes like those, he would have made a successful cop. No suspect would have lasted long when forced with an interrogation with Foshay. They undoubtedly would have caved and offered up whatever confession would get the man's gaze to lessen up.

"I'm, very serious," she said, though the smile lurking at the corners of her mouth would have said different. "Is there any way you could tell us how or why Excalibur would be in Boston, and if it is indeed here, where is it?"

"Not right off hand," he said after pausing to think. He was obviously intrigued, and she noticed the doubts he had shown a few moments before had all but vanished. "Let me do some research tonight, though, and I might be able to come up with something for you."

"We are under a bit of a time constraint," she said, disappointed. "The IRA has the document, and their hired gun is actively looking for the sword too. Right now it's a race to see who gets there first, and they have a head start."

"I understand, Agent Sommers. Give me tonight, and I will do my best to get you the answers you need."

She looked at Ambrosius but he remained silent. His behavior through this whole meeting had been so peculiar and borderline rude that she was not all that surprised when he chose not to say anything. Instead of waiting for the British agent to chime in, she made the decision to give the professor the time he requested.

"Alright Professor Foshay, you've got until tomorrow."

"Great. Why don't you and Agent Ambrosius stop by my office at the university tomorrow, shall we say around 10am? Hopefully by then I will have something for you."

"Okay," she said, sliding out of the booth the same time as the professor.

"I will see you both in the morning. Now if you will excuse me, I have a long night ahead of me." He shook her hand before making his way back through the bar and out the double doors. She watched him go with a renewed optimism of her own.

"Well, chatty Kathy," she said to Ambrosius, who was still seated at the booth. "I'm beat."

"The professor was more interesting and helpful than I gave him credit for," Ambrosius said.

"Yeah, he could prove to be the key to this whole crazy mess," she said. "I'm not sure how they do it back in merry old England, but here in the States when you have a face to face with someone who might have valuable information, it is fairly customary that you actually participate."

"You seemed to have things well under control, and as you made it clear to me, this is your investigation," Ambrosius said with a mischievous grin.

"Well, your poor excuse for wit aside, I'm going back to my room to slip into something more comfortable, like a coma. Why don't you meet me in the lobby at 8am and we will go from there?"

"I will see you in the morning then, Agent Sommers."

"Don't stay up too late," she said playfully.

She could not help it, but she was looking forward to seeing the professor again, to see how he would react on his home turf, so to speak. She found herself excited at the prospect of not only seeing Foshay, but possibly getting the information that would let her know where Excalibur was going to be found.

CHAPTER 16

The Ghost took a cab back into downtown Washington D. C., and felt a sense of déjà vu as he found himself standing in front of the brick building which up to recently had been the residence of the translator, Steven Jackson. It had barely been a day since he was last in this spot. He smirked as he remembered how enjoyable his last visit had been.

The wind was blustering, and the early evening had brought with it lower temperatures and an increased chill. The fact his breath appeared in rivulets of frosted mist was evidence of that. When a new breeze kicked up, he shivered involuntarily. He was not in the best of moods, and the cold weather only added to his displeasure even if it did match his demeanor.

At this moment he would have paid big money to be back at his estate in the London countryside, sipping a large brandy and sampling the delights of a young and naïve patron he had managed to seduce from his nightclub. Instead, he was stuck retracing his steps. He had wanted to be well on his way to finding Excalibur by now, but thanks to his own eagerness which had so obviously worked against him, Jackson had pulled a fast one and sent him on a fool's errand.

His smirk turned into a mask of pure hatred when he thought about how he had been so easily duped by the old codger. He wished Jackson were still alive so he could kill him all over again. It would not have been a nice and tidy death, either. He would have made sure the old man begged for a mercy which would not be delivered before the end came.

Thoughts of his imagined revenge continued to run through his head as he walked up to the apartment building's entrance. The intense hatred helped in fighting off the cold. Unlike his last visit, the streets and sidewalks were almost completely deserted. This worked in his favor, he knew. If someone spotted him entering the building a second time, they might recognize him as someone who was out of place. From his experience, those kind of suspicious characters often got reported to the authorities.

He could have fallen into the warm embrace and welcoming grasp of his magic, but since no one was around, he would not need to expel that kind of energy. He may have to call upon the bracelet's power soon enough once he was inside, but that would not be a problem. If all went well, he would be able to locate the information he required fairly quickly, and then be on his merry way before anyone was the wiser.

He entered the building and found himself in the outdated lobby once again. Everything looked much like it had on his first visit. One would never have known a violent crime had been committed a few short floors up from this very spot.

Like the streets outside, the lobby was quiet and devoid of life. That could change at any time, so he did not dawdle. What head start on Blackburn he thought he had was now gone. It had dwindled away thanks in part to Jackson's lie.

"Crafty old goat," he muttered quietly.

He begrudgingly respected the man for being able to out smart him even in the face of his demise. The feeling was fleeting, however, as he still wished he could have one more chance at slitting Jackson's throat and watching his life's blood pool at his feet.

He pushed the elevator button and heard the loud humming and creaking along with a disconcerting grinding noise as the cables were shaken from their stillness and the elevator descended from its perch on one of the higher floors. It landed with an audible thud, and after a longer than necessary pause, the doors slid open with a groan. He shook his head in disgust. Everything about this place screamed ancient. It insulted his modern sensibilities, and it only served to make him hate the dead translator even more.

Since Jackson's apartment was still undoubtedly considered a crime scene, he decided to draw upon the bracelet's power. It would not help his cause if he happened to stumble across any of the building's other residents trying to get a peek at the violence which had taken place under their noses. Or, worse yet, a stray investigator burning the midnight oil and working the case.

He felt the now customary tingling sensation throughout his body, and knew the magic had taken effect. He was now invisible and could go about his business without any worry about being seen or recognized. He could slip in and back out of Jackson's apartment without having to worry about being disturbed.

He was happy to see his worries were for naught, as the fourth floor was deserted. The other tenants were probably settled in for the evening, relaxing before they went to bed so they could get up early for a new day of their pathetic, meaningless lives. The thought made him want to retch. Just the idea of leading such a mundane existence abhorred him.

The door to Jackson's apartment criss-crossed in yellow police tape, marking the spot as an active crime scene. Whoever had posted the yellow tape had been careless enough to leave a large gap at the bottom, which would easily allow him enough room to duck under. The locked door, however, was a problem he would need to rectify.

The last time he was here, he had simply walked into the apartment after Jackson himself had opened the door. Now, he would have to put some of his other talents to work. A Boy Scout he was not, but their motto of always being prepared definitely applied to him.

He smiled inwardly as he removed a small black case from his coat pocket. Inside was everything he would need to pick any number of locks, ranging from a common padlock all the way up to the most sophisticated electronic locks used by high profile security systems. One look at the regular key lock on the apartment's door, and he knew there was not going to be any level of difficulty involved in getting around it.

Removing two small silver items which resembled miniature dental picks, he knelt down to eye level with the doorknob. He inserted the tools into the lock and after several seconds of maneuvering them around, he heard an audible click. Leaving the picks in place, he gave the handle a testing turn. Much to his satisfaction, the door opened.

He waited a few seconds, staring into the darkened interior. Nothing seemed amiss, but he wanted to make sure the place was completely empty before going inside. Once he was positive the apartment was clear, he removed the picks and replaced then in the case, slipping it back into his pocket. Then, bent over low enough to get under the police tape without disturbing it, he let himself in. He quickly and as quietly as possible shut the door behind him.

The interior of the living space was nearly pitch black. The only light came from the glow of the streetlamp outside, causing some odd shadowy images on the ceiling and wall across from the window, but he barely noticed. He was death incarnate and a darkened room did not bother him. In fact, it was where he was most comfortable.

The apartment was unnaturally still. This was the same sensation every residence took on when the person living there died. It was as if whatever made a place a home died with its owner. All that was left was an empty shell which would have given a normal person the creeps, but to him was a compliment to a job well done.

He withdrew from the magic which concealed him and made his way to the Jackson's office without hesitation. If any real answers as to the sword's current whereabouts were to be found, it would be there.

Even though the place was dark, he could still see where the police and detectives had disturbed many items in their desperate search for clues. Jackson had been a neat and tidy person; what some people might refer to as fussy. As a result, his apartment had been immaculate in its cleanliness. Now, however, the place looked like a lazy housekeeper had neglected his or her duties and had hastily tried to clean up before being discovered.

The investigators handiwork could be seen most clearly in the office, which looked like it had been ransacked. Either that or a small and contained explosive device had been detonated. If Jackson could have seen this mess in his private little sanctuary, he would have suffered another major coronary.

The Ghost walked over to the desk, figuring any information Jackson had on his translation would probably be found there. On his previous visit, he had not paid much attention to the room in general. He'd sat quietly, and even napped as Jackson went about his business. It was not until Jackson had seemingly finished the task that the Ghost slipped out of the magical cloak of camouflage the bracelet provided.

Once Jackson blurted out New York City as the sword's location and then had the audacity to die, he had left in a hurry before properly double checking the information. This lack of attention to detail had cost him valuable time. In his haste to get started, he had grabbed the document, thinking it would have whatever details he would need, only to discover Jackson had left no other clues with it. Now he was back completing a job he should have done more thoroughly the first time. This breach in his personal protocol was near unforgivable, and he could only hope it would not cost him in the end.

He turned on the polished silver desk lamp, hoping no one on the street would notice the soft glow coming from a dead man's apartment. It was then he noticed what looked like mini plastic easels not far from his feet. They were the same color yellow as the police tape marking the front door, with black numbers printed on both sides. It was a wonder he had not stepped on them when he had crossed through the room in the dark.

Upon closer inspection he could see the little easels were actually forensic team tools marking several brown and red spots which had dried onto the office's carpet. He grinned maniacally. The spots were the blood splatter from his interrogation with

Jackson. He was on the verge of continuing his inspection of the desk and its drawers when a large cluster of the forensic markers on the floor on the other side of the desk caught his attention.

He stood on his tiptoes so he could peer over the edge of the desk and saw a large garnet-colored stain which looked like it had been applied by a small paintbrush. He was stunned by the realization that what he was seeing was a message.

He walked over to read Jackson's last words scrawled desperately into the carpet more clearly. After seeing what had been written, especially the city name Boston, he was both happy, and angrier than he had been in a long time. In one last great act of defiance, the translator had not only tricked him, but had enough presence of mind to tip Blackburn off as well.

"Bastard!" he said yelling into the silence of the empty apartment. "I hope you're roasting in the deepest pit of hell, old man!"

He was so angry, he was trembling, on the verge of losing control. He took several deep calming breaths, and when he felt the fire in his stomach begin to subside knew he had kept his temper from boiling over. Now that he was able to think clearly once again, he chuckled. Jackson's failure was now complete. The message the translator had left for Blackburn had also found its way to him.

He now knew the city where the fabled sword Excalibur was hidden, but did not know the exact location. Boston was a large city and one of the oldest in the country. There were any number of places the sword could be, and without any kind of reference point, he had no idea where to start. He could spend days if not weeks trying to piece together the puzzle of the blade's secret resting place.

Then it dawned on him, this was exactly what Blackburn must be doing right now. Thanks to the dead translator's last message, Blackburn knew to go to Boston, but not where to find the sword.

The Ghost had a rather pleasant image of the fat agent stumbling around the city, looking like a complete fool, overturning every rock his obese carcass came across. The mirth of the moment was short lived, however. He knew how resourceful Blackburn could be, and the man no doubt was working on some kind of plan.

The document was the key, he knew. Those fools of the *Na Ri`Laoch* along with the powers that be at the Agency believed it was some kind of map which it may very well be, but it might also lay out exactly where the sword actually was.

It was not until he'd examined the paper while on the plane that he realized he had no way of reading it. The actual translation had to still be here, somewhere in Jackson's apartment, and more specifically, here in this room.

From what he was able to recall, Jackson had spent most of his time working on the computer, occasionally standing up to flip through some books located on the shelves directly behind the desk.

Since he had not found anything important in the drawers, the most logical place to look next was the computer itself. He seated himself in the leather chair, which, he noted, was much more comfortable than the one he used in his own office back at his club. He made a mental note to rectify that matter when he returned.

As the system booted up, he had a momentary flash of panic when he realized the information might be password protected, but as the system finished loading, and the desktop came up without any problems or requests of password confirmation, he calmed down It only reaffirmed how much of an incompetent fool Jackson had been. The man had a state of the art computer system with which he used to translate material for the most covert agency in the world, and the trusting old coot did not even bother to create a simple password.

The Ghost spent the better part of the next half an hour running through the computer files without any success. As the minutes ticked by, his frustration grew. He felt ready to put his fist through the flat liquid crystal display monitor, and then toss it out of the nearest window. If he did not get what he was looking for soon, Blackburn might stumble across the sword by sheer blind luck, and that would complicate matters. He could not let that happen.

He was about to give in to his violent temper and lash out at the computer when he noticed an icon in the lower right hand corner of the monitor on the taskbar. He had completely overlooked it before, but now it seemed to be shining like a beacon, calling out for his attention. It resembled a tiny version of the Rosetta Stone, and he knew he had found what he had been so desperately looking for.

He manipulated the mouse so the pointer was directly over the icon and double clicked it. Immediately the special program Jackson used for difficult projects came up onto the screen. It looked unremarkable at first. Disappointment nearly took his breath away and threatened to unlock the fury he had already repressed more than once this evening. Then he saw a program file named simply "Agency". He clicked the file eagerly, anticipating he would finally have the desired translated version of the precious document, but found only more confusion instead.

Inside the file was a series of names with what appeared to be dates listed after them. He scrolled down until he saw Blackburn's name, but the date after it did not make any sense. According to the numbers, something had been referenced with the corpulent Agent's name on March 19, 1973. Why would Jackson care enough about a translation he did over thirty years ago that he would keep Blackburn's name and date all this time? Unless, maybe, the numbers were not a date at all.

He looked at the numbers as they were configured on the screen, 3-19-73. Perhaps there was some kind of password after all. Or, even more likely, a code. He scanned the room for any indication that there might be a safe hidden somewhere, on the off chance the numbers were a combination. He had a knack for spotting items of that nature, but he came up empty.

He surveyed the entire room, taking in every minute detail he could. His gaze came to rest on the bookshelves directly behind him. This was the same area he remembered Jackson pulling books from while working on the document's translation.

He skimmed the titles, trying to glean any helpful piece of information and figure out what he was missing. He had never heard of any of them as they all had to do with ancient languages and cultures.

The answer was here. He felt it so strongly, he could almost taste it. It was like having the answer to a question right on the tip of your tongue, but being unable to spit it out.

There were books of all sizes on the six different shelves that made up the bookcase from floor to ceiling. He looked back at the computer screen, and could see the name of his arch nemesis and the mysterious numbers staring back at him, taunting him. He could almost hear the mocking sounds of Jackson's laughter from beyond the grave. What was the connection?

He looked back and forth between the computer and the bookcase several times before an idea crept into his head, then felt like an idiot for not seeing it sooner.

"It can't be that easy, can it?"

He went to the third shelf and traced his finger down the row of books lined up like well trained soldiers, counting each one as he touched it. When he got to the nineteenth, he stopped This particular book just so happened to be the tallest on the shelf, long enough, in fact, to conceal a standard size sheet of paper.

The Ghost could only shake his head in amusement. What an utter fool Jackson must have been to utilize such a ridiculous method of trying to conceal his work.

He tugged the book free from its perch. It put up a minor resistance, wedged tightly between its two neighboring books. The cover showed a glossy picture of green grass covering rolling hills. The old idiot had actually hidden the document's translation in a book detailing the history of the Gaelic culture and language. He might as well have put up a large red neon sign with an arrow.

As he opened the book up, the spine crackled with age. The ancient translator could have probably related to that before his untimely demise.

On page 73, he opened the book all the way. There, resting comfortably in the fold, was a white sheet of computer printer paper.

He removed the sheet, and tossed the now useless book on the desk. He had what he wanted, his treasure in the form of a single piece of paper.

A large grin spread across his face. He had the name of the city, and now he had the exact location of the sword.

Excalibur's hiding spot was somewhat of a surprise, but nothing that would pose a major problem for him. All he needed to do to put the puzzle together was go to Boston and collect his reward. Then he would snuff out Blackburn's miserable life like the flame of a candle. That was the part of this whole devious scheme he was most looking forward to. Finding Excalibur would be pleasurable, but the dispatching of Agent Reggie Blackburn would be the most gratifying.

He folded the sheet of paper and slipped it into the same inside pocket of his overcoat as the lock picking tools, still grinning like a court jester. The only dilemma facing him now was to decide whether he should try and catch a flight out to Boston later this evening or wait until morning.

The lure of a good night's sleep won out, and he decided to check into a plush hotel. He would sleep in and eat a hearty breakfast, but, first, he would celebrate this evening success.

A muffled rattling sound cut through his reverie like a hot spoon through ice cream.

He knew instantly that it was the front doorknob being turned, that someone had just entered the apartment.

Without hesitation, he called upon the magic of the bracelet and fell into its comforting embrace. Knowing he could not be seen, he moved from the office into the hall. From there he would be able to see who else was now with him in Jackson's apartment.

At first all he could see was the shadow of someone moving around the front room. When this new visitor came into view he immediately recognized the large frame of the last person he expected to see.

He felt a rage like no other encase his body. He wanted to spring into action and do what he did best. It would seem this evening's celebratory festivities were about to begin a little earlier than he could have imagined.

CHAPTER 17

Blackburn drove straight to Jackson's apartment building.

He knew he shouldn't be driving after as many beers as he'd consumed. His head was still a little fuzzy from the alcohol, but he felt like he was thinking clearly for the first time this evening. If he was going to find anything which would be of use to Sommers and her investigation, it would be back at the scene of Jackson's gruesome death.

Luckily, traffic was light. The longer this took, the better the chances of Sommers running into the Ghost, and he could not in good conscience let that happen. Sommers was good, and she was as tough as they came, but the Ghost was a danger she was unprepared to handle even if she thought differently.

The sound of Paul McCartney's voice filled the silence, The Beatles song *Yesterday* pouring through the radio's speakers. Reggie barely paid attention, as his mind was still on the way he and Sommers had parted. He could not shake the feeling the damage he had undoubtedly caused to their friendship might be irreparable.

He had grown accustomed to the loneliness which was an unfortunate side effect of being in the employ of the secretive Agency. He worked alone, lived alone and even socialized alone. Sommers was the first real friend he'd had in more years than he cared to remember, a kindred spirit. She was as dedicated to the cause of justice as he was. She was also the only person he had run across in his 44 years who was even more sarcastic than he was. He had not fully realized how important her friendship had become. He would do anything within his power to salvage that friendship even if it meant breaking every rule in the book. It was the least he could do to save the only friend he had.

This case seemed so innocuous when he had found the document in the run down apartment of the IRA terrorists. He had been so sure it was the perfect one for Sommers to cut her teeth on. The unexpected twist of Jackson's murder and the introduction of the Ghost into the fold however, had really upped the ante.

He could have kicked himself for not anticipating the danger Sommers was now facing. He, better than most, understood the true nature many of the Agency's cases took, how every single one inevitably took a turn into the realm of the bizarre. He had lost count of how many investigations had gone bad before getting better. It was the nature of the beast, so to speak.

But who could have ever foreseen the involvement of the Ghost? This was not the type of thing the former agent turned assassin would be a part of.

That was what scared Reggie the most. If the Ghost was not a part of the hunt for Excalibur to further his own endeavors, then it meant he had ulterior motives, and that could not be good for anyone else involved. Why else would he come out of seclusion for something with no real profit in it?

He parked, made sure he had his ID in case any law enforcement professionals were still at the crime scene, and jogged across the street. He was embarrassed to find himself out of breath when he reached the building's front stoop.

"I gotta lay off the late night pizza runs," he muttered, between gasps of air.

Deciding that, under the circumstances, four flights of stairs would be fatal, he took the elevator. A wave of sadness hit him when he saw the yellow tape around Jackson's door.

He had known the translator a long time. They had worked together on several occasions. Until now, he had been too caught up in the case for Jackson's death to really sink in on a personal level. Standing out here in the quiet hallway looking at the police tape, he had the overwhelming urge to grieve.

Jackson's death was so needless and made no sense. It was unimaginably cruel as well, but that was how the Ghost operated, one of the characteristics which made the assassin so dangerous. As a stone cold killer, the Ghost had no regard for human life.

There was no way Reggie was going to let Sommers face that kind of monster alone, especially after seeing what the murdering bastard had done to Jackson, who was nothing more than a helpless old man.

He plodded down the hall, his feet heavy as the weight of his decision to break protocol rested rather precariously on his massive shoulders. He was out of breath again when he reached the door, though from nervous tension this time.

The Agency had zero tolerance for those who could not follow their guidelines. There was too much as stake to turn a blind eye to those who could not play by the rules. The one tenet above all was that once an agent was given a case, they were on their own. It was there way of maintaining the absolute secrecy the Agency held so dear.

And here he was, intruding on an investigation not assigned to him.

With his big meaty hand, he wiped his brow. Beads of sweat caused from stress were dripping into his eyes causing them to sting. He had not thought it would be this difficult. Then again, when Sommers was involved, nothing was ever easy. A grin spread across his mouth as he flashed on how much a pain in his backside she could be.

"Ah, dammit, Sommers," he said. The grin turned into a large toothy smile as he pulled the yellow crime scene tape down, wadded it into a ball, and slipped it into his coat pocket.

The door was not locked.

He did not think any of the seasoned officers from the Washington D.C. police department would make that kind of careless mistake. It could have been someone from the coroner's office when they had removed Jackson's body, but this too was highly unlikely.

His free hand reached for the reassuring presence of his Agency issue firearm. He pulled it free from its holster, and let the gun dangle casually at his side.

There was something not right about the whole scene. The hair standing up on the back of his thick neck was proof enough of that.

He took one cautious step into the apartment, then another, half-expecting some sort of ambush to take place at any second. His muscles tightened from the tension of having his nerves so on edge. His grip on the 9mm also tightened, and he switched the handgun's safety to off.

There was no obvious sign of another person. As far as he could tell, he was here alone, though every investigative fiber in his body was telling him different.

The only way he was going to assuage those feelings was to do a room to room search. He did his best to make as little sound as possible, at which he was surprisingly adept for a man of his considerable size, as he moved into the kitchen.

Seeing Blackburn rummaging around was the absolute last thing the Ghost had pictured after hearing the door to the apartment scrape open. He had not been sure what or who he would find, but he had been certain this was not it.

His hatred for the man a few feet away from his hiding spot in the hallway was so intense it radiated out of every pore in his body. Blackburn represented everything he, as a powerful international player, abhorred. Blackburn had been the only man to come close to capturing him, a personal slight to his ego he could not let go unpunished.

He wanted to kill the agent so badly he could almost taste the violence he would unleash. He'd savor it like an expensive fine wine. It was all he could do to keep himself in check and not rush out to the living room and pummel the object of his rage to death with his bare hands.

The only thing holding him back was that he did not want Blackburn's death to be over so fast. He wanted to make it last at least long enough to hear the man plead to be allowed to die.

He could tell by the tension in Blackburn's body that the agent was wary, definitely had his guard up. This was clearly evident by the gun being clenched like a security blanket in Blackburn's pudgy hand. It would not matter, however. The imbecile could not shoot what he could not see. The Ghost could slip into the living room as quiet and ethereal as the wraith like figure he was nicknamed for, and take Blackburn by surprise; incapacitating him.

He reached around his back and grasped the finely honed knife he kept hidden on his black leather belt. It was the same blade he had used to remove Jackson's pinky finger and still had some of the translator's blood dried on the blade. One quick and heavy blow from the hilt to the base of Blackburn's skull would take the mammoth of a man off his feet and render him unconscious. Then, the fun could really begin.

He was on the verge of making his move when a nagging thought pushed to the forefront of his brain, begging for an answer.

"Why aren't you in Boston?" he asked in a silent whisper.

Like a jolt of electricity, the answer hit him. Jackson had left the message, but died before he could specify where. Blackburn had come back here for the same reason the Ghost had, to find the sword's hiding spot.

He wanted to laugh out loud, and would have if not for the fact it would tip Blackburn off. They had always thought alike, that was why the agent was a worthy adversary, why Blackburn had almost caught him. It was also yet another reason why he needed to be eliminated, but maybe now was not yet the time. There still might be more to this game in need of being played out.

As he continued to watch Blackburn stumble around in the darkened living room like the bumbling fool he was, the Ghost tried to reason out the curveball this unexpected appearance had thrown him. He knew he could kill Blackburn right now without much difficulty, but something was holding him back. There was more to this story, and he would need to figure it out before he would be able to experience the happy ending he was longing for, the ending which had him standing over the lifeless corpse of one Agent Reggie Blackburn.

If Blackburn was here, that meant someone else must be working the investigation in Boston. The pretty woman he had seen with Blackburn when he had been staking out the translator? She was obviously an agent in training, and from the way she and Blackburn had interacted, undoubtedly his protégé as well.

If he really wanted to torture Blackburn, he would leave the man alive long enough to first witness the untimely demise of the female agent. Then he could dispose of Blackburn, take the sword, and live happily ever after.

He smiled like a kid at Christmas morning as he watched Blackburn move into the kitchen. The stupid agent was so predictable, doing a room to room sweep of the entire apartment. This would give him enough time to leave Blackburn a message, and then exit the premises before the fool was any the wiser.

He returned to the office. It was all he could do to stifle the gleeful laughter he felt building. Things were going far better than he could have ever hoped for.

After clearing the kitchen, Blackburn returned to the living room. He could not shake the feeling that he was not alone. He also had the unnerving feeling he was being watched, even hunted. He tightened his grip on the 9mm. There was no way he was going down without some kind of a fight. He was anything but helpless prey.

He made his way down the hall, stepping cautiously into a spare bedroom which looked more for show than functionality, and smelled musty from disuse. He guessed Jackson did not entertain overnight guests, or any guests for that matter, very often. Still, he had to be thorough in his search.

As he was about to check the closet, as cliché as that was, a soft rustling from out in the hall made him freeze in his tracks. It was the sound of a light footstep walking on carpet. Reggie had to fight down the urge to go charging into the hall like some sort of superhero ready to catch the bad guy.

He stood statue-still instead, listening to the ensuing silence and hoping to catch any other sound. When he did not hear anything else, he took a quiet step of his own toward the hallway. When he heard the next sound, that of the apartment door being shut as someone exited, he did take off at a full and heedless charge.

Like a bull in a china shop, he ran headlong back into the living room, banging his shin against an end table and causing the lamp stationed there to fall to the floor. Thanks to a spin move any NFL halfback would be proud of, he was able to stay on his feet, but still almost crashed into the door shoulder first. If he had, with the momentum he built up along with his massive weight, he would have taken the door off its hinges and landed flat on his face.

Instead, he flung the door open so hard he still almost ripped it out of its frame. With his gun raised before him, ready to fire if necessary, he shoulder rolled out of the apartment and came to one knee in the corridor ready to shoot. He was agile for a big man, which made the maneuver all the more impressive.

It was a good plan, except that the hallway outside Jackson's apartment was completely deserted. Whoever had exited the apartment was nowhere to be found.

The adrenaline rush of excitement intertwined with the potential for danger left him momentarily breathless. He lowered the gun, and got back to his feet, remaining on guard because this whole scenario was having a very Ghost-like feel to it. If this was the case, then things could get real messy quick.

The elevator was still sitting on this floor from when he had ridden it up. His shin throbbed from where he had smacked it on his mad dash through the apartment. He looked toward the stairwell, but knew if the mysterious intruder had taken the stairs, by the time he could get there and check it out, the intruder would be long gone.

The only thing that made sense was for him to return to the apartment and resume his search for any clues as to who the intruder was, and for anything that could help Sommers.

This time, he did not bother with the rest of the apartment, but made directly for Jackson's office. If anything helpful was to be found, it would be in there. Plus, he was positive this was where the intruder had also focused their search.

The office was a mess from the homicide detectives and forensic team. This was not unexpected. What was out of the ordinary however was the pale glow coming from the monitor sitting on the desk. Reggie's heart rate spiked. Whoever had been in the apartment had evidently been trying to crack into Jackson's computer.

He moved around to the other side of the desk to get a better look at the screen. He nearly dropped to his knees as the air in his lungs was blasted out of his chest by the shock of what he saw.

There, written on a blank Microsoft Word document, was a message addressed to him.

Dear Agent Blackburn:

It has been fun watching you creep around this apartment. Though, I do hesitate to use the word "creep" as someone with an ass as large as yours cannot truly "creep" anywhere. Anyway, I wanted to let you know I was around. It would be rude of me not to say hello to an old friend like you, after all.

By the way, don't waste your time looking for the document's translation. I already have it, and will be arriving shortly to collect Excalibur. I thought it would only be sporting of me to give you fair warning however, that I intend on paying your pretty little female friend a visit and showing her my special attention before I complete my business here. That is, unless you can stop me.

See you in Boston.

Sincerely,
The Ghost

For the second time in a matter of minutes, Reggie charged back through the apartment and out the door.

If he played his cards right, he should be able to make it to Boston by early morning. He was not an overly religious man, but he prayed out loud that it would not be too late.

Sitting in yet another dingy little diner much like the one from which he'd first spotted Blackburn and his pretty little pet, sipping an even worse cup of coffee, if such a thing was even possible, the Ghost watched with cruel humor as Blackburn came bursting out of the apartment complex. He laughed loudly as the fat agent literally sprinted to his car.

The other patrons could only stare uncomfortably at the strange visitor. None of them had the nerve to ask what was so funny, for fear of actually finding out. He ignored them like the worthless peons they were.

He finished his cup of coffee, tossed some money on the table, and left without really paying much attention to the way the other diners turned their heads away from him as he walked by.

He had more important details to attend to.

He too was in a hurry. He only had an hour to catch his flight. It would seem he'd indeed be flying out of this poor excuse for a Nation's Capitol after all, except instead of New York, he would be touching down in Boston.

CHAPTER 18

She relaxed on the beach, squishing the cool moist sand between her toes. The light breeze felt good against her face. So did the cool spray from the ocean. The familiar scent of the sea made her feel as safe as if she was snuggled up in her favorite down comforter. It made her feel at peace, like she was home.

The sun was just starting its journey across the sky to where it would inevitably set in a magnificent array of orange and crimson. At the moment, however, the sunshine sparkled like precious gems on the large expanse of blue ocean which stretched all the way to the horizon.

Thinking she would take a quick swim before the sun went down, she stood up, brushing the sand off her lap with both hands. She had to pause and take in a deep breath, so moved by how perfect the moment was. She was on the verge of jogging across the beach and down to the water so she could jump into the welcoming embrace of the ocean, could almost feel the cool water running across her bare skin, when the scene was disrupted by the obnoxious chirping of the bedside alarm.

Amy Sommers rolled over on her side so she was facing the evil device, which had ripped her away from the pleasantness of the dream, and forced her back to consciousness here in the cold reality of her hotel room. After a few seconds of the maddening alarm echoing through her sleep deprived mind, she had had enough.

She slammed her hand down on the digital clock with its bright red numbers, which seemed to be mocking her as they let her know it was 6:30am. The force not only shut the buzzing alarm off, but also knocking the clock completely off its perch on the nightstand. It landed with a crunching thud on the floor. All she cared about was that it had finally stopped the incessant noise.

She sat up and shifted her feet out from beneath the blankets and onto the floor. Exhaustion had completely taken over her body, and she felt like she had barely slept a wink. Her muscles ached like she had just gone three rounds in the UFC with "The Iceman" Chuck Liddell. She knew from experience the only cure was to get up, move around, and consume as much coffee as was humanly possible.

"God, I hate mornings," she said, leaning over and putting her elbows on her knees so she could rub the sleep out of her eyes before attempting to stand up. It was moments like this she missed being the second shift homicide detective back with the LAPD, where going into work early meant not stopping for lunch first.

As punctual as Ambrosius had shown himself to be, she knew if she did not hurry and get a move on, the British agent would undoubtedly show up at her room wondering what was taking her so long. Then he would look at her in the perturbed manner she had seen him use on more than one occasion already in the short time they had been working together. She had no desire to be made to feel like a rank amateur by the uptight agent this early in the morning. It would not set a good tone for the rest of the day.

With that in mind, she went directly to the shower, where she let the hot water ease some of the tension out of her body. The steady stream of steaming water massaged the knots out of her muscles, especially in her shoulders and upper back, allowing her to finally stand erect. It felt so good, if she'd had more time, she would have spent the entire morning in there. As it was, she rinsed herself off as quickly as possible and went back to the dresser where her luggage still sat from the night before. She had been so tired she had not even bothered to unpack.

Representatives of the Agency or law enforcement specialists in general were supposed to look the part of being a professional. She just was not feeling it today, and decided on comfort instead of style. She was trying to locate a mythical sword and avoid an assassin, not walk the runway of a fashion show in Milan. She slipped on a regular pair of blue jeans with a white long sleeved turtle neck shirt. Knowing the weather was likely not to improve, and more snow was probably on the way, she pulled on her black boots. Lastly, she slipped into a black blazer, which covered and hid her shoulder holster nicely.

She spent the next fifteen minutes fixing her hair and make-up, never spending all that long fine tuning herself for the outside world's viewing pleasure. It was hard enough to be taken seriously in the law enforcement field simply being a woman, but if you looked like a dainty super model, you had no chance of being accepted. Instead of being treated like a cop, you became the object of desire, and that was the kiss of death. If you were perceived as weak or helpless, then you immediately became a liability. She was not weak or helpless; a point she had proven time and time again.

A quick glance at the clock, still lying on the floor where she had swatted it to, told her she was ahead of schedule. She still had a half an hour before she was supposed to meet Ambrosius.

She thought about calling Reggie, even though she was still angry. Her cell phone was sitting on the dresser next to her suitcase where she had tossed it before going to bed. She wanted to talk to him, but halfway across the room, she talked herself out of calling. As much as she wanted to forgive the big idiot, her pride and sense of duty would not let her. This was her case. She worked hard to earn it, and he was out of line with his over protective big brother stunt. Still, she would have liked to bounce a few ideas off him.

As it turned out, the decision was made for her. When she picked the phone up, and flipped it open to see if she had any messages, the screen was dark. The battery had gone dead, and she had forgotten to plug it into the charger. Now she would be stuck without a phone for most of the rest of the day.

"I hope you have a usable phone, Ambrosius. If not, we really are going to be on our own," she said.

Since she was ready, she decided to head down a few minutes early. Maybe she could even beat him, and be the one to utilize a disapproving look towards the other's tardiness. This thought put an extra spring in her step as she grabbed her overcoat and exited her room.

She practiced her looks of admonishment she planned on using on Ambrosius in the reflective surface of the shiny brass control panel on her way down in the elevator. She was looking forward to needling the stuffy agent much like she did Reggie. It was one of the perks of the job as far as she was concerned.

It was all for naught when she spotted the British agent casually leaning against the check-in desk. He looked dapper as ever in a charcoal gray Armani suit, as rested and at ease as she wanted to be, and this only served to infuriate her even more.

"Damn," she said, loud enough to garner a few looks from other hotel visitors within earshot.

"Why are you so sour looking this early, Agent Sommers?" Ambrosius asked as she approached.

"Nothing," she said, feeling a little like a child who had been scolded. "Let's just get started."

"Would you like to get something to eat before we meet with the professor?"

"Yeah, I could eat," she said. "Besides I don't think having my stomach growling like an angry jungle cat would be a good way to get in the professor's good graces as he hopefully explains where our sword is at."

Ambrosius smirked. She followed him to the restaurant, unable to shake the feeling she was losing control of this case, and that somehow Ambrosius was now taking charge. There was definitely a new sense of purpose to the guy this morning, and if she was not careful, she might get left in its wake.

They ate a decent breakfast in relative silence. At one point Ambroisus did inform her he'd had their car brought around, and it would be waiting for them when they finished eating. She was glad he had thought of that detail, but again she felt like she was a step behind and losing ground.

From the very start of their partnership back when Ambrosius made his unexpected entrance at her apartment, she had sensed an underlying purpose to his being a part of this investigation. She had the feelings it was more than just finding the sword. He'd played it pretty cool up to this point, but now that they were possibly on the verge of discovering the fabled blade's location with help from Professor Foshay, chinks were developing in Ambroisus' otherwise steadfast armor of crisp professionalism. The calm indifference he seemed to wrap around himself like a security blanket, and wanted her to believe was the real him, was beginning to wear away, and signs of his true nature were starting to show through.

She considered confronting him on it, but discarded the idea. If she pushed too hard, he would merely shut down and re-establish the distance he had been working so hard to maintain. Hopefully, given an ample amount of time, he would trust her enough to explain his ulterior motives, but until then she would let the issue drop. She would rather have him focused and enthused about working the case instead of cold and distant. She was going to need his experience and knowledge to see this investigation through.

"Do you think Professor Foshay will have found anything to help us discover Excalibur's whereabouts?" Ambrosius asked.

The question was out of character for him, and it led credence to her belief that there was something more to this case than simply finding a historical artifact. Since she had just scooped her last bite of scrambled egg into her mouth, she had an excuse to pause and finish chewing before she could reply. This gave her time to come up with what she hoped would be a reassuring comment.

"I can't honestly say," she said . "If anyone could however, it would be the professor. He seems to know his stuff, and was genuinely interested in helping us. If anything else, maybe he can at least point us in the right direction."

Ambrosius nodded in agreement, and in somewhat of a resignation to the fact there was no way to know until they actually met with Foshay. He then slipped back into the introspective silence she had witnessed for the majority of their morning meal.

Her coffee had cooled considerably, but it still tasted like the sweet nectar of the gods. She lamented not having her favorite travel mug to take with her, but figured if absolutely necessary, she could stop off on the way and get a cup to go. There had to be a Starbuck's around here somewhere.

Ambrosius moved what was left of his eggs Florentine around the plate with his fork. He still appeared deep in thought, but with the caffeine starting to kick in, she was ready to get moving. She had no intention of sitting around waiting for Ambrosius to snap out of his personal little reverie.

"Hey, earth to Ambrosius," she said, waving her hand in front of his face. "Are you done eating or what?"

"Huh? Oh…uh…yes. I am ready as soon as you are, Agent Sommers."

"Good, then let's go," she said standing up.

Ambrosius followed her lead, but she could see the man was still distracted. It was starting to make her fell a little anxious herself.

"Are you ok?' she asked. "It's like the lights are on, but nobody's home with you this morning."

"I'm quite all right, Agent Sommers. This case has brought back a few…memories for me. If we are able to succeed in finding Excalibur, it could mean the end of a long journey," he said.

"Well, speaking of the journey, why don't we get moving on it," she said, trying to keep the mood light. She was reassured when he smiled back at her.

True to Ambrosius' word, their car was waiting for them right out in front of the hotel. She was still unaccustomed to this kind of preferential treatment, but could find herself getting used to it rather quickly.

Of course, back in Los Angeles, she had never needed to worry about dashing across a parking lot through freezing temperatures and then having to wait for what felt like an eternity for the car to warm up before getting any kind of heat. Then again, being a part of the Agency in Washington meant she never had to worry about her gender getting in the way of fair and equal treatment. With everything she had seen and experienced in her short time with the

Agency, they appeared to have no hidden political agenda. Their only concern and duty was the innocent people they protected.

After adjusting her seat and strapping on her seat belt, she put the sedan in gear and pulled out of the Hilton's lot.

"Do you remember how to get there?" Ambrosius asked.

"Yeah, the professor gave us directions last night before he left, remember."

"I do, but that was not my question. I wanted to make sure *you* knew where you were heading."

"Is this your way of telling me you wanted to drive?" she asked, defensively feeling the blood rush to her face.

"Not at all, Agent Sommers. Besides, you Americans have the nasty habit of driving on the wrong side of the road," he said smoothly. He paused, then added a last dig which she knew was meant to irk her. "It's quite uncivilized of you."

"Why you stuck up British blue blood," she said, acting as if she was truly hurt by the mock insult. "It's no wonder we kicked your snobbish hides back across the ocean, or should I say the pond."

"Touché," he said, accepting defeat.

She could not help but smile at how deftly Ambrosius had been able to not only get her frustrated to the point of anger, but then defuse the situation with an offhand joke. It was nice to see him acting more like the agent she had arrived in Boston with instead of the gloomy and distracted guy who had sat across from her during breakfast.

The traffic was congested as the morning commuters made their way to work, though it was nothing like what she had experienced back in Los Angeles, and it moved along at a good pace. The large stone edifice that could only be Boston University came into view after only ten minutes.

She drove around the large campus until she came to 725 Commonwealth Avenue, the address for the College of Arts and Science. The whole school had an old European design which she was sure Ambrosius found to his liking, though he did not say anything. It reminded her of pictures she had seen of some of the older prestigious Ivy League Universities like Harvard or Yale. Somewhere in that impressive-looking structure was Professor Foshay's office, and hopefully the information leading to the hidden location of Excalibur.

There were several empty spaces in front of the building. They were clearly marked as faculty parking spots, but she pulled into one anyway. She was in a hurry and figured if anyone decided to make a stink, she could always flash her badge.

Though the outside of the college had a medieval castle look to it, the interior had been updated and decorated to modern standards. A heavy silence fell over the place, like being in a large library.

Professor Foshay's office, Room 115, was down the hall, around the corner, and the first door on the left. The quiet began to grate on her nerves and close in on her, making her feel claustrophobic. Where before she'd been reminded of a library, she now had the ominous feeling of being in a morgue, or, even worse yet, a tomb.

What is it about this case? No matter what, things always turn to the topic of death.

She could only hope this was not some portent of what was to come.

They found Foshay sitting at his desk, poring over several books which lay open before him, so focused on his materials he did not even notice them arrive. Sommers waited a few seconds more to see if he would look up, then knocked loudly on the door frame.

The sound cut through the oppressive silence like a deer rifle in a meadow. The professor jumped, knocking books to the floor. She felt bad for startling the man, but when he looked up and met her stare with his intense eyes, all was forgotten. In fact, she forgot to speak, and it was Ambrosius who stepped up.

"Professor Foshay, it's Agent Sommers and Agent Ambrosius. May we come in?"

"Oh, yes, of course. Come in and please don't mind the mess," the professor said.

The office was not overly large, and what space was available was crammed with books, some of which looked to be pretty old. Sommers was no expert by any means, but guessed that many of the ancient-looking tomes were collectables and probably valuable. There were no decorations other than a poster-sized portrait of a man dressed in Renaissance clothing. It hung on the back wall behind the desk, giving the appearance that the man was overlooking the office.

"That's Sir Thomas Malory," Foshay said, evidently noticing and answering her unasked question. "He is considered by some, myself included, to be the father of Arthurian legend. It was his book, *Le Morte d'Arthur*, which brought the stories to the forefront of the literary world."

"Ah, I see," was all she could think to say, interrupted by a snort of derision from Ambrosius.

"You disagree, Agent Ambrosius?" the professor asked.

"Let's just say, I have a different perspective, Professor," Ambrosius said.

"If you say so.," When neither she nor Ambrosius did not ask anything else, he offered, "Please, have a seat."

The chairs were surprisingly comfortable. Sommers thought she recognized the design as being ergonomic, and wondered how many students had sat in this same seat and faced the professor's intimidating gaze. Under the right circumstances, the man's eyes could be inviting, but she would bet her paycheck if the guy was angry and dressing down a student, those same eyes could put the fear of God in a person.

"I'm sorry for the disorganized jumble you see. I kind of lost track of time, and forgot it was so close to our appointment. I am usually a little better prepared for any guests.," the professor said with a sheepish grin.

"No problem, Professor," she said. "If you think this is bad, you should see my apartment."

"Yes, well maybe the next time I'm in the neighborhood," he said.

She was so taken aback her voice caught in her throat. It became one of the rare moments in her life when she did not have a snappy comeback. Instead, it was Ambrosius who recaptured the moment and put everything back in perspective.

"Maybe you two can set up a social gathering at another time. We are here strictly on business. Were you able to come up with any information for us?"

"Uh…yes…well…um…" He stammered and tried to regain his composure.

She took a measure of comfort in his face turning a nice shade of crimson which undoubtedly matched her own. She could tell his comment had been completely out of character for him, and getting caught by who he thought was an FBI Agent was probably tantamount to getting caught feeling up your high school sweetheart by her father. If she was not so embarrassed herself, she would have laughed at the predicament they now found themselves in.

"To answer your question, I would have to say yes and no," Foshay said.

"I think I might have been able to answer half of what you asked for last night, and I may be able to help with the second half even though I do not have a definitive answer."

"What do you mean?" Ambrosius asked.

Sommers heard the concern creeping into his voice. She knew, because she was experiencing a similar sensation.

"For starters," the professor began, "I believe I know how Excalibur may have gotten here in the U.S. and specifically Boston, but I was unable to find any mention of a specific location."

Ambrosius slumped in his seat, defeated, and clearly disappointed. Sommers could sympathize. She too had expected to walk out of this meeting with the answer in her grasp. Still, Ambrosius seemed to be taking the news rather hard.

"Why don't you tell us what you've got?" she said, keeping one eye on Professor Foshay, and the other on Ambrosius.

"There are many references to Excalibur sprinkled throughout the history of the British monarchy. This is not surprising, as I am sure many of the English kings would have claimed to be in possession of the sword to help justify their own reigns. I am also sure there were many replicas forged, and then passed down from generation to generation. This is actually pretty common knowledge."

"How does any of that help us?" she asked.

"I was getting to that," the professor said in what she guessed was a tone he reserved for an impatient student.

She could not help it, but this thought made her smile, which she knew the Professor would notice.

"According to legend, Sir Bedivere threw Excalibur back into a lake where it was caught by the Lady of the Lake." He launched into what she figured was his lecturing voice. "So I based my premise on: what if Bedivere didn't throw the sword back, but instead kept it? Even in the legend, it says it took him three times before he could bring himself to give up Excalibur. What we do know is that following these events, Bedivere becomes a hermit and dies shortly after."

"Is it weird for a knight to suddenly become a hermit?" she asked. "Sounds like the work of a guilty conscience to me."

"Very strange behavior indeed," the professor answered. "The only explanation I have is maybe he did keep the sword, and passed it on to the monarchy in hopes of healing the land. From there things get kind of sketchy and there is not much mention of Excalibur until it turns up in the hands of King Richard I, the Lionheart, around 1190. King Richard, it is also widely rumored, was a distant cousin to Sir Bedivere."

At this point in the conversation, Ambrosius was listening intently to every word the professor said. He appeared to be on pins and needles as Foshay divulged what he had learned.

"Now, in 1190, Richard arrives in Sicily on his Crusade to the Holy Land. Supposedly he is carrying Excalibur with him as a good luck talisman. Of course historians believe the sword is merely a replica of some sort, but what if it wasn't? Once in Sicily, Richard is met by the French Army, led by their king, Philip II. Together these two armies besiege the city of Messina; capturing it.

The leader of that area during this time is a man named Tancred, who is often referred to as Tancred of Sicily. The two armies stay in Messina until Tancred is forced to sign a peace treaty sometime in 1191. As a part of this treaty, Tancred's daughter is promised to Richard's nephew; now get this, a man called Arthur of Brittany. That's just a little too coincidental for my liking. How about yours?" The Professor finished with an excited flourish.

"Agreed," she and Ambrosius said at the same time. She looked over at her partner who returned the look with an upraised eyebrow.

"Yes, I know, I owe you a Coke, or some kind of nonsense to that effect," Ambrosius said in the dry tone she had come to expect from him. This in turn made her laugh out loud.

"Thanks, Ambrosius, I needed that," she said once she stopped laughing. The look of disdain he aimed in her direction nearly started her on another fit of laughter, but she was able to catch herself. "I'm sorry, Professor, please continue."

"That's quite all right Agent Sommers." He stifled a laugh of his own behind the charade of a fake cough. "As I was saying, Arthur of Brittany married Tancred's daughter and Tancred was named the legal King of Sicily. As a gift, Richard gives Tancred Excalibur, thinking that it is only a sword forged by one of his weapon makers and not realizing it is the real deal."

"This is all very interesting, but how did Excalibur get here in Boston?" she asked.

"Patience, Agent Sommers, I'm getting to it. Now, shortly after this marriage, Philip suddenly pulls his army out of Messina and returns to France somewhat unexpectedly. As I figure it, he didn't return empty handed."

"You mean...," she began but did not finish.

"I think Philip realized what Tancred was given, somehow gained possession of Excalibur, and took it back to France with him. There it stayed as part of the French monarchy's treasury for centuries. Then, in 1764, none other than America's own Benjamin Franklin is dispatched to England by the Colonies in an effort to oppose the Stamp Act. Once his duties in England are finished he begins a tour of Europe in what many believe is really a mission to drum up support for the war which is inevitably coming. This tour takes him to France in 1767 where he begins a love affair with the French people. He gains a near celebrity status, and befriends King Louis XV. Now, back in the Colonies, things are really heating up. Franklin goes back to England, where he stays until 1775 helping out the revolutionary cause as a politician. During this time he asks his biggest fans, the French, for help in fighting England. What does the French king do? My guess is, as a dig at his old nemesis, the British, Louis gives Franklin Excalibur. Franklin takes the sword back to the Colonies with him when he returns in early May of 1775, soon after the first fighting of the war takes place. That same year on November 10th thanks to a resolution from the Continental Congress, the United States Marine Corps is born, and the commanding officer carries with him what is rumored to be a magic sword. Guess what city he is from? That's right, right here in Boston. Of course we all know what happens with the Revolutionary War."

"That is quite a tale," she said, when it was clear the Professor had nothing more to add.

"Tell me about it. I spent the better part of the night piecing it together."

From the dark circles under his eyes, she believed him. She looked over at Ambrosius, but he was deep in thought. No doubt mulling over all that they had just heard. It was quite a story, but it did answer the question of how Excalibur might have come to be in the U.S.

"Well that does seem to all add up," she said.

"Yes, but it still does not help us in regards as to where Excalibur is now," Ambrosius said.

"I do have some theories as to that," the professor said.

"It would have to be someplace that can be dated back to the Revolutionary War era. We know it's not sitting in a museum somewhere."

"Huh, Revolutionary War era," she said, her voice loaded with sarcasm. "How many of those are there in Boston? Hundreds?"

"Not as many as you might think," he said, ignoring her sarcastic tone. "I think we should start our search with churches, especially some of the Catholic ones. Many of them date back to the 1700's."

"How do we know this marine officer didn't keep Excalibur after the war, and it's now sitting in a trunk in the attic of his great-grandson however many times removed as some lost family heirloom?" Ambrosius asked.

"I don't believe that would have happened. For one, at the very least, Benjamin Franklin knew what the sword was, and I am guessing so did the rest of the Founding Fathers. They would not have allowed such a weapon to be lost. They would have kept it in case it would be needed again. Why they decided on Boston as the place to keep the sword, I don't know, but it would be someplace where it could be safe and private."

It made sense to Sommers, but did little to help them actually find the sword. Something else he'd said finally sank in.

"What is all this 'we' talk?" she asked, already knowing what the answer was going to be.

"Come on, Agent Sommers, if there is even a remote possibility Excalibur is real, I have to see it. I have spent my entire professional life studying Arthur and his legends. You have to let me be a part of this."

"Absolutely not. That is out of the question, Professor," she said. She could sympathize with Foshay, but there was no way the Agency would agree to letting a civilian tag along.

"Agent Sommers, let's be reasonable here. You need me," the professor said. She could hear the pleading in his voice. In a few minutes she would not be surprised if he dropped to his knees and begged.

"Why is that Professor?" she asked.

"I know Boston. I grew up here. At the very least, I could be your guide."

In reality, he made a good point. It would be helpful to have someone lead them around the city. It would definitely save them time, and that could prove to be invaluable. But there was also the matter of the Ghost to consider.

"Professor Foshay, I understand your desire to want to be a part of this investigation, but this is a FBI matter. I cannot accept responsibility for your safety," she said, hoping that by hinting at a possible danger, he would be discouraged. Her warning fell on deaf ears.

"I accept any and all risk involved, Agent Sommers. This is a chance of a lifetime for me. I have to take it." He put the full focus of his eyes on her. She felt the pulling at her heart strings increase, and the walls of rejecting his wish crumbled.

She looked over at Ambrosius for support, but he was no help. He merely returned her look and shrugged. "I don't think it's a good idea, but it could also save us time."

"There you go, Agent Sommers. It's two to one," Foshay said, and she could tell he was clinging to Ambrosius' statement like a lifeline.

"That may be, but as lead Agent my vote is the only one that counts," she said. "I can't believe I am agreeing to this, but get your coat, Professor. We've got a sword to find."

CHAPTER 19

Reggie Blackburn had driven straight through the night, making stops only to fill up on gas and caffeine. He was exhausted beyond his endurance due to the lack of sleep and because of how the high level of energy his fear for Sommers' safety was taxing his body.

He had tried reaching her on her cell phone, but so far had only managed to get in touch with her answering service. His imagination was playing horrible tricks on him as to why she might not be able to pick up, but he knew with the Ghost around, nothing was too far-fetched.

He could only hope he had beaten the crazed murderer to Boston, and could find and get to Sommers first. At the very least, he would be there to offer whatever protection he could against such a dangerous adversary. He had almost captured the Ghost once upon a time; maybe this time he could stop the assassin once and for all.

Frustration mingled with fear was fraying what was left of his already shot nerves. If he had only acted sooner, he would not be in this hellish prison of his own making. If anything happened to Sommers, he would never be able to forgive himself. It would be his fault, and he would not be able to live with that kind of guilt.

Sommers was tough. She would put up a nasty fight. She would lose, but she would not go down quietly. He held on to that thought. If he was not able to find her before the Ghost, he would have to count on her tenacity to hold out until he could arrive. Despite the pure terror he was feeling at the prospect of Sommers facing down the Ghost alone, he managed a smile thinking of the fight she had in her.

If the Agency stuck to routine, Sommers and the British agent would have rooms at the Hilton on Broad Street. He had stayed there himself a couple of times while working cases in the Boston area.

He gave his old blue sedan a little more gas, and it responded by speeding down the Interstate. He had to find her before the Ghost did. He just had to. It was no longer a question of losing his job; it was now a matter of losing his very soul if he failed to save her.

The plane touched down on the runway of Logan Airport with the screeching of tires and a quick jolt, causing the Ghost to lurch forward in his seat. He barely noticed. His thoughts were too focused inward on the success of his current mission to be bothered by something as mundane as the landing of an airplane.

He had slept soundly for almost the entire flight, and felt completely refreshed. He was ready to hit the pavement running, so to speak. The only major decision he needed to make was whether he wanted to locate the sword first, or make a social call to Blackburn's attractive protégé. Both options appealed to him and he decided to think on it over a good breakfast.

He glanced down at the black leather bag sitting on his lap. Inside was the now translated document detailing Excalibur's whereabouts. This was his trump card, and what allowed him to be so nonchalant. He knew Blackburn was on his heels and might even already be in Boston. He seriously doubted it, but the fat fool had proven himself to be resourceful in the past.

With no idea where to even begin to search for the sword, Blackburn would no doubt try and find the female Agent first, being the big Boy Scout he was. This would give the Ghost ample time to eat and plot out his next move. He could picture the look of pure heartbreak on Blackburn's face when the fool of an agent realized he was too late to make any kind of a difference.

This could prove to be an extremely profitable and lucrative excursion indeed. In one swoop, he would have eliminated the one true thorn in his side, gained possession of perhaps the most lauded magical sword in the entire history of such weapons, and earned an obscene amount of money from some two-bit terrorist group. He could not help but smile like the cat that had just eaten the canary.

The pilot's voice came through the loudspeaker, saying that he hoped everyone had enjoyed their flight. This was the signal for everyone to get up, gather their belongings along with their overhead luggage, and begin their exit from the plane, and the Ghost elbowed his way to the head of the line. Naturally, this caused a few dirty looks from his fellow first class passengers, but he could care less. Had they known who they were glaring at, and known he was capable of reaching into his inside jacket pocket, removing the gold ink pen he always carried, and the gouging out the eyes of each disgruntled passenger, they would have all minded their own business. As it was, he let their disrespect slide. He had other matters to attend to, and far more important prey to hunt.

With the recent snowfall, he decided on renting something with four wheel drive instead of a luxury car which he usually chose. After giving the rental car clerk at the desk one of his many credit cards featuring yet another one of his identities, he drove out of the airport and into the city of Boston in a comfortable blood red Trailblazer. It was not exactly his first choice of vehicles, but the color had sold him and so it would do.

The rumbling in his stomach reminded him of how hungry he was. He decided on a well earned breakfast before his visit with Blackburn's female friend. He would need all the energy he could get to carry out his macabre plans he had in store for her.

His eyes shone with a light only pure malice could cause as he stepped on the gas pedal, speeding him on his way to a morning filled with a breakfast fit for royalty and murder.

Only the loud vibrating sound and sensation of the sedan's tires slipping onto the grated shoulder of the road snapped Reggie Blackburn back to alertness. He lost count how many times this happened, and resorted to slapping himself in the face as hard as he could to stay awake.

Thankfully, the storm had petered out and the roads were clear. Not that it would have mattered if they were drifted over; he would have found a dog sled and team to get him to Sommers if that was what the situation called for. His friendship with her deserved no less.

He let out a sigh of relief as his destination came into view. He was physically, mentally, and emotionally exhausted, and seeing the hotel was like spotting the finishing line of a race after running a marathon. Of course, if Sommers had already left, then his journey would continue. Still, seeing the hotel felt good.

He pulled into the parking spot closest to the main entrance, then sat and took a couple of deep breaths to clear away some of the fogginess which settled over his tired brain and collect himself before continuing. He knew he looked as disheveled as he felt, but his only thoughts were to the safety and well-being of Sommers.

It was at that moment he noticed movement out his driver's side window. His reaction time was sluggish due to his tired state of mind, but when he was finally able to get his eyes focused enough so his vision was no longer akin to looking through bathroom glass, he was stunned by what he saw. There, walking out of the hotel and moving towards a black Agency car, were Sommers and the Brit she was working the case with.

A sense of utter relief flooded through his body, so intense he almost began to weep in release. The entire drive, after seeing the message left by the Ghost, he had feared the worst. It was that fear which had kept him going through the night. Finding himself here and seeing that Sommers was safe was emotionally overwhelming.

Before he could get out of his car, she'd gotten into hers and pulled away. Reggie swore, fumbling the gear shift of his own car into reverse. Sommers turned right out of the parking lot and began accelerating down the street. He quickly backed out and hit the gas in an effort to catch up. He had not driven all night to get to Sommers only to lose her now.

He followed her to Boston University, where she must have been following up on the lead concerning the literary professor he had given her. He smiled in spite of the tension he was experiencing. Sommers was nothing if not thorough when it came to an investigation.

It took him a couple of trips around the small lot before he found a parking spot of his own. He was lucky enough on his second pass; a young woman exited the building and drove away, freeing up a space for him to pull into. He paused while the old blue sedan idled, unsure if he should go ahead and follow Sommers into the building or wait for her to exit. If he went in, it could potentially damage whatever interview she was conducting with the professor. Knowing Sommers like he did, he decided it would be better to wait. She was already not happy with him, and if he barged in on her now and ruined her chance of finding a new lead, he would more than likely find himself on the wrong end of her service revolver. This caused him to snort out a chuckle, even though he did not like sitting and twirling his thumbs out in the car while Sommers was potentially in danger. It was highly unlikely the Ghost would make an appearance and attempt something here at the University. It was not the assassin's style. Still, he did not want to take any unnecessary chances. Until the Ghost was stopped, they all were at risk no matter where they were.

After fifteen minutes of waiting, he was having a hard time staying awake. It was well over twenty-four hours since he had last slept, and it was finally catching up with him.

"Maybe I should go in after her before I drift off into a coma."

He was seriously considering doing just that when the sound of another vehicle pulling into the parking lot caught his attention. He peered out the window at a black stretch limousine, which seemed out of place here at the University. It did not even bother trying to find an empty space, but slowed to a halt directly in front of the College of Arts and Sciences building's entrance. No one got out. It gave Reggie a bad feeling. He did not think it was a coincidence that whoever was in the limo decided to show up at the same time Sommers was here.

Reggie reached under his suit jacket into his shoulder holster, removed his weapon, and rested the firearm in his lap casually as he watched the limo. He could feel the coldness of the metal through his pants material.

He'd barely noticed a silver Suburban cruising through the lot, even when it stopped in his row, effectively blocking him in. He'd barely noticed the two men exit the vehicle.

But, when one of them knocked on the passenger's side front window of his car, he noticed. The rapping startled him so that he raised the 9mm and almost fired at the man in mirrored sunglasses.

The second man had apparently hung back, but now moved to the driver's side. Reggie, seeing that he was basically surrounded, lowered the gun, but made no move to either exit his car or roll down any of the windows. Whoever these guys were, he did not plan on making things easy for them.

By their dress and demeanor, he was reminded of the Secret Service Agents he sometimes had dealings with. Both of the men wore expensive navy blue suits with matching overcoats. They both also sported military style haircuts as well as mirrored glasses which effectively hid their eyes. If they'd had earpieces and talked into their cuffs, he would have thought the President was nearby. As it was, he guessed they were some sort of private security force hired by whoever was in the limo.

Neither one was brandishing any kind of a weapon, but that did not mean they were not armed. If it came down to it, Reggie was pretty sure he could take both men out before they would be able to get to him, but from the way they just stood there waiting for him, he did not think it would come to that.

After a few more seconds of no one wanting to take the initiative to make the next step, he decided enough was enough. Still keeping a tight grip on his firearm, he pushed the button on the control panel built into the armrest of the driver's side door and waited as the window slowly descended. A blast of cold air rushed in and nearly stole his breath.

"Can I help you guys?" he asked.

The one by the driver's side door bent over. Reggie stared at his own image reflected in the man's sunglasses.

"Agent Reggie Blackburn." It was more a statement of fact rather than a query. "Would you please come with us?"

"I don't know what this is all about, but I'm not going anywhere," he said.

"Sir, it is very important we speak with you. We know Agent Amy Sommers is inside, and once she exits the building, we will be asking her to join us as well."

"What is this all about, and who are you?" he asked when they failed to identify themselves.

"I know this is somewhat unconventional, Agent Blackburn, but it is very important you trust and come with us. We have information which could prove extremely beneficial to you and Agent Sommers. Please trust us on this."

He did not know why, but something about the man, the way he spoke and his whole very proper attitude, made Reggie inclined to believe him. Even though he had been given next to nothing in the way of an explanation in who his visitors were and how they seemed to know so much about him and Sommers, for some reason he did trust them.

"What the hell," he said, re-holstering his sidearm. "But this better be good."

"Trust me, Agent Blackburn, you will not be disappointed."

He turned off the sedan's engine and opened the door. "Lead the way," he said.

He was not surprised when they began leading him not to the Suburban, but to the black limo. Reggie followed closely without saying a word, though a number of questions were racing through his head.

Once they got to the limo, the young man he had spoken with opened the rear passenger side door, and made a motion with his hand, signaling that Blackburn should get in. He shrugged his shoulders, and decided to go with the flow.

"What the hell," he said again, before ducking his head and climbing into back of the limousine.

—CHAPTER 20

Amy had never seen a person move so fast. When she agreed to let Professor Foshay tag along on the hunt for Excalibur, he jumped out of his chair. He rushed around his office trying to gather his belongings as quick as he could, before she had a chance to change her mind. It was like watching a home movie on fast forward. She half expected the next time the professor spoke, he would sound like one of the Chipmunks.

Agent Ambrosius was indifferent to the professor's obvious excitement He looked bored with the whole situation. She was having a hard time keeping up with Ambrosius' mood swings at this point, so did not even bother to make a comment.

"I think I have everything, Agent Sommers," the professor said, and it was only mildly disappointing to hear that his voice had absolutely no chipmunk quality to it.

He had two books tucked under one arm and a folder overflowing with papers in the other hand. He had also slipped into a black Navy pea coat and a Boston Red Sox baseball cap.

"All right then, if Agent Ambrosius can find a way to tear himself away from the moment, we will be on our way," she said.

She hoped her little jibe at Ambrosius would render some sort of reaction, but she was disappointed. No comment or snappy comeback; he merely stood up and waited for her to lead the way out of the office. As she neared the main reception area, she saw a man in front of the glass doors, effectively blocking the exit. From the way he stood with his legs slightly apart and hands clasped behind his back, she immediately pegged him as some kind of security officer. Though he was wearing mirrored sunglasses, she got the distinct impression he was staring directly at her.

"Where should we begin our search, Professor?" she asked, more to see how the guy with the mirrored glasses would react than to get an actual answer.

As expected, the stranger in the expensive dark blue suit turned his head as if he too was waiting for an answer. That is, until he unexpectedly spoke up instead, and responded to her question.

"I believe I may be of some assistance with that, Agent Sommers."

If she had been unnerved before by the stranger's presence, hearing him speak her name so casually was downright shocking. She had absolutely no idea who he was, and was one hundred percent sure she had never seen him before, yet here he was talking to her as if they had known each other for years. It creeped her out. She could feel goose pimples rise on her skin. She had a horrible intuition that the guy was actually the Ghost she had heard so much about, and considered going for her gun. If not for the sound of Ambrosius' voice, she may have done just that.

"Is this a friend of yours, Agent Sommers?" Ambrosius asked.

The caution in his voice made her feel a little better about being so on edge. She was not overreacting. If Ambrosius' instincts were rankled by this unknown guy's presence too, then her own instincts had been correct.

"Not likely," she said, taking a step backwards. If something bad was about to go down, she wanted to be able to move quickly.

"Please, be at ease. It was not my intention to startle you, Agent Sommers, or you, Agent Ambrosius," the man said, raising both hands like he was surrendering.

"Okay, Criss Angel, you want to tell me exactly how you know our names? Or should I see if dodging bullets is part of your little magic act, too?" Sommers did not like being left out in the dark and was starting to lose her temper.

"If you would be so kind as to join me and my associates, all will be explained," the man said, keeping his voice calm and even. "Of course, you are welcome to join us as well, Professor Foshay."

By the surprised look etched across the Professor's face, she could tell he did not know who the obviously well informed man was either. This upper hand, combined with the way he presented and carried himself with such confidence, told her that whoever the guy was, he was a professional, and that had the potential to make him even more dangerous than he was letting on.

She looked through the glass. He had mentioned associates which meant there was at least one other person around somewhere. Though she did not see anyone else in the parking lot, there was a long black stretch limo parked in front of the doors. She could only assume this was where the mysterious associates were waiting.

"I can't speak for anyone else here, but I'm not going anywhere until you tell me who you and your 'associates' are, and how you know our names," she said.

"I agree," Ambrosius said from behind her.

She continued to size the guy up. If he was stupid enough to try anything or attempt to make any kind of sudden hostile movements, she was going to take him out. There was too much at stake to spend time playing guessing games. One person involved in this case was already dead, which only upped the ante for the rest of them. She had no intentions of ending up like Steven Jackson.

"Who I am is irrelevant, as is the identity of my associates. I am sure you do not know any of us. I can assure you, however, that neither I nor my associates mean you any harm. In fact, I am quite certain you will find what we have to say to be extremely helpful."

"You'll understand if I am a little skeptical," she said. "How do we know if we can even trust you?"

She spared a glance at Ambrosius and the professor seeing similar questions mirrored in each of their eyes None of them were about to follow this guy or his unknown associates anywhere without a few more assurances.

"All I have to offer you is my word, Agent Sommers. I promise you that it is as unbreakable as any promise I could make you. I guess it is up to you to decide if that will be assurance enough. I am not here to force you, Agent Ambrosius, or even Professor Foshay to do anything or go anywhere. I am here more as an ambassador, offering you a chance at perhaps getting everything you wanted as far as your current investigation is concerned."

He had made no threatening move as of yet, but she knew from experience that did not mean one was not coming. She had met many chameleon like criminals; those who could adapt to any social situation. Generally speaking, some of the worst cases she had the misfortune of working were committed by suave and charming gentlemen like the one now standing before her.

Still, she did not get that same kind of dangerous vibe from him. Either he was good as his word, or smoother than anyone she had ever run across, and he was absolutely right in saying only she could decide which it was. This effectively put all the responsibility right in her lap.

"Can you tell us where it is you would like us to go?" she asked, hoping to get at least one piece of information before she made up her mind.

"I'm sorry, Agent Sommers, but at this point all I can offer is the assurance that this is not some kind of elaborate set up, and I can also assure you it will not be a waste of your time."

She shook her head in frustration. Basically, she and her two colleagues were being asked to take a leap of faith. If she had been back with the LAPD, there was no way she would have gone anywhere under these conditions, but now as a member of the Agency she was forced to utilize whatever resources became available, and that included taking a ride in a limo with complete strangers to an unknown destination.

She looked over at Ambrosius. He shrugged noncommittally, putting the ball in her court. It was her case and therefore her decision to make. She knew the British agent would go along with whatever she decided.

"What the hell," she said, after pausing long enough to reason through all the options available to her. "I guess we're in."

"Excellent," the man said. "If you three will please follow me, I will escort you to your ride, and we can be on our way."

With that, the guy turned and walked out the door. She, Ambrosius, and the professor followed quickly behind.

Reggie was surprised to find the back of the luxury vehicle completely empty. He had been under the impression he would be joining at least one other person, but found himself alone. He assumed there was a driver, but the glass partition separating the front and back was tinted a dark black, making it impossible to see through.

This was not the first time he had ridden in a limo, but this one was definitely the most luxurious. With its plush and comfortable leather seats, fully stocked minibar, and a state of the art entertainment system that looked as if it would take a NASA engineer to operate, he had to admit he was impressed. Whoever or whatever organization these guys worked for, they were extremely well funded.

The opulence of the limousine did not take his mind off Sommers or the potential danger they all faced with the Ghost coming to Boston. Having the opportunity to speak to her, face to face, was really the only reason he even agreed to get in the limo in the first place.

As the time ticked by, his patience began to wear thin. He was tired, stressed, and worried all at the same time. He made up his mind; if Sommers did not come out within the next couple of minutes, he was going in after her. He was done taking chances with her safety.

Every passing second brought the Ghost closer and closer. Soon enough, the one-time agent would strike.

He was leaning over to grab the door handle and let himself out when he heard the sound of approaching feet. He paused, frozen in mid reach, and heard the unmistakable sound of Sommers' voice. He could recognize that sarcastic tone anywhere.

As expected, the stranger in the mirrored sunglasses walked directly up to the awaiting limo and opened the rear passenger side door for them.

"Well if this is some elaborate trap we are being taken to, at least we are going in style," Sommers said.

"If it is a trap, it really doesn't matter how we get there. The end result will still have us just as dead," Ambrosius said.

She looked over her shoulder relieved to see a smile tugging at the corners of his mouth. He had, at least for the moment, dropped his melancholy and returned to the dry-humored agent she could better relate to. "I don't suppose I could get you to tell us where we are going?" she asked again, figuring it would not hurt to try one more time.

Her reflection, staring back at her from the mirrored lenses, was like something out of a cheap carnival funhouse, all exaggerated and distorted. The guy, to his credit, stood as motionless as a sentry under her scrutinizing gaze. This spoke volumes to her about the man's professional training. He gave off the aura of someone with a true sense of duty.

"I promise you, Agent Sommers," he said. "You would be sorely disappointed if I ruined it for you now."

It was not so much what he said, but how he said it, that took her aback. His voice had taken on the tone of someone trying not to give away a well planned surprise. Ambrosius and the professor looked as puzzled as she herself felt. With a shrug, she decided not to keep whoever was inside the limo waiting any longer.

"What the hell," she said as she ducked her head and entered the limo.

From the corner of her eye, she noticed the man smiling, and slowly shaking his head, with an expression like he had just been told the same joke twice.

CHAPTER 21

Stunned, Amy froze with her head and shoulders inside the car, one foot on the door frame, and the rest of her still out in the cold.

While recapturing her wits, she attempted to finish climbing into the limo. Unfortunately, in her confusion, she stumbled, lurched forward awkwardly, and landed almost face first in Reggie Blackburn's large lap.

"I gotta say, Sommers," he said. "You really know how to make a guy feel welcome."

Too shocked and embarrassed even to come up with a sarcastic retort, she dropped onto the seat across from Reggie and stared open-mouthed at him as Ambrosius and Professor Foshay got in after her.

Ambrosius took a seat next to Reggie and the professor sat next to her. The limo was large enough for them all to sit comfortably, but she still felt cramped, even claustrophobic, but after a couple of deep breaths the moment passed. She wanted to say something to Reggie, but, thanks to her graceful entry, she found herself tongue tied.

The door closed and locked. The limo pulled forward to begin making its way out of the parking lot.

"I take it you're all right Agent Sommers?" Ambrosius broke the tense, confused silence. She could have kissed the British agent for taking the initiative, even if it was a reminder of her embarrassing landing. "That was quite a nasty spill you took."

"Yeah, nothing wounded but my pride," she said, sparing a look over at Reggie.

"Speak for yourself, Sommers; that was my crotch you head butted," Reggie said. "A few more inches and it would have been disastrous."

"Really, a few more inches," she said, between sarcastic snorts of derision. "You'd think you would be used to the need of a few more inches when dealing with that area of your body."

Reggie leaned his head back and bellowed out a laugh that was good to hear. By the circles under his eyes, she could tell Reggie had not slept in some time. He appeared disheveled as well. His laugh went on longer than she would have thought, as if it was more of an emotional release filled with relief than due to the humor of her comment. The last time they had spoken, the conversation hadn't been friendly. She'd left him at the airfield back in Washington with both of them going their separate ways, wondering if their friendship might be over.

"Now that's the Sommers I have come to know and barely tolerate," Reggie said, once he had his laughter back under control.

"Excuse me," the professor said. "You two know each other?"

"Unfortunately," she said, and then smirked when she saw the look of disgust settle onto Reggie's red face.

"I take it that means this are not the associate we are going to meet," Foshay said.

"Hardly," she said before Reggie could answer. "Professor Foshay, this is Special Agent Reggie Blackburn."

"I'm just along for the ride like the rest of you," Reggie said after her introductions.

"Speaking of that," she said. "Why are you here?" She knew the Agency's strict noninterference policy, so his unexpected appearance was more than a little unnerving.

A look of dark concern moved across Reggie's face. He settled back in his seat and took a long, nerve-calming deep breath. She, Ambrosius and the professor waited with rapt attention to hear Reggie's explanation. The worry lines around his eyes deepened as he seemed to collect his thoughts in preparation. Whatever had transpired was serious enough that he'd apparently dropped everything and drove straight through the night. His exhaustion, both physical and mental, was clearly marked by the sunken in look of his otherwise alert eyes as well as an emotion she thought she would never associate with her friend and mentor, fear.

The limo drove on. She had no idea where they were going, and thanks to the darkened windows, was unable to see much as well. Not that she would have known where they were headed, unfamiliar as she was with Boston. They were basically at the mercy of their hosts.

"Tell me what happened, Reggie," she said.

After a slight pause, which felt to her like an hour, Reggie began speaking. He told how he had gone straight to his favorite pub after their argument at the airfield, then returned to Jackson's apartment in hopes of finding something useful. He described in exact detail his run-in with the Ghost, along with the message he discovered on Jackson's computer. He finished by telling them of his drive to Boston, and how he had tailed them from the hotel, which led to his own meeting and invitation from the stranger with the mirrored sunglasses.

Sommers felt a knot in her stomach. Reggie's fear of this Ghost character was almost tangible, it was so intense. So was his relief from the worry that he might not arrive in time. He had risked everything to come here and stand by her side.

It made her anger over their last meeting seem petty. Reggie was the one true friend she had ever had in her entire adult life. He had proven that fact all over again by these most recent actions.

She again found herself to be speechless, which, for her was as close to an impossibility as it could get. Twice in the span of less than an hour was akin to getting struck by lightening twice during the same storm. Once again, it was Ambrosius who broke the silence and asked the question on everyone's mind.

"So, this Ghost is here in Boston right now as we speak, and he knows Excalibur's location?"

"Yep," Reggie said.

"Who is this Ghost person?" Professor Foshay asked.

He had been so quiet, plus all her attention had been focused solely on Reggie's story, that Sommers had forgotten the professor was even sitting next to her. Hearing him speak now made her jump. She hoped no one else had seen her frightened rabbit imitation.

"He's the bad guy," Reggie said. "Think of Hannibal Lecter, but without the appetite."

"Ah. Sorry I asked."

Sommers felt for the guy. She liked Foshay, and knew this was a lot for him to take in. She wondered if he was beginning to second guess his desire to come along. Then again, she wondered if she was having second thoughts herself, as well.

So much for letting the rookie get broken in slowly. Apparently she had jumped into the proverbial fire feet first, but truth be told, she would not have it any other way. Danger was simply part of the job. You either dealt with it and moved on or you were in the wrong line of work.

The limo slowed and made another turn. By the sound of tires moving over loose gravel, they were now heading down some kind of trail. Or, better yet, a private driveway. The tinted windows continued to foil any efforts to get a glimpse outside. Sommers thought it was like trying to see through muddy water at night. This was just another reminder of who was in control for the time being. Had this been a card game, she would have folded her hand a long time ago, with the odds so stacked against her.

She casually slipped her right hand inside her coat and touched the reassuring grip of her sidearm. The gun felt good in her hand, and helped remind her she was not completely helpless. She felt even more reassured when she noticed Reggie was doing the exact same thing. They shared a nod of understanding.

They came to a stop. Another vehicle door opened and then closed somewhere behind them. Sommers wondered if this was a courtesy escort or was it some sort of security protocol to make sure she and her companions did not try to commandeer the limo and escape.

It did not come as any real surprise when the passenger side rear door opened, and Mr. Mirrored Sunglasses greeted them.

"I hope everything was to your satisfaction," the man said.

"Oh yeah, everything was just peachy," she said. "Now you want to tell us just where in the hell we are?"

"Why don't you see for yourselves, Agent Sommers?" He took a step back and gestured with his arm in an inviting manner.

The bright sunshine hurt her eyes after being in the darkened interior of the limousine for such a long period of time, and she was momentarily blinded. It took a good twenty seconds before she was able to adjust to the sudden introduction of light and her vision returned to normal. She had a sudden flash of sarcastic insight, wondering if this was why their hosts favored the mirrored sunglasses.

When her vision fully returned, she looked around, then sucked in a deep breath and shook her head in astonishment.

"Wow!" she said. She looked at her companions and they all nodded in unison, agreeing with her shocked exclamation.

They stood in the shadow of a castle, replete with stone turrets and banners flapping in the breeze. She even spotted a portcullis with a large black iron gate pulled open so only the pointed tips were showing like the open mouth of an evil creature. If she did not already know better, she would have sworn they were all somehow transported to the English countryside. It was like she had stepped back in time to the Middle Ages.

The gravel sound she had heard was actually a long lane that ended in a circle drive directly in front of the gate. The stones were pure white limestone, gleaming magnificently in the afternoon sun, so white they made what snow was still on the ground look dirty in comparison.

She looked over at Ambrosius and saw an odd dreamy expression on his serious face., "Make you feel a little homesick does it?" she asked.

"More than you know, Agent Sommers," he said in a far off voice. "More than you know…"

"Welcome to Chateau Nicholas," Mirrored Sunglasses said.

"All right, I gotta admit it, I'm impressed," she said.

"If you will all follow me please, we can get inside and out of this chill air."

They did followed their guide through the open gate and into the lush courtyard of the chateau. She took notice of three black Cadillacs also parked in the circle drive. She did not know if these were the rides of more guests such as herself and her companions or if these belonged to the promised associates they were going to meet with.

The courtyard was immense, large enough to host a high school football game. It was well taken care of and landscaped to perfection. Even this late in the year and with the near freezing temperatures of the last few days, there were still some flowers blooming prettily.

A large fountain with a circular pool dominated the center of the courtyard. Rising up out of the middle of the pool was a perfectly crafted granite sculpture of a woman's hand holding a sword, as if the feminine hand was thrusting the sword up from some mysterious depths. The four of them stood side by side, staring at the sculpture.

"Is this what I think it is?" Sommers asked.

It was Ambrosius who decided to answer. "Yes Agent Sommers, that is exactly what you think it is."

She had been unsure on what to expect from this impromptu excursion, but she had not thought in a million years to see such an obvious symbolic reference to the exact same fabled sword she was desperately trying to locate. She could only shake her head again, the case continuing to baffle her as it led her down its path full of twists and turns.

"I told you this would not be a waste of your time," Mirrored Sunglasses said. "Now, if you will follow me, I promise you will find more surprises inside."

He led them across the courtyard to the front entrance of the chateau. Sommers could not help turning around and looking over her shoulder at the depiction of Excalibur. The uneasy feelings she had been experiencing were slowly but surely starting to subside. They were replaced by a renewed sense of optimism. Maybe this was the break she had been hoping for since arriving in Boston.

The entrance was an enormous oak door, rounded off at the top, adding to the old world charm of the place. There was a black cast iron knocker set slightly above center. Mirrored Sunglasses lifted the iron loop and slammed it down on the awaiting metal plate loudly three times. Immediately after the third knock stopped echoing, the heavy door was pulled open from the inside, and they were invited in by a man dressed like a stereotypical gentleman's butler, complete with black tails and white gloves. She had the sudden desire to call the man Jeeves, but was able to utilize some self-restraint before embarrassing herself.

They stepped over the threshold and into a large parlor; complete with marble floors and a winding stairway carved out of the same stone. It was breathtaking in its beauty and craftsmanship. The sight was overwhelming as well, and she wondered if that was at least partially the point. Anyone entering this place would find themselves at a distinct disadvantage. Even now, she felt small and insignificant in comparison to the grandeur of the chateau.

"If you would like, Mr. Dawson will take your coats," Mirrored Sunglasses said, motioning towards the older man she thought of as "Jeeves." His voice almost boomed in the amplification of the large open space.

So, Jeeves has a name. At least someone attached to this organization does, she thought.

They slipped out of their winter coats, and handed them over to Mr. Dawson. Their guide waited patiently as they did this not removing his own overcoat or glasses.

"Now, if you please," Mirrored Sunglasses said. "We are going up the stairs and to the right. My associate is there waiting for you."

"Well, I for one can't wait to see what's next," she said.

"Hear, hear," Reggie said from behind her.

The sounds of their shoes on the expertly crafted marble steps echoed, rolling like thunder across the chateau. When they reached the top of the staircase, they turned down a rather lengthy corridor. In a stark contrast, their feet made a "shushing" sound as they moved across a soft and plush crimson carpet. The walls were covered in either elaborate tapestries depicting knights in battle or portraits of distinguished looking men and women so detailed they looked as if they could climb out of their respective frames. Also, every so many feet was a full scale suit of armor. She was no expert, but she had a pretty good idea they were authentic, and not replicas.

She would have liked to stop and inspect the armor as well as the artwork a little closer, and from the way the professor was slowing down before each piece, she knew he felt the same. Mirrored Sunglasses never slowed, however, as he moved down the long hall. He stopped at the fifth door and turned to look at them.

"My associate is waiting for you inside," he said.

"You're not joining us?" she asked.

"Not at the moment," he said, and she got the impression that he fully expected to be apart of whatever unfolded. With a polite nod, he turned and retreated back down the hall.

"Well, let's not keep our host waiting," Reggie said.

"Indeed," said Ambrosius under his breath. He seemed anxious to find out what all the cloak and dagger secrecy was all about. Sommers felt the exact same way.

"Shall we?" she asked.

"Take us in, Sommers," Reggie said.

"You're such a gentleman, Reggie, letting the only woman walk into the great unknown," she said.

"Yeah, because you are so helpless and all," he said.

"Can we break up the sarcasm festival, and find out what is behind door number one?" Ambrosius asked.

The dry wit of his tone made them all laugh out loud, even if it was more of a nervous laugh than anything due to humor. Leave it to Ambrosius to put things in perspective in his own special way.

"All right Ambrosius, you win," she said. She grabbed the bronze door knob, twisted it, and opened the door.

She led them into what looked like a medieval version of a boardroom. Instead of a long rectangular conference table, however, the room was dominated by a circular one. The irony of the symbolism was not lost on her or her companions. They all shared another knowing look.

At the rear of the room was a large stone hearth big enough for two people to stand side by side in. A fire blazed and the burning wood crackled, adding a sense of comforting warmth to the room. The roaring fire did not capture her attention so much as the man sitting with his back to it did. He was middle-aged, casually sipping wine from a crystal goblet and smoking a Churchill style cigar. The smoke he exhaled floated lazily upward, where it formed a mini cloud above his head.

"Hello, Agent Sommers," the man said. "I am sure you would like some answers."

"You got that right," she said. Her reply came out a little more strained than she would have liked. If the man sitting before her was as perceptive as she was giving him credit for, then he would have definitely picked up on it.

"Well for starters, let me introduce myself. My name is Thomas Nichols."

The name meant nothing to her beyond a faint ring of familiarity. Their host was a distinguished and handsome man. His hair had gone an almost complete gray, though there were still a few strands of a darker color still fighting the good fight. She put him in his early to mid fifties though he seemed to radiate the energy of a much younger man. His gaze was intense, and she could feel the aura of his self-confidence behind it.

"Nice to meet you Mr. Nichols," she said. "You already seem to know my name, and I'm guessing I don't need to make any introductions with my friends here as well."

"No, that won't be necessary. If you, Agents Ambrosius and Blackburn, and Professor Foshay would please join me, maybe I can answer a few of your questions."

She made no move to sit down, and was pleased when the others followed her lead and remained standing. She was not about to put herself or anyone under her protection into a vulnerable situation without at least some kind of reassurance that no harm would befall them.

"You want to tell me just how it is you know so much about us," she said. This was a statement, and almost an order, instead of a question.

Nichols took a long puff on his cigar and smiled mischievously. Sommers did not care much for what she saw in that smile. It reminded her of the Cheshire Cat from *Alice in Wonderland*. This was a man who was used to playing at secrets, and one who was used to holding all the cards.

"It is our duty to know such things, Agent Sommers," Nichols said.

His use of the word "our" was not lost on her. It implied there were more men at his disposal.

"And just who are you?" she asked. "What exactly is your duty?"

"We are the Franklin Knights, Agent Sommers, and we are the guardians," Nichols said. "We knew of your arrival in Boston almost immediately. We knew you would search out the good professor there eventually. We also know there is another, less savory, individual in our fair city, though I do not believe we need to concern ourselves with him just yet. It is our duty to know this information. Trust me, Agent Sommers, I can help you if you let me."

She glanced at the others. Reggie had concern etched on his face. Ambrosius appeared tense like a cat ready to pounce. The professor looked as out of his depth as ever.

"How exactly can you help me, Mr. Nichols?" she asked.

"For starters, I know where Excalibur is."

It was like someone sucked the air out of the room. A collective gasp escaped the four of them at roughly the same time. She felt a little light headed, and without thinking about it, she moved over to the nearest chair, pulled it out, and sat down at the round table. Ambrosius, Reggie, and the professor all did the same.

"Mr. Nichols, you clearly have our attention," she said when she was able to find her voice again.

CHAPTER 22

The Ghost brought the toothpick he was holding in his right hand to his mouth and began working to free a miniscule piece of ham which had lodged itself in between two of his molars.

Terrorizing innocent victims always seemed to go better on a full stomach. A delicious omelet of grilled ham, white asparagus sweet pepper, and onions, and potato hash mixed with the perfect blend of Chimay blue and basil was all topped of by a magnificent cup of French-brewed coffee. Sel De La Terre, his favorite five star restaurant in Boston, had really outdone itself.

The food had re-energized him, now he could focus his full attention on the tasks at hand. By the end of this day, he would have possession of Excalibur, Blackburn would be dead, and he would be several million dollars richer. Life was indeed good.

Carrying the case in his left hand, he crossed the street to his awaiting vehicle. The Trailblazer's lights blinked on and then off in response to his pushing the red unlock button on the black fob connected to the key ring he'd removed from the front pocket of his black Caraceni designer slacks. He picked up his pace as he approached his awaiting chariot. He was definitely feeling giddy at the prospect of wrapping up all his loose ends before the day was out.

He carefully laid the case containing the now translated document on the passenger's seat. With the care he took, one would have thought it was a fragile piece of glassware instead of an attaché case designed to withstand the impact of an explosive device.

He had spent the time it took to fly from Washington D.C. to Boston catching up on some sleep as well as studying the document. With the use of his laptop computer, he scanned the internet for maps and information, and was certain he knew exactly where the fabled sword of Arthur was hiding.

King's Chapel. A more appropriately named place, there could not be, he thought. Now, it was only a matter of going and claiming his prize.

In all his worldly travels, he'd only been to Boston a handful of times, and thus did not know the city all that well, beyond the locations of the best nightclubs and five star restaurants. His internet research had helped pinpoint the address of King's Chapel. It was on the corners of Tremont and School Streets in South Boston, in one of the oldest districts in the city. If his calculations were correct, that part of Boston dated all the way back to the Revolutionary War era. It was there the first part of his journey would come to an end.

He carefully scanned the different street names as he drove, until he came to the corner of School and Tremont. There on the corner was King's Chapel.

It was really not all that impressive in his estimation, reminding him of a smaller, shabbier version of the Supreme Court. Instead of a bright white marble, however, the Revolutionary War era place of worship was made from what looked like a dull gray granite. The chapel was nothing awe-inspiring, but if the document sitting on the seat next to him was to be believed, what was hidden somewhere in the depths of the chapel's basement made this place special.

He pulled the Trailblazer around to the side of King's Chapel and utilized the public parking. From there he was able to get a good look at the cemetery which shared the land and was part of the tourist attraction associated with the centuries old chapel.

Many of the headstones had been faded by time and the harsh elements so the names and dates were now unreadable. Several of the grave markers were elaborate with handcrafted scrollwork from a bygone era. The attention to detail was magnificent, and under different circumstances he may have taken a moment to appreciate the craftsmanship. Something else had caught his eye however, and left him with an uneasy feeling. The entire front of King's Chapel was covered with scaffolding as a large restoration project of sorts was obviously under way.

The presence of construction workers scurrying about the scaffolding caused a nagging in the back of his mind. He would have to proceed with caution, all of his senses on full alert.

He chanced a look at the bracelet on his wrist, and briefly considered drawing on its power. But he still had the confrontation with Blackburn to think about, and when he finally met up with the agent, he wanted to be at his full strength. Instead, he popped the clasps on the case and removed a copy of the translated document. He folded it long ways one time, and slid it into the same inside pocket which contained the directions to the chapel.

It was a short walk from the parking lot to the entrance of King's Chapel. Despite the snow and cooler than normal temperatures, there was still a good sized crowd out front. He could make out the restoration project workers, staff, and a number of tourists. He knew from checking the chapel's website that tours were offered regularly as long as a religious service was not in session. He had been banking on no such service, and from the number of people milling about waiting for the tours to begin, knew he had guessed right. All was going according to plan.

His idea was a simple one. He would join a tour like the rest of the peons, and then, once inside, he would slip away. He would then make his way to the basement and search until he found Excalibur. If anyone stopped him, he could easily claim he had simply gotten lost. If all else failed, he would call on the magic and make himself invisible to those around him. He would only do that if it was his final option, however.

He realized he probably did not look like a typical tourist, but at this point, so close to obtaining Excalibur, he did not really care. He was focused with a single minded determination on the recovery of King Arthur's legendary sword. If the idiots happened to notice him or notice something out of the ordinary, he would give a thought to dispatching them at a later time.

Seeing a crowd of those very same peons starting to gather at the entrance, he quickened his own pace to catch up. He wanted to get inside as soon as possible. The sooner he could get his hands on Excalibur, the sooner he could be on his way, and the sooner he could exact a measure of his own style of revenge against Special Agent Reggie Blackburn.

When the heavily polished oak front door opened, the crowd was ushered in by the tour guide that time forgot. The Ghost had no idea how old this shrew was, but she looked ancient. The old crone began launching into her well rehearsed spiel as the dozen or so of the group filed in.

"King's Chapel is one of the oldest in the entire country. It was first built in 1687…"

The old woman's voice sounded like someone stepping on dry corn husks, but he did not pay her much attention. As soon as he had entered the chapel he began scanning the area.

There was no doubting the chapel was old. The interior had that feel of having seen countless decades. The weight of having experienced so many years had settled into every nook and cranny of the place. Some wear and tear had begun to show, and as a result, the restoration project had moved inside as well. When he noticed more scaffolding filled with workers doing repairs to one corner of the high vaulted ceiling, he once again experienced the same nagging sensation in the back of his mind as before. He was not sure why but something was setting off his instinctual warning bell.

As the tour guide droned on, he and the rest of the group made their way down the center aisle, moving toward the altar. One of the construction workers climbed down the scaffolding carrying a bucket filled with liquid of some kind. The worker, who was covered in plaster dust, disappeared through a door located directly under the scaffolding.

The Ghost watched with curiosity piqued. The group of tourists moved to another part of the chapel, but he remained rooted to his spot. After a couple of minutes, the worker returned through the same door except now the bucket he carried was empty and most of the plaster dust had been brushed off. There must have been some kind of washroom or utility room behind the door. If he had to guess, he would say the entrance to the basement would be in that general direction as well.

He glanced over his shoulder at the group of people he had walked into the chapel with. They were enthralled by the information the old guide was spewing, and no one had noticed he had not bothered to join them. In fact, they were not paying any attention to him at all.

Without any further hesitation, the Ghost began making his own way to the other side of the chapel where the door was located. He walked calmly and confidently, giving off an air of a person who knew exactly where he was going. He hoped this would make anyone who did happen to notice his presence and register the fact he was somewhat out of place think twice before speaking up and questioning him.

As it turned out, no one appeared to care what he was doing, because he was able to get to the door without incident. He tested the knob, and, finding that it was not locked, let himself in.

He was surprised to find a well lit hall instead of some sort of janitor's closet or work station. From what he could see, there were several doors lining both sides of the hall all the way down until it ended in a T-section.

The sound of a toilet flushing off to his left grabbed his attention. He heard a faucet being turned on and off, followed by the noisy blowing of an electric hand dryer. Signs marked the two doors as public restrooms. The sounds were emanating from the ladies' room.

When the sound of the dryer kicked off, he quickly stepped towards the men's restroom. Whoever was in there might find it suspicious if he was loitering in front of the ladies' room.

Sure enough, he heard the sound of the door opening as he stepped into the men's room. Luckily, it was empty. He stayed close to the door, listening intently. He heard footsteps as the lady who exited the bathroom walked down the hall. He waited until the sounds had faded into nothingness, and then counted to an even fifty before leaving the men's room.

The hall was deserted once again. He looked around for any type of security cameras or devices, but did not spot any. He snickered in derision at how trusting these fools were. Granted, from what he had seen of King's Chapel, the place contained little of value. Still, he had expected far more security in a place which was hiding one of the most famous historical relics known to man.

The lack of security protocol did bother him, but he pushed the anxiousness it caused out of his thoughts as he made his way down the corridor. He paused before each door, hoping to find some sign to the basement. So far all he'd found were the bathrooms, offices of various chapel employees, and one large boardroom. He was not discouraged, however, as he knew he must be close. He was in the inner workings of the chapel, and it was only a matter of time before he would find what he needed.

When he reached the T-section, he turned right, onto a much shorter hallway that came to a dead-end. He could see a large red box hanging on the wall in the center of the right-hand side. A single door was on the far side of the box. As he moved closer he recognized the red box as that of a fire hose encased in glass to be broken in the event of an emergency. This brought a knowing grin to his face.

He passed the fire emergency equipment with barely a glance. The door was marked "Employees Only" and had a sign with what looked like blue stairs etched on it. This was clearly the entrance into the chapel's basement.

He tried the gold-colored lever in place of a regular round door knob, and as he thought, found it locked. He took another look around and, seeing no one, removed the same tools he had used to let himself into the translator's apartment. With the same practiced ease, he picked the lock in mere seconds. The grin on his face grew even wider as he saw cement steps leading down into the darkness below.

He flicked the light switch located just inside the door. When the soft yellow glow filled the stairwell, he quickly shut the door behind him so the light would alert anyone who may happen to wander by. He waited, listening for several seconds to make sure no one was already in the basement, and to make sure he had not inadvertently tripped some alarm when he had picked the lock and opened the door. Only silence answered him, so he cautiously began his descent.

The bulb created a semicircle on the hard unfinished floor after the last step. He stood bathed in the light, waiting for his eyes to adjust to the darkened basement. As it stood now, he could only make out dark shapes and shadows. He had no sense of direction or depth yet, and therefore was not sure how large the basement even was. It could be one huge open space or several rooms used for various storage space.

He reached into the inside pocket of his coat and removed the folded sheet of paper. He wiped his brow with the back of his hand. The basement was overly warm, and he could hear the soft hum of what he guessed was the furnace from somewhere in the shadowy dark.

He looked over the translated directions. Satisfied, he returned the paper to his pocket, and took a couple of steps into the dark. His eyes had adjusted as much as they were going to and he could now make out rows of shelves and workbenches creating a labyrinth. Every available space was used for storage of boxes, old furniture, and what appeared to be nothing but plan old junk. The basement was immense, appearing to go forever much like the ocean does to someone seeing it for the first time. Finding the sword was going to be more difficult than even he had anticipated.

He ventured a glance at the ceiling. It was only a couple feet above his head, giving the basement a claustrophobic feel. Several bare light bulbs sat in fixtures with pull strings hanging down. He moved over to the closest of these lights and gave the string a hard yank. With a loud clicking, the immediate area was filled with the same yellow glow as the stairwell. He continued to make his way through the maze of shelves, turning on lights as he went. He had an excellent sense of direction, moving to what he knew to be the northern corner. This, according to the document, was where he would find Excalibur.

The cellar was dry, which was surprising for how old it was. This was a credit to the long dead mason workers who toiled away several centuries ago laying the chapel's foundation. Of course the basement had been updated since then, but the initial groundwork had been laid in the 1700's. The absence of moisture meant there was no mildew or mold. There was, however, a fine layer of dust covering everything in sight. A musty smell accompanied the filth, giving the basement the feel of an ancient tomb.

The Ghost brushed at some of the fine dust which clung to his coat. He'd inadvertently bumped into what appeared to be an old piano bench piled on top of old office furniture in the style of something out of the 1970's. After removing the dirt, he cursed under his breath and continued on his way, trying to avoid touching any of the refuse as he passed.

Even though several lights were now on, most of the basement was still encased in shadows. He still could not see an end to the rows of junk. He chanced a look back, but the stairs were now lost from sight. At this rate he would need a survival kit and compass. With all the junk down here, he had no doubt that if he looked long enough he would find whatever survival gear he needed. The thought did not give him comfort.

As he continued to make his way to the north corner, it was like stepping backwards through time. Every aisle he turned down was another decade or era. He figured when he finally made it through the maze of junk to his destination, he might truly run into items which had been stored down in this infernal hole since the place had been built. He would not be surprised if he even came across the bleached bones of the original builders left here after a cave in of garbage.

After what felt like a ridiculous amount of time had passed, he spotted the brick wall marking the end of the basement. He still had to double back and take a separate aisle before the mounds of junk opened up. There was not much light here. He looked around for one of the overhanging bulbs, but there were none nearby so he would have to make do. He cursed himself for not having the foresight to bring along a flashlight. He always prided himself on being so well-prepared for all contingencies, but not this time.

He unclipped his cell phone from his belt and flipped it open. Using the glow from the display screen, he slowly traced the phone down the corner, scanning the ancient bricks. Approximately halfway down, he found markings carved into one of the bricks. He moved his face to within inches of the wall in an attempt to get a better look. He even ran his finger across the spot in question. Feeling the grooves made by whoever had carved the small sword symbol into the brick, his mood picked up considerably.

As per the translated directions, he slid his hand to the brick directly across the corner from the one with the sword marking. He pushed on one end and felt it move slightly. He pushed harder, causing the mortar to crumble. As if it was on a swivel, the brick swung out long way at its center. He then put his hand on the part of the brick now jutting out, and shoved it back into the wall until it was flush.

There was a pause in which nothing happened, and he began to wonder if he had done something wrong. He was considering consulting the instructions again when a grinding noise reverberated across the basement. It sounded as if some large creature was clearing its throat after waking up from an extended nap. He held his breath, and waited to see what would happen next with impatient anticipation.

A section of the wall started to move inward. There was a large release of stale air, filled with dust that enveloped him in a grimy cloud. The smell was nauseating, and he found himself trying to cough and sneeze at the same time. Neither function was successful, and he continued to choke on the thick dust-filled air.

The cloud finally dissipated enough for him to catch his breath. After sucking in a lungful of cleaner air, he saw the hidden door was now completely revealed. A six by four foot section, which only seconds before had been perfectly hidden as part of the brick wall, now stood partially open. According to the document those Irish fools had brought with them to this country, Arthur's sword Excalibur was lying in wait in the hidden room beyond.

With his excitement mounting, the Ghost reached out with both hands and pushed. The wall swung easily inward, almost knocking him off balance. He had expected it to be heavy and unwieldy, yet it moved as smoothly as if it was attached to well-oiled hinges.

He stepped into an eight-by-eight room. The walls were made from similar bricks as to the rest of basement. There was no light save for what little filtered in from outside. This caused some exaggerated shadowing throughout the chamber, but he could make out the stone altar in the exact center of the room.

Thinking the raised stone dais to be akin to a sarcophagus, he walked over, preparing to push a heavy stone lid. As he approached, he saw that it was all one piece. There were no seams visible. He wondered if, like the door to the chamber, there was some sort of hidden catch or lever. Then he noticed two forked metal rods set into the top of the altar, and a sinking feeling began to settle over him.

The metal rods were placed far enough apart and fashioned in a way that would be perfect to hold a broadsword. He refused to admit he might have been duped, and did his best to convince himself maybe this was some elaborate distraction to fool anyone who might have stumbled onto the secret door by chance.

In the blue glow from the phone he looked again at the paper. When something on the floor caught his attention, he knelt to get a better look, and felt whatever hope he had of still finding Excalibur in this room come crashing down.

There in the dust he could make out a set of footprints different than his own. They were partially covered by dirt, and had been there for some time. At least a few years. Someone had been in this chamber sometime within the past few years, and removed Excalibur.

An overwhelming fury swept over him. He stood, the paper slipping from his hand, and threw his cell phone with every ounce of strength his angered state could muster. The small piece of modern technology shattered into state-of-the-art shrapnel as it connected with the unforgiving brick wall.

He burst back out of the chamber in a blind rage, and shoved the first thing he reached. Metal shelving filled with years worth of forgotten junk toppled over, echoing with the sound of a mini avalanche. Like a petulant child, he continued to kick and hit anything in his path, yelling out his frustration in one long stream of vile curses.

When his anger was finally sated, and he was once more controlled by reason and rational thought, he was able to regain his composure. He still trembled from the aftershocks of his temper tantrum working their way through his system. He found himself standing amidst deposed shelves and broken knick-knacks from another decade. Realizing how much noise and commotion his tirade had undoubtedly caused, he knew he had to get out of this underground prison and the King's Chapel now.

Haste was more important than stealth. He made his way haphazardly through the maze of refuse to the stairs leading up and out of the basement. It took longer than he liked, as he had to double back after turning down wrong aisles to find himself at dead-ends. Finally, he emerged into the soft yellow light marking the staircase.

He climbed up the steps two at a time. No one was in the small hallway. He half walked and half jogged around the corner and down the longer corridor. He could see the door which would allow him access back into the main worship area. He was not about to take any chances.

A man in a well-tailored suit stepped out of the same men's room he himself had hid in a short while ago. The man looked up in time to see the Ghost's fist come slamming down into his temple, and crumpled to the floor as if someone had pulled his plug and let all the air out.

The Ghost continued through the door, not slowing down at all after eliminating the potential obstacle and witness. Back under the scaffolding being used by the restoration project workers, he remembered the uneasy feeling he had experienced upon first seeing them, and now understood why. With the King's Chapel undergoing a major facelift, whoever else knew about Excalibur had removed the blade out of precaution, so it would not be accidentally discovered.

The tour he had entered with was nowhere to be found, not that he cared. He made his way up the aisle until he exited out the front door. The sun momentarily blinded him after spending all that time in the darkened basement. It took a few seconds before he got his bearings back, and he returned to the parking lot and his awaiting vehicle.

Once he was inside the Trailblazer another fit of rage overtook him. He pounded his fists into the steering wheel until a slippery wetness ran down his wrists. The sight of the garishly red blood dripping onto his pant legs was enough to quell the tide of his anger.

He had unwittingly been outmaneuvered, and that was unacceptable. Someone was going to pay. An evil grin replaced the dangerous scowl on his twisted face. He still had Blackburn and his female companion to deal with. Maybe their luck would be better than his and they could lead him to Excalibur. Or give it to him; he was sure Blackburn would trade the sword for the woman's life. All was not lost, he would simply have to adjust his timetable.

Hearing the sound of sirens nearing the chapel, he knew it was time to leave. He fired the SUV up, actually passing a police cruiser as he pulled back onto Tremont Street and drove away. He did not spare a second glance, however; he had work to do.

Unnoticed by the Ghost as he made his hasty retreat out of King's Chapel, a worker who had previously placed a phone call now placed another.

After dialing, the worker waited for his superior to pick up on the other end. When the superior did, he passed on his information.

"Yes, our second party has fled the premises, and he left empty handed."

"I see," a voice on the other end said before hanging up.

The worker closed his phone, slipped it back into the front pocket of his work overalls, and returned to his job of repairing an area of water damage to the chapel's ceiling.

CHAPTER 23

"I can see I have managed to render you somewhat speechless, Agent Sommers," Nicholas said.

"I think you caught all of us," she said, motioning with her hand to encompass her three equally shocked colleagues, "with our proverbial pants down, Mr. Nicholas."

The older gentleman smiled at her rather blunt summary of the situation. His smile seemed sincere and he appeared to be genuinely amused, which managed to alleviate some of the tension she'd felt. She was not a hundred percent positive quite yet, but she hoped she could trust this man.

"Who or what are the Franklin Knights?" Professor Foshay asked.

Leave it to Foshay to ask the pertinent question. This afternoon had taken such an unexpected turn that Sommers thought her brain might be on some sort of sensory overload. She was grateful the professor was at least still paying attention. She turned to look in his direction, and when he met her eyes she gave him a smile and a nod to show her appreciation.

"The Franklin Knights, Professor Foshay, are the guardians and caretakers of the very sword you all have been looking for. It has been our charge for over 200 years to protect Excalibur and its secrets." Nicholas took another long puff of his cigar, exhaling a cloud of aromatic smoke.

"I don't understand," Reggie said. "If your...organization has known about Excalibur for all these years, why keep it hidden? Why not give it to a museum or even to a government agency for safe keeping?"

Amy had been thinking something similar, and now turned her attention to Nicholas to see how he would respond. Their host did not answer right away. Instead, he slowly leaned back in his chair and stared at Reggie for several long seconds before answering.

"The simplest answer to your question, Agent Blackburn, is that the duty given to my great-great-grandfather by Benjamin Franklin himself was to guard the sword until such a time it would be needed," Nicholas said.

She was on the verge of posing her own question when the professor slapped his open palm onto the top of the table.

"Of course!" the professor said, his voice rising in excitement. "I knew your name sounded familiar. Your great-great-grandfather was Samuel Nicholas, the leader of the Continental Marines, wasn't he?"

"Very good, Professor Foshay. He was indeed the very same man you just mentioned," Nicholas said, a large friendly smile moving his face as well.

"I'm sorry to intrude," Ambrosius said, "but what does any of this have to do with Excalibur?"

Good old Ambroisus, she thought. He had been quiet up to this point, not all that out of character for him as she had personally witnessed his many mood swings over the last few hours, but the man's own excitement was starting to again show through the chinks in his prim and proper veneer.

"Ah, my good Agent Ambrosius," Nicholas said. "It has everything to do with Excalibur."

"Why don't you fill in the blanks we seem to be missing for us, Mr. Nicholas?" she said.

"It would be my distinct pleasure, Agent Sommers," Nicholas said. He set his cigar in the crystal ashtray next to his wine flute, and sat forward in his chair, giving nothing away. "I am sure the knowledgeable professor here has already filled you in on the events leading to Excalibur's arrival in this country, so I will not bother with those details."

"Yes, according to Professor Foshay," Ambrosius said, motioning towards the professor, "the sword's last known location was in the possession of you ancestor, Samuel Nicholas, but after that, Excalibur seems to have been lost to history."

"Not quite," Nicholas said. "As you know, Benjamin Franklin brought Excalibur home with him when he returned from his travels abroad. This was shortly before the outbreak of the Revolutionary War in May of 1775. Later that year, in early November, the United States Marine Corps was born at Tun Tavern in Philadelphia when the Continental Marines were formed. My great-great-grandfather, Captain Samuel Nicholas, was put in command. He was quickly promoted to Colonel and given four officers to serve under him."

"Why is that significant?" she asked, interrupting their host's explanation.

"All in good time, Agent Sommers," Nicholas said. There was the hint of a mischievous gleam in his eyes before he continued. "Now, naturally, the Marines that Samuel Nicholas was in charge of were not like the elite fighting force the Marines are today. They were more like an undercover protection service. Some of their first assignments were covert operations in which they assisted the Navy. The Continental Marines participated in the first naval battle between an American squadron and the British Navy in 1776. They also fought at the Battle of Princeton against General Cornwallis' main army. Most importantly, however, they had the task of ferrying and protecting the Continental Army, including General George Washington, across the Delaware River at the Battle of Trenton. In all of those instances, along with all their missions in-between, Samuel Nicholas carried Excalibur with him, and in all of those instances, the Continental Marines were never beaten."

The significance of Nicholas' last statement was not lost on her or her companions. No wonder a terrorist organization would want to get their hands on the sword. Yes, according to legend Excalibur granted the rightful owner the right to become king of Britain, but even if that particular bit of lore proved to be false, the terrorists could cut an unstoppable and bloody swath through England on their way to the throne.

"This history lesson has been fun and all, but when do we get to the part where you and your merry band of knights come in?" Reggie asked.

"Let the man finish, Reggie," Sommers said, shooting him a stern look which he ignored completely in true Reggie fashion.

"Thank you, Agent Sommers, but I was just getting to that part," Nicholas said. He took a sip of wine before launching into his story anew. "Once the war was over, there was no further need of the Continental Marines. In 1785, they were disbanded. Samuel Nicholas traveled to Philadelphia accompanied by his four officers to return Excalibur to Benjamin Franklin. Unbeknownst to Nicholas and his men, a select group of this country's forefathers had met and discussed this very subject, and decided Excalibur would not be returned to the French, to Britain, or anyone else. Instead, it was to be kept safe in case it would be needed, especially if the English tried to retake the Colonies. It was left up to Benjamin Franklin to decide how and who would keep Excalibur's secret. Naturally, Franklin turned to the one man he had already entrusted the sword to – my great-great-grandfather Samuel Nicholas. Thus, the Franklin Knights were born."

"That's quite a tale, Mr. Nicholas," she said.

She looked around the room. Everyone was busy mulling over all the information they had been given. She was sure there were at least a thousand questions swimming around in each person's head, but no one seemed sure how or where to begin.

"I can't believe after all this time and study I have put into Arthurian legend, Excalibur has been right here in Boston under my nose," the professor said.

She had to smile at the sound of astonishment in his voice. For him this must be akin to someone who had spent the bulk of their professional life searching for Bigfoot only to find themselves accidentally stumbling across the beast as it slept in their back yard.

"That does bring up the question as to how Excalibur came to be in Boston," Reggie said.

"And its current location," Ambrosius added.

"Would you mind elaborating further for us, Mr. Nicholas?" she asked.

Before Nicholas could reply however, the muffled sound of the William Tell Overture emanated from the his jacket. The sound was so unexpected it left her momentarily speechless.

"If you will excuse me for a moment," Nicholas said. He then reached into an inside pocket and removed a small black cell phone which he answered. "Yes...I see." Worry lines appeared on his brow. "Call me back when he leaves." He hung up, frowning in a moment of trepidation, albeit a brief one. "Let's see, where were we?" he asked.

"You were about to tell us how the sword got here in Boston," she said, deciding to let the phone interlude pass for now.

"Ah yes. Thank you, Agent Sommers. After accepting the job they had been given, Samuel Nicholas and his officers left Philadelphia and came to Boston. This is where most of them were originally from, so it was where they would hide and protect the sword. Only those five men knew its location. That secret has been passed down from father to son for generations, as has the charge of keeping Excalibur safe until such a time its power is once again called upon. Our group has grown over the years to include watchers, and even soldiers in case their services are ever needed. But only the descendents of the original five men, designated as Caretakers, know where Excalibur is."

"So you know where it is right now?" Ambrosius asked in an excited whisper.

"I am one of five current Caretakers," Nicholas said. "Mr. Grant, who served as your guide here, is another."

"And you will take us to the sword?" Sommers asked.

"Yes, Agent Sommers. It has been decided that you will be given the duty of returning Excalibur to its rightful home."

"After all these years of keeping the secret, you're willing to just hand it over?" Reggie asked. "I'm sorry, but what's the catch."

She had to admit Reggie had a good point. She had been so caught up in the initial fervor of fulfilling her mission that she did not bother with thinking the whole thing through.

"Yeah, Mr. Nicholas. Why would you give me, or us," she said, motioning, "the sword whose secret you and your organization have taken so seriously for the last 200 plus years?"

Nicholas smiled sadly before answering. "Trust me, Agent Sommers, this decision was not made lightly. This conclusion was reached only after much debate. The moment the document surfaced, those of us in charge knew our time was limited. If Excalibur fell into the hands of terrorists, the results could and undoubtedly would be catastrophic. We are simply not equipped to handle such a threat. Recent events have made that fact even more abundantly clear."

This last statement left her a little confused. "Has something happened, Mr. Nicholas?" she asked, thinking of the phone call Nicholas had gotten a short while ago, and also wondering if it had anything to do with the Ghost. She looked over at Reggie and saw the same concern mirrored on his face.

"Nothing unexpected, Agent Sommers," Nicholas said. "It seems our mutual adversary has finally made an appearance."

"Are you talking about the Ghost?" she asked, and was embarrassed by the quiver in her voice.

"The one and same," Nicholas answered.

"We knew it was only a matter of time before our paths would cross with his," Ambrosius said.

"We can't let him get his hands on Excalibur," Reggie said.

"Don't worry, Agent Blackburn," Nicholas said smugly. "This Ghost is in for a bit of a surprise, and Excalibur is currently in no danger of falling into the vile clutches of this rather unsavory fellow."

"What do you mean?" she asked.

"The document was not currently accurate. We moved the sword to a new location a several years ago due to an unforeseen restoration project taking place at its original location."

She sat back in her chair and let out the nervous breath she had been holding. Reggie gave an audible snort of nervous laughter while the professor and Ambrosius sat in silence. The tension which had swept over the room at the mention of the Ghost was released as quickly as it had come.

"Again, I have to ask, why me?" she asked when the feelings of relief subsided.

"Honestly, Agent Sommers, we did not have a lot of options and we wanted to move quickly. If anyone would have the means of protecting the sword, it would be the Agency. My associates and I knew you and Agent Ambrosius would eventually seek out Professor Foshay, seeing as how he is the foremost expert in Arthurian legend. It was a slight surprise to also find Agent Blackburn there as well, but his presence only adds to our knowledge that Excalibur will be kept safe."

"Will you take us to the sword?" Ambrosius asked.

"Mr. Grant is standing by to do just that. But first, I need assurances from you that Excalibur will be returned to its rightful owner, and that it will be kept safe so as not to fall into the hands of those who would use its power for evil."

"Sir, if given Excalibur, I can guarantee it on my life," Ambrosius said his voice as serious and grave as she had ever heard it.

"Then the charge passed down to me from my great-great grandfather Samuel Nicholas, given to him by Benjamin Franklin, I know pass on to you: Agent Sommers, Agent Blackburn, Agent Ambrosius, and Professor Foshay."

The enormity of the man's words settled on her shoulders like a shroud. By the serious and dedicated looks on the faces of her three companions, especially Ambrosius, she knew they felt the weight of responsibility too. Something very important had passed to them, and they were not about to falter for any reason.

Nicholas' cell phone cut through the silence again. A similar scene as before played itself out. Nicholas carried on a brief conversation, then returned the phone to his pocket. This time, however, a look of amusement moved across his face instead of concern.

"It would seem your Ghost has realized his mistake and left empty handed. From what I have just been told, he was not very happy upon his departure."

"That is not going to bode well for someone," Reggie said.

"Yeah," she said, heeding Reggie's warning as thoughts of the translator's body and how he had been tortured before he died flashed before her eyes. "Let's just hope its not us."

"Mr. Nicholas, if you would be so kind to tell us where Excalibur is now, we can get started," Ambrosius said. "The quicker we get the sword, the quicker we can get it far away from men like this Ghost and his employers."

"Of course," Nicholas said as a knowing and mischievous smile played at the corners of his mouth. "Do any of you follow baseball?"

—CHAPTER 24

The Ghost drove aimlessly through the congested streets of Boston, trying to decide how best to proceed.

He spotted a business which piqued his interest, an internet café nestled between a mom and pop dry cleaners and a shabby looking bakery. With its offering of modern technological advances, the small coffee shop looked about as out of place as a python in a bunny cage.

"Always Online Café," he said reading the name of the bright blue neon sign hanging out front. "Let's hope so."

The place was as empty as the many parking spaces outside proclaimed it to be. The Ghost was pleased. He did not need some pimply-faced computer geek who had been updating a Facebook page in hopes of adding more friends to a list that would never fill the empty space the geek had in his real life looking over his shoulder as he worked.

After his failed excursion at the King's Chapel, the document enclosed inside the Halliburton was nothing more than a worthless piece of paper. The mere thought of the time he wasted searching the chapel's basement made his blood boil all over again.

He sat as still as petrified wood, both hands gripped tightly around the steering wheel, as he tried to get his emotions under control. After several deep cleansing breaths he felt his fury slowly drift into mild irritation and finally dissipate into the reserved calm he was more accustomed to.

The Always Online Café was not very big, the lighting was low and seeing as how he was the only customer, the place was quiet.

A twenty-something guy sat behind a register, reading an astrophysics textbook. He did not bother to look up until the Ghost was standing directly across from him. "May I help you?"

"Yes you can," the Ghost said coldly. "I need to use one of the computers, and I would also like a cup of whatever you have that will pass for coffee."

"That I can do, Sir. Please have a seat anywhere you like. The coffee will cost you $1.25 and there is a $5.00 an hour charge for use of the computer and internet."

"I may be a while, so just run a tab for me."

"No problem, Sir. Help yourself to a computer, and I will bring your coffee out shortly."

He chose a spot close to the entrance but off to the side for privacy. The computer was a newer model Dell, but basically a child's toy compared to his Acer Travelmate back in London. It would serve his purpose however, and that was all he was interested in.

After reaching over for his cup of coffee and taking a sip, he made a face of pure disgust as the bitter flavor reached his taste buds. He looked back with pure malice over his shoulder at the young man, who had retreated behind the counter and resumed his studies. He did not know who he would have to kill to get a decent cup of gourmet coffee in this country, but he was giving serious consideration to finding out.

A scene of some tropical island served as the wallpaper on the monitor, a harsh reminder of the chilled temperatures outside. The Ghost opened an internet search engine and went to work.

It took him barely an hour to get what he was looking for. He smiled gleefully as Special Agent Reggie Blackburn's private Agency cell phone number appeared on the computer screen. Even though he had not been active with the Agency for years, the backdoors he had installed into their security systems were still there. He would have to remember to utilize this little trick of his more often for future reference.

He punched the number into his own cellphone so he could save it, shut everything down, paid his bill without leaving a tip on the principle that the coffee was horrid, and exited the internet café.

Once back in the Trailblazer, with the heater on, he took out his cellphone again.

With a deep breath to focus his thoughts, he scrolled down his contacts list until the number for Blackburn came up, and he pushed the "send" button.

Fenway Park, Blackburn thought. *Who would have ever guessed...?*

Mr. Grant, their initial guide, would drive them to Fenway Park and oversee Excalibur being transferred to Sommers. His grandfather several times removed had been a lieutenant under Samuel Nicholas, making him part of the inner circle of the current Franklin Knights.

The butler, Mr. Dawson, had brought their coats and the four of them stood quietly in the chateau's foyer, lost in their own respective thoughts, as they awaited the arrival of Mr. Grant. Reggie read a myriad of emotions in their expressions, including excitement, disbelief, and subtle hints of fear. He couldn't be the only one wondering what had become of the Ghost.

This case was finally coming to a head, and if all went as he hoped, he and Sommers would be back in Washington before the day was out. Then he could start to untangle the mess he was undoubtedly in for letting his personal friendship lead him into interfering in an active case.

An ominous wave of foreboding crashed over Reggie as his cellphone began to vibrate. He hesitated before answering, but the device would not be denied.

It was a number he did not recognize. He turned his back and took several steps away from the others so they would not be able to listen in on his conversation.

Once he knew he was out of earshot, he said, "Agent Blackburn." "Reggie, my old friend, it's been a while," the Ghost said.

He actually cringed when he heard the words and the all-too-familiar voice. His worst fears were about to be fully realized.

The only response he seemed to be able to come up with was a shake of his head in stunned disbelief which of course was a futile gesture. He'd known this moment would eventually come. As soon as he learned the Ghost was also searching for Excalibur he knew their paths would inevitably cross.

"What do you want, Granderson?" was all he could manage, anger causing him to clench his jaw tightly.

"Easy, big fella," the Ghost mocked. "You're going to give yourself a stroke. I'm sure your blood pressure is already a touch on the high side. Besides, you already know what I want."

He heard the tone in the Ghost's voice take on a razor's edge. "You can't have it, and no matter what you try, I'll stop you."

"Really, Reggie, there is no need for this to escalate to open hostility. I would hate for *people* to get hurt because you do not want to play nice and share."

The way the Ghost emphasized the word "people" put him on alert. It had clearly been a warning, and he spared another look at Sommers, knowing exactly what "people" the killer was alluding to.

"Don't even think about --"

"Don't pretend to think you can give me orders, Blackburn. Those days are long behind us, and now I'm the one in charge."

He heard madness in the Ghost's voice, and knew there would be no reasoning with the man. He would have to choose his own words carefully or he might accidentally set the lunatic off on a violence spree.

"You know I can't give you the sword, Granderson."

"Poor Blackburn, always playing the hero. Except, this time, your lack of compliance could lead to someone else becoming the dead martyr. Look, I'll make it easy for you. Just tell me where the sword is and I will get it myself. Once I have it, I'm gone, and you will no longer have to worry your fat face about me. But mark my words and mark them well, Reggie. If you deceive me in any way, your lady friend will die in an excruciatingly slow and messy way, but not before I've had my fun. You know I always make good on my threats."

There it was, out in the open. If he did not give the Ghost Excalibur's location, Sommers' life was forfeit. The Ghost would indeed make good on his threat. Whatever power the guy had at his disposal, Reggie knew he was no match for. He could only protect Sommers to a certain degree. If the Ghost wanted to get to her, he eventually would, and there was nothing Reggie or anyone else, in the Agency or otherwise, could do about it.

"By your pause I'm going to surmise that you are considering my proposal and your options, Reggie old buddy. Let me simplify your options. You don't have any. Give me the location or the woman dies in a lot of pain."

Reggie knew the Ghost was right. His only real option was to give Granderson the sword's location and hope he could get there before his adversary did and put a stop to this madness once and for all. It was a long shot and in all honesty a horrible plan, but it might be enough to save Sommers.

"All right, Granderson you win."

"Truly, Reggie, was there ever any doubt I wouldn't?"

"It's somewhere in Fenway Park. Don't ask where because I don't know. I'm on the verge of being taken there myself."

"I see. This could prove rather interesting them, couldn't it?"

"There, now you know the sword's location, but also know this," Reggie said, his own voice taking on a steely edge. "I'm going to do everything in my power to stop you."

"I wouldn't have it any other way, Reggie old friend. I'm actually looking forward to it."

He was ready to fling one last insult at the Ghost, but the line went dead. Trembling with rage, it took him several attempts to replace his phone back into its clip.

Mr. Grant and their ride had arrived. Reggie walked back to the others, still with no idea how to proceed.

"You okay, Reggie?" Sommers asked. "You look a little shaken."

"Yeah, I'm fine. I'm just anxious to get this case over with," he said, which was more true than anyone knew.

"You and me both," Sommers said.

He was the last one out the front door. The sunshine did nothing to brighten his mood. All he could think was that, no matter what happened next, the Ghost must be stopped.

By any and all means necessary.

CHAPTER 25

The atmosphere inside of the limousine was mostly positive as the lights of the stadium appeared in the distance. There was a sense of hopeful optimism. Except for Reggie, Sommers noted.

She had been watching him closely ever since he received that phone call, and he had become more sullen and withdrawn with every passing mile. She considered broaching the subject, but paused.

If there was something going on she needed to know about, she was sure Reggie would tell her. Until he decided to open up, she would give him some space. The vibe he gave off was creeping her out, though. It almost reeked of fear.

"We're coming up on Fenway," Mr. Grant said.

He was in the back with the rest of them, having changed out of the well-tailored suit he'd worn when she first met him into more casual attire: khaki slacks, a lightweight white shirt, and a black mid-thigh length leather jacket. She still wasn't sure how much they could really trust the guy. So far, Grant had not given up any information either through his words or behavior. He was as much an enigma as the rest of this case. He was friendly enough, but only to a degree, managing to keep a professional distance which made him seem aloof.

Who would have thought this case would end at a baseball stadium? Nothing about this search for Excalibur had been simple, so why would actually getting the sword be any different?

"What made you and your associates choose Fenway Park?" Professor Foshay asked. "It seems like such an odd choice."

"The Nicholas family is part owners of the Red Sox franchise, which gives Thomas Nicholas access to the stadium," Grant said. "The restoration project of the King's Chapel meant we had to move quickly. Fenway Park provided us with an easy solution. Besides, it has been a boon for baseball fans in this town."

"What does that mean?" Reggie asked, the first words he'd spoken since their brief conversation back at the chateau.

"It could be mere coincidence, but Excalibur was moved to Fenway in January of 2004," Grant said.

"I don't understand," Professor Foshay said.

"The Red Sox won the World Series in 2004. Their first since 1918," Reggie said.

"Wait a minute, they won this year too," she said, catching on.

"Correct, Agent Sommers," Grant said. "They have also been in the playoffs every year since the sword was moved."

"And you think Excalibur being at Fenway is responsible for the Red Sox's resurgence?" Professor Foshay asked.

It was Ambrosius who answered. "It has long been rumored that anyone who carries Excalibur into battle is unbeatable, so it is not much of a stretch to believe its power could affect this sport team just by its proximity to their field of battle, so to speak."

"Great," she said with a sarcastic chuckle. "If the Red Sox Nation gets wind of what we're up to, we'll have the whole city after us."

"Yeah, just think of the trouble we would have if the Cubs fans in Chicago knew about this," Reggie said, and they all laughed.

Despite the much-needed round of laughter, Sommers found that her cop intuition was up and running, warning her deep down in her gut that things might get rough before all was said and done.

As the oldest stadium in professional baseball, Fenway Park did not offer all of the modern amenities of many much newer parks built in the last few years. One of those perks Fenway lacked was easy and accessible parking. The Red Sox fans must have faced a traffic nightmare after each game. The logistics of 30-40 thousand people trying to cram their automobiles onto the already overcrowded Boston streets was something she did not even want to think about.

Their driver avoided the insufficient parking situation by taking them around to a gate at the rear. It opened onto a small lot capable of holding maybe forty cars. Sommers realized it was the players' entrance, deserted now with baseball season over, but she could well imagine the crowd of autograph seekers who must swarm to this lot like moths to an open flame.

The limo took an open spot closest to an entrance which lead into the stadium. She felt the luxury vehicle idle as it was put into park, and then was a little surprised when the engine stopped completely. Apparently the driver was not going to wait with the car like in the movies, but must be planning to attend their little part as well.

"What about security?" Ambrosius asked as the limo stopped.

Sommers turned to look at the Knight, awaiting his answer.

"Security will not be a problem," Grant said, his smug tone expressing total confidence. "One of the perks , if you will, of being part owner of the franchise is that Mr. Nicholas has sole rights to contract his company out to provide private security for the stadium."

"So, this means…," she said, trailing off, hoping Grant would get the hint and fill in the blank.

"This means," he said, "all security officers within Fenway Park were handpicked by Mr. Nicholas himself. They are all loyal to our cause."

They exited the limousine one at a time, with Mr. Grant being the last. He had a quick word with the driver, who looked like a Secret Service clone, before taking the lead and walking towards the stadium's entrance. They went single-file, with Amy, Ambrosius, the Professor, and Reggie following Grant. The driver moved into a rear guard position and followed as well.

They moved into a narrow, dimly lit tunnel, illuminated by a single light bulb hanging uncovered several feet above their heads. The tunnel was worn, and had obviously seen its fair share of decades. Amy had to take a second to catch her breath as she realized they were walking down the same passage that baseball icons like Babe Ruth and Ted Williams had used.

The slamming door echoed, loud enough to startle her. The already dark passage became encased in shadows. Grant opened another door ahead of them. Light poured through from a brightly-lit room. Sommers looked over her shoulder, past Professor Foshay, at Reggie. He was definitely on edge and worried. His odd and nervous behavior had her concerned. It was not like him to be so skittish. She saw his eyes darting around, searching every crack, crevice, and corner where a shadow had come to roost.

They emerged into the much heralded Red Sox clubhouse. At this moment, Sommers knew, she was the envy of every baseball fan in Boston. She was a moderate sports fan at best, but even she could not help but feel the thrill of excitement as she looked around.

The lockers stood like sentinels, though were now all empty; the players having packed their belongings at the end of another successful season before scattering to their winter homes awaiting spring. The carpet was the same color green as the lockers and crunched under their feet as they moved through the room. A large Red Sox logo was woven into it at the exact center of the room.

Though Fenway Park itself was quite old, the clubhouse had been modernized. There were several large screen plasma televisions, along with plush furniture that seemed to be calling out to her to come sit and relax. It was a good thing Grant kept them moving because if there had been any type of pause, her self-control would have broken down and she would have launched herself onto the nearest sofa.

Grant never slowed, however, as he led them into an adjoining training room full of work-out equipment. The free weights and machines were state-of-the-art and would be the envy of any public gym in the city. They proceeded into what was obviously the equipment storage facility. It looked like a mini warehouse, with every piece of baseball equipment imaginable and some she would have never imagined, packed on shelves and racks. The rows of bats, gloves, and uniforms made her feel as if she had somehow stepped right into an obsessed Little Leaguer's dream.

Grant turned. "We are going to a sub-basement. It will be darker and the steps are old and narrow, so everyone please watch your step."

He strode over to the far right corner and waved them forward. In the tile floor were a metal ring and concrete circle around a lock, and a black line that made up the seam of a trapdoor. Grant pulled a silver chain from under his shirt from. Attached to the chain was a small key. It reminded Amy of the key she had used on her locker back when she was with the LAPD. Grant knelt, inserted the key into the hole in the center of the pull ring, and gave it a twist. She heard the sound of the lock's tumblers clicking into place.

She tossed a questioning look Grant's way as he grabbed the ring with one hand and easily pulled the trapdoor open.

"We made a few updates and modifications when we first brought Excalibur here," Grant said by way of explanation.

"Well then, let's get this party started," she said.

"By all means." He stepped onto the stairway leading down.

She watched as Grant disappeared into the darkness, hearing the creaking and groaning of the aged steps as they accepted his weight. After sharing a look with her companions and receiving a nod of approval from Ambrosius, she began her descent.

The steps led down about six feet. Using what light seeped down from the equipment room above, she was able to maneuver down the ancient staircase without incident. As soon as she touched down on the hard concrete of the sub-basement's floor, she could hear the protest of the stairs as whoever was next in line began their descent.

When they were all at the bottom of the steps, Grant produced a small hand held flashlight and led them down a narrow hall.

"It's just up ahead," he said.

Behind them, the stairs creaked again, probably the old staircase resettling after having been unused for so long. Sommers focused on the small circle of light from Grant's flashlight, which had come to rest on a steel door with an electronic keypad.

The metal of the door gleamed. It looked so out of place in the decrepit sub-basement she had to wonder why no one had noticed it before. Then she remembered that Fenway's security force was in the employ of Mr. Nicholas and his Knights.

She held her breath in anticipation as Grant punched in the code on the number lock. There was a slight pause where nothing happened, and she experienced a flash of paranoid fear that this whole journey was for nothing, but in the next second the red sensor light on the keypad flashed green and the lock released with an audible click.

Grant grabbed the lever on the door and pushed it down, allowing the heavy steel door to swing inward. He stepped across the threshold and was quickly gobbled up by the absolute darkness of the chamber's interior. She wanted to follow, but hesitated. It was not until a light switched on from within that she let out the breath she had been holding.

One by one, they moved into what looked like a bank vault. The light was provided by two sets of fluorescent bulbs set into the ceiling. The cinderblock walls and concrete floor were painted a battleship gray, giving the room a bunker feel to it. In the center of the room was a wooden table. On the table was a large metal container about six feet long.

The air in the room was stale and humid, and only grew worse with everyone's increasingly rapid breathing. She looked around at her three companions, hoping to see their anticipation and excitement matched her own. Ambrosius was sweating profusely like he was sick with a fever, Professor Foshay looked almost giddy with a silly grin spread across his face, and Reggie kept staring over his shoulder nervously.

"I hope you understand the level of responsibility you are about to take on by accepting Excalibur, Agent Sommers," Grant said.

"Trust me, Mr. Grant," she said. "I have seen up close and personal what people are willing to do to get their hands on this sword. I don't enter into this lightly, but it is the task I have been given. It's my duty to see Excalibur gets to the Agency safely, and I mean to do just that."

Grant appeared reassured by her comments and with a barely perceptible nod of acknowledgement moved over to the box. The container had a key and combination lock set into it. When Grant finished manipulating the locks on the box, he went around the opposite side of the table so he stood behind the container, facing them. She could feel the tension mount as Grant paused, making her think it was for dramatic effect. Then, with a quick flourish of movement, lifted open the lid.

She caught a brief twinkle as if something gleamed in the light, but other than that was unable to see the contents. No one spoke or even breathed as Grant reached into the box, grabbed hold of something, and pulled forth the sword Excalibur.

She was not sure what she expected, but the heavens did not open up, angels did not sing, and lightning did not flash from the sky. Instead, Grant stood there bathed in artificial light, holding a fairly ordinary looking blade.

Rather anticlimactic, she thought, and had to admit she was actually a little disappointed.

The sword itself was nothing all that special to look at. It looked like a standard broadsword any number of medieval warriors or knights would have carried during that era. She was about to move in for a closer look when she heard Reggie voice the same question rolling through her mind.

"Is that it?"

"Yes, Agent Blackburn that is it," Ambrosius said in a voice filled with reverent awe. "That is Arthur's sword. That is Excalibur."

His tone of almost religious fervor gave Sommers the urge to genuflect, though she did not see what was so special about this sword that would cause such a reaction. To her, the sword Grant held was the same as others she'd seen on display at museums. Heck, this whole thing could be an elaborate hoax, and the sword could be nothing more than a Hollywood prop, for all they knew.

As she was beginning to second guess this whole scenario, she felt a pressure on her waist like she was being grabbed from behind, followed by a sharp sting along her throat. In stunned disbelief, she saw a hand holding a wicked looking knife materialize as if from thin air.

"Good work, gentlemen," said a voice as smooth and calm as the death it promised. "Now hand over Excalibur or your pretty little friend here dies."

CHAPTER 26

No one immediately reacted. The Ghost's unexpected appearance had thrown them all for a loop.

"What the hell…" Sommers said, instinctively beginning to pull away from the knife at her throat.

"Easy now, Agent Sommers," the Ghost said. "I don't want to kill you…yet. But don't think for one second I won't slit your throat and bleed you right here and now."

The confidant tone in the man's voice left no question as to the validity of his threat. She had participated in countless interviews and interrogations during her career, and had absolutely no doubt the man would do exactly as he said if she continued to struggle. His perfect calm left her chilled and she froze in place.

"Very good, Agent Sommers. I see Agent Blackburn has trained you well."

The Ghost had pure malice in his voice when he mentioned Reggie's name, an obvious hatred and longing for retribution that went deeper than mere rivalry. The way Reggie stared at her captor with obvious hatred spoke of a betrayal both men felt and wanted resolved.

She shifted her eyes to gauge how the others were handling this new drama. The driver stood motionless, waiting to take his cue from Grant, who had not moved and still clutched Excalibur tightly in his hand. Ambrosius seemed to be in a deep concentration. The professor was scared, as well he should be. It was several long seconds before Reggie finally spoke. "Well, Granderson, I'm glad you showed. To be honest, I didn't think you had it in you."

She felt the pressure around her waist increase and the tip of the knife dug into the soft skin of her throat, drawing a small bead of blood as the Ghost tightened his grip in response to Reggie's taunting words.

"I'm going to enjoy watching you suffer, Blackburn. I've waited a long time for this, and make no mistake this time I will kill you."

"Then let's get this over with," Reggie said. "Let the others leave, and you and I can settle this alone like we should have done years ago."

"Fine with me, but I want the sword first. Once I have possession of Excalibur, your pretty little partner here and everyone else can walk away."

She did not believe that for a minute. The Ghost had no intention of letting anyone walk out of here if he could help it.

"I suggest, Mr. Grant, you do as he says and hand over the sword," Reggie said.

The look Grant leveled at Reggie said there was no way that was going to happen. He would sacrifice her and everyone else in this room if it meant keeping Excalibur safe. Grant was a soldier willing to die for his cause. Unfortunately, if they did not come up with a viable plan soon, they might all share that same fate.

"Look, he said he would let you go if you give him the sword," Reggie continued.

"I don't care what either of you are saying," Grant said angrily. "Excalibur is going nowhere."

"I said give him the sword!" Reggie shouted, lunging over the table at Grant.

Reggie's unexpected maneuver provided Sommers the opening she was waiting for. When Reggie moved as if to wrestle Excalibur away from Grant, she heard the Ghost's sharp intake of surprised breath. His grip around her waist loosened and the knife at her throat dipped.

She did not hesitate as she fell back onto her self-defense training. As soon as she felt the pressure let up, she brought the heel of her shoe slamming down into the Ghost's shin with as much force as she could muster. She was rewarded by the man's grunt of pain. His leg buckled. She drove her elbow into his stomach, forcing a rush of exhaled air, and then dove to the ground as far away from her attacker as she could get. As she hit the floor, she was already reaching into her coat to free her gun.

At that moment all hell broke loose.

She scrambled up to one knee, bringing her firearm to bear in hopes of getting off a quick kill shot. Chaos reigned all around her. The Ghost took the same knife he had been holding to her throat, and plunged it up to its glossy black hilt into the chest of the man who had been their driver. The man staggered back a step before toppling over face down nearly on top of her. The impact of the hard floor caused the blade to continue on its deadly path, the bloody tip protruding from his back.

She tried to scream a warning as the Ghost turned his deadly attention onto Ambrosius. Her voice was lost in a sudden gust of wind which stole the air from her lungs. The strength of the gale picked up the Ghost and flung him over her head and against the far wall. The brackets of one set of fluorescent lights snapped, and they came crashing down on top of Grant, who dropped Excalibur. The other set of lights began to flicker on and off, adding a strobe light effect to the surreal scene.

Ambrosius held both arms out in front of him with his index fingers and thumbs forming a triangle. He shouted a word she did not comprehend and what looked like a bolt of white lightning shot forth from the triangle. She felt her hair stand up and the air crackled as the bolt of electricity flew past her and exploded against the far wall. The concussive force of the blast knocked her backwards onto the floor as she tried to rise to her feet.

A gun fired, joining the incessant ringing in her ears. She thought the sound came from the direction where Reggie had been standing. She tried to stand again, but her head was spinning and yellow dots danced before her eyes. Someone grabbed at her arm and she saw Professor Foshay kneeling at her side. He was speaking, but she could not focus on what he was saying and so the words were lost as he helped her back to her feet.

Ambrosius attempted to close the distance between himself and the Ghost, who was against the far wall where the wind had blown him. Smoke wafted up from a nasty looking burn on his left arm. Reggie had ducked behind the table, using it and the metal box which had contained Excalibur as cover.

Foshay tried to drag her in the direction of the open door and the relative safety of the hall. Her ears finally popped and her hearing returned in full in one loud confusing wave of sound: Ambrosius chanting in that same strange guttural language, Reggie shouting for the British agent to get out of his way so he could get a clear shot.

She was shocked to find she still had her own firearm in her hand. Meanwhile, the Ghost produced a handgun of his own from beneath his scorched coat. Sommers pushed Professor Foshay aside and took aim. She was shaking, afraid she might hit Ambrosius by mistake, but if she did nothing, the assassin was going to have a perfect kill shot lined up.

She squeezed the trigger. The discharge was thunderous. The bullet flew wide, pinging the wall a foot from the Ghost's head, startling him. Ambrosius abruptly stopped chanting, his concentration apparently disrupted.

She was hurriedly lining up another shot when the Ghost lived up to his name and vanished.

"Everyone out now!" Reggie screamed. She had never heard him so close to panic and it frightened her.

"I'm not leaving without Excalibur!" Instead of panic, there was an unmistakable sound of desperation behind Ambrosius' British accent.

Sommers did not know what to do. The last few crazed moments had left her dazed and confused. She heard a painful groaning and saw that Grant was regaining consciousness. He had a nasty gash over his left eye, the blood from it turning his face into a crimson mask.

The chamber grew eerily silent and calm, like the weather right before a severe thunderstorm unleashed its fury. Sommers trembled from the strain, her adrenaline beginning to subside.

She knew from experience that within a few seconds the shaking would stop and she would once again be in control of her senses.

Then another gun shot rang out, and Reggie disappeared in a red mist.

"NO!" Sommers screamed. Professor Foshay tackled her to the ground.

Several more shots fired in rapid succession. Foshay grunted, and she felt a warm dampness soak into her clothes. Ambrosius began chanting again and the air became charged with some unnamed energy. She saw Reggie's legs sticking out from behind the table. She heard the wind return, growing in intensity. But then it was cut off as yet another shot rang out, this one from a different gun. In his confusion, Grant had fired at Ambrosius, mistaking the British agent for the Ghost.

Sommers pushed against the floor, trying to shift Foshay's weight enough so that she could scramble to her feet. The professor grunted again, but at least she knew he was still alive. She was not so sure about Reggie however.

A final shot sounded as if it came from directly behind her. Grant's head snapped back as if he had been kicked. She could see a perfect bloody circle between his eyes before he slumped to the ground.

She had lost her weapon when Foshay tackled her. As she was about to retrieve it, she felt the warm metal of a recently fired gun press into the back of her head.

"I don't think that's a very wise idea, Agent Sommers," the Ghost said.

She froze.

Ambrosius ... where's Ambrosius? He was nowhere within her line of vision.

"Don't bother looking for your friend," the assassin said, as if reading her thoughts. "That fool I just killed took care of him for me. Bad luck for you, as he was the only one who might have had a chance to stop me."

Her heart sank down into her gut. Foshay gasped in pain as he tried to roll to a sitting position, but the Ghost kicked him like punting a football. The professor went sprawling, unconscious. Her instinct was to turn and fight back against the Ghost, but she knew she would be dead before she even would have the chance to look him in the eye. She was no good to anyone dead. The only way out of this with even a chance for survival was for her to play it cool.

"Take the sword," she said, and hated the fact she sounded as if she was pleading. "We are in no shape to try and stop you. Take Excalibur and go."

"Oh, I intend to, but first I have some unfinished personal matters to attend to."

Bright white light exploded behind her eyes as the Ghost slammed the grip of his gun into the back of her head. She fell forward onto her hands and knees, not quite losing consciousness, but she was in nowhere near any shape to prevent what happened next.

The Ghost circled around to where Reggie was still lying on the floor and fired four times at point blank range into his massive chest. She wanted to scream with rage, but her over-taxed body rebelled and all she could manage was a choking sob of despair. Reggie's body jerked with the impact of each shot. The look of pure unbridled joy on the Ghost's face was something she knew would haunt her nightmares for the rest of her life.

When the gruesome execution was finished, the Ghost moved to Grant's body and retrieved Excalibur. Sommers tried again to rise to her feet, but it was useless. She fell from all fours to a sitting position with her legs splayed out before her. The pounding in her head matched the beating rhythm of her heart.

She was spent both emotionally and physically, and had nothing left to offer in way of resistance as the Ghost approached. She did not even try to fight as the assassin raised his handgun level with her head. With another vicious grin, he pulled the trigger. She waited for the bullet to rip through her skull, putting her out of her misery, but all she heard was the "click" of an empty clip.

"I guess it's your lucky day, Agent Sommers," was all the Ghost said before striding out of the chamber with Excalibur.

She sat motionless until the sound of footsteps faded. Then she rolled over and threw up, every painful heave increasing the already overwhelming pounding in her head. She knew there was no way she would be able to get up, so she half-crawled, half-dragged herself to Reggie's body.

She knew before she got there he was already dead. When she saw the ruin the assassin's gun had turned Reggie's chest into, it became all too real and she could not hold back the tears. Despite the blood, she rested her head on Reggie's now still chest and sobbed uncontrollably.

She remained that way until the Boston Police showed up and called for the paramedics.

—CHAPTER 27

As the large British Airways Airbus A321 leveled out after its take off, the Ghost eased back in his seat, relaxing. He could not think of any other moment in his life he felt so content. He knew he was smiling like a school boy holding the hand of his first crush, but he did not care. The events of the last few hours had left him feeling truly happy for the first time in years.

He leaned his head back onto the soft cushion built into the headrest of his oversized first class seat. Closing his eyes, he called forth the images of Blackburn's last moments on this earth. The way the man lurched like he was being shocked on an operating table as each bullet pierced the bloated body had been a thing of beauty. It had not quite been the death the assassin had envisioned for the man he hated above all others, but it would suffice. Seeing the light fade from Blackburn's eyes to the dull emptiness only death brings was satisfying enough.

Excalibur was his, and at the moment secured safely in the cargo hold. He had not wanted to give the sword up, but there was no way in the post 9/11 era he was going to be allowed to bring a weapon of any kind, much less a broadsword, with him to his seat. But he'd felt so good after killing Blackburn, he had not even minded handing Excalibur over to the airline attendant. It was a good thing he had disposed of his firearm in route to the airport, however.

All he wanted to do now was return to his club in London and collect his fee from those fools of the *Na Ri` Laoch*.

If there were no further delays, he would be landing at Heathrow in seven and a half hours. Things could not have gone smoother.

His only regret was leaving the female agent alive. It was unlike him to leave loose ends, but this one was minor. He had Excalibur and Blackburn was dead. He had achieved both his objectives when taking this job. It was irrelevant that Agent Sommers had survived.

He knew the Agency and was confidant that his former employers, for all their blustering, would not come after him. It was not their style. If this Sommers proved to be the meddlesome type, he would eliminate her as well.

As he enjoyed the mental images, he frowned slightly. It did nag at him that he could not recall seeing the body of the other man. The one who, like himself, had access to some sort of magic. He had seen the strange British agent get shot and fall to the ground, but could not remember noticing him after that.

When the flight attendant came by and took his drink order, he dismissed the whole notion. He was not going to let such a trivial matter invade his glory of putting an end to one Special Agent Reggie Blackburn.

As he recalled the blood pouring from the wounds in Blackburn's chest, he closed his eyes and settled for a nice long nap. He deserved it after a successful and productive day's work after all.

The pressurized interior of the private plane did little to help the constant throbbing in her head. Amy leaned back into the leather seat, closing her eyes, hoping she would be able to sleep for the hour it would take to return to Washington and her meeting with Director Smith.

The events of the last 48 hours were a blur. Her only reminders were the continuous ache in her head and the gut-wrenching sense of loss she felt throughout her entire body. The image of Blackburn lying so still on the cold floor of the chamber flashed across her memory and she had to choke down a lump of emotion beginning to build in her throat. She knew if she let one tear slip out the floodgates would open, and she would not be able to stop.

She remembered waking up in the sterilized room at Massachusetts General Hospital, feeling like she had been run over by a steamroller like Wile E. Coyote in the old Bugs Bunny and Roadrunner cartoons, except that she did not have the ability to peel herself off the ground and re-inflate her body. She still felt flat, as if everything inside her had been forced out, leaving her completely empty or better yet, hollow.

She'd suffered a mild concussion as a result from being pistol-whipped by the Ghost. Apparently, she was not as hard-headed as everyone believed. She had been out cold for close to 24 hours, with the doctors becoming increasingly concerned, until she showed signs of waking up.

When she did wake, it was not all that surprising to find she was not alone. Sitting in her private hospital room was Professor Foshay, sporting a few bandages of his own where a bullet had been surgically removed from his right shoulder. Thomas Nicholas, the incognito leader of the Franklin Knights, was also there. Both men had seemed pleased to finally find her coming around, but the feeling was not mutual. Seeing them only made what had happened all too real, and even though it caused her head to hurt so bad she saw white spots dance around her vision, she broke down and cried.

She appreciated the fact neither had tried to pat her on the back and tell her everything was going to be all right. Instead, the professor had gotten up and closed the door to her room so she could have some privacy to grieve. Though it must have been incredibly awkward for the two men, they sat quietly, waiting for her to regain her composure. Unfortunately, she remembered thinking, that was something she was unsure she would ever be able to do again.

Once her crying subsided to an occasional sob, Nicholas asked her what had happened. She told him everything, though it took a while due to her having to frequently pause every so often to stop herself from breaking down again. Foshay helped fill in when she could not speak, and together they were able to relate everything which had transpired at Fenway.

Nicholas listened to their recounting of the events without saying a word. When she finished, the older gentleman nodded his head and thanked her. He asked about Excalibur. She explained that, from what she remembered, the Ghost had taken the sword. Again he simply nodded. She could see the deep sadness in the man's eyes. She recognized the emotion immediately because she was feeling the same despair herself.

Nicholas informed her that he had arranged for her to return to Washington the next day, with a driver to pick her up here at the hospital and Nicholas' own private plane to fly her home. She had thanked him and tried to apologize for her failure, but he waved her words away.

"I am sure this isn't over quite yet, Agent Sommers," Nicholas had said, before exiting her room leaving her wondering if he had really been there at all.

She recalled how haggard the professor looked. The energetic sparkle in the man's eyes she'd so marveled at was gone. In its place was a pallid haunted look that almost made her cry anew. She sincerely hoped the special gleam would return, because if she thought for one second she was responsible for *that* loss as well as losing Reggie, she would collapse within herself and never find her way back out.

She vaguely remembered speaking on the phone to the same Agency assigned aide who had flown with them to Boston, telling him that she was returning to Washington tomorrow and needed to report to Director Smith immediately upon her arrival. He'd assured her everything would be arranged and a car would be waiting.

When she hung up her phone she broke down again. This time Foshay did comfort her by sitting next to her on the bed and wrapping his arms around her. She did not argue and instead buried her face into his chest and wept until a nurse entered. The nurse gave her pain medication for her head and a sedative to help her rest, which did not take long to go into effect. The last thing she remembered was Foshay tucking her in before sleep overtook her.

The next morning she had awakened to find her clothes had been pressed and dry cleaned. This had been another gesture from Thomas Nicholas. The pain in her head had subsided to a constant dull ache, and she had to fight down nausea as she dressed. Professor Foshay showed up shortly after and when she signed herself out of the hospital, he waited with her until the promised driver arrived.

She had deeply appreciated the fact the professor had walked her to the car and volunteered to ride along with her to the airport, which she'd readily accepted.

They spoke little as the driver made his way to a private airfield where Nicholas' plane was waiting. Sommers was not sure if they had grown closer or drifted farther apart after all that had happened. She liked Foshay, and under different circumstances may have even pursued him socially, but with the loss of Excalibur, the disappearance of Ambrosius, and of course Reggie's death she had nothing in the way of emotions to offer anyone. The professor deserved better than that.

They'd walked hand in hand to the awaiting plane. She was thankful for the small comfort.

Before boarding she gave the professor a business card with her home number hand written on the back. He looked at it briefly before slipping it into a pocket.

"If you ever need me, call me," she said.

"Will I ever see you again?"

"I don't know, Professor, but I certainly hope so."

"So do I, Amy Sommers. So do I."

She could tell he'd wanted to lean in and kiss her, but she had not given him the opportunity. She was still too emotionally numb to let herself give in to that kind of desire. Instead she flashed a forced smile before entering the plane. She had not even watched out the small window as the plane had taken off.

Now, on her way back to Washington, she thought on their last conversation, however brief it had been, and almost smiled. Almost.

The plane touched down a short time later. She was thankful she had been able to get at least a little rest. The trauma of the last few days was catching up to her, and she was past the point of regular exhaustion. After the meeting with Director Smith, she was planning on holing herself up in her apartment and sleeping for a week.

She made her way to the now familiar Agency black sedan. As she settled into the backseat she did not bother with any attempt at small talk or friendly banter with the driver. Instead, she closed her eyes hoping to catch a few more Z's before having to face the director.

Her thoughts turned to Ambrosius, whose disappearance was still unexplained. She had never figured him to be a coward, and was certain he had not run away. There had to be some other explanation. She vaguely recalled him chanting, being able to utilize some sort of power, but the specifics were lost to her. Maybe his mysterious exit from the fighting was somehow linked to those inexplicable abilities.

It felt as if she had just closed her eyes when motion of the sedan coming to a stop woke her up. She recognized the parking deck which marked the entrance to the Agency's underground headquarters.

They were here, and she didn't know if she should be feeling relieved or worried. For all she knew after the debacle her first case had turned into she would soon find herself among the unemployed. What really bothered her was she was no longer sure if she even cared.

After going through the procedure to board the elevator, she looked into the camera lens, took a deep breath, and took the first step to what could possibly be the end of her career.

"Agent Amy Sommers to see Director Smith."

She nearly threw up all over the elevator as it whisked her away to her destination. The speed of the ride increased the pounding in her head, but thankfully it did not last long. When the doors opened up, she staggered out into the lobby she knew led to Director Smith's office.

The secretary smiled at Amy and motioned for her to go ahead. Behind the secretary's smile she could sense pity, and for some reason she had the sudden desire to punch the poor woman square in her face. The last thing she wanted right now was to be pitied. That would tarnish Reggie's memory if everyone sat around feeling sorry for her. She could not, *would* not accept that.

She was starting to get angry as she approached the door to Director Smith's office. This quickly deflated however as the door swung open and Director Smith stepped out to meet her.

"Agent Sommers, I'm glad to see you appear to be recovering from your injuries."

The man's presence still commanded respect, so part of her wanted to snap to attention and salute. Another emotionally damaged part of her wanted to throw her arms around him and apologize for her failure as she wept. Instead she settled on a simple response.

"Thank you, sir."

"Please, Agent Sommers, come in and have a seat. I'm sure you are exhausted after everything that has happened."

She did as instructed and winced slightly as the Director closed the door behind her. The sound was eerily similar to what she guessed someone driving the nail into the coffin of her career might sound like. She was about to speak on that very subject when it dawned on her the director had known about her injuries. She had not mentioned anything when she had phoned the Agency back in Boston.

"Sir, how did you know...," she began, trailing off as the director held up his hand.

"It seems you have made some very well informed friends, Agent Sommers. I was contacted by a Thomas Nicholas who told me everything after he had gotten the story from you. I have some agents doing a follow up investigation to help piece the whole story together as we speak. I know about the Ghost. I know about

Excalibur, and ..." At this point he paused. "I know about Agent Blackburn as well."

Amy felt tears welling up in her eyes. The wound caused by Reggie's death was still too fresh, and the mere mention of his name was enough to bring the pain to the surface. She did not want to appear weak in front of the director, so she lowered her head, hoping to shield his view of the tears spilling from her eyes down her cheeks.

She heard Director Smith move around behind his desk and sit down. From the way he paused she guessed he was waiting for her to regain some self-control before he continued.

"I'm sorry, Amy," Director Smith said, surprising her by using her first name. "I'm sorry for your loss. Agent Blackburn, Reggie, was my friend too. I am also sorry you were put in such a dangerous situation for your first case. If anyone is to blame for Reggie's death, it's me."

Hearing him speak so genuinely only made her have less restraint. She covered her face with both hands as she became overwhelmed with grief. This was the last thing she wanted Director Smith to see, but she could not stop the emotional tidal wave from crashing around her.

"What happens next?" she asked, her voice shaking.

"To be honest I'm not entirely sure," the director said. "I am going to put you on extended leave, however. You need some time."

Anger was the catalyst she needed to get her emotions back under her command. She had fully expected to come in to the director's office and at the very least get suspended, or worse, fired. Yes, she was in pain over the death of her best friend, but she was not some first year cadet who needed to be coddled. The director's words had the stink of her being placated.

"What about Excalibur?' she asked, almost demanding an answer. "What about bringing Reggie's murderer to justice?"

"I understand your ire, Agent Sommers, but it is misguided. It is standard procedure to put agents on extended leave after working a particular traumatic case. I am treating you no different. I know you feel a sense of duty towards Reggie and I commend you for that, but for the time being I am ordering you to go home."

She was about to protest further when the director cut her off by holding his hand up.

"This is nonnegotiable, Agent Sommers," the director said, and then she noticed a mischievous look in the man's eye. "Now, how you spend your time on leave is up to you."

She had her mouth open ready to argue when the director's last statement sunk in. She quickly closed it and stared at her boss. Had he inadvertently given her permission to work the case on her own?

"If you are ready, Agent Sommers, I will have someone meet you outside and take you home."

She nodded, not knowing how else to respond. This meeting had gone nothing like she had prepared herself for, leaving her completely confounded. She felt like she was on autopilot as she got up and started out of the office.

"Oh, and Agent Sommers," the director called from behind her. "Please be careful."

"Yes, sir," she said.

The car was waiting for her as she stepped off the elevator. She breathed in the cool afternoon air. She really did not feel like going home and being alone, but had nowhere else to go.

She watched the shops and various other buildings as the sedan passed each one, mulling over what Director Smith had said. Or, more what he had implied. As the sedan came to a stop in front of her building she decided right then and there she was going after the Ghost. Excalibur could be damned as far as she was concerned, but the Ghost would pay. She owed that much to Reggie.

She made her way upstairs, remembering how happy she'd been just a few short days ago, Reggie had saved her from the mind-numbing training by assigning her first case. Now everything had come crashing down like a house of cards.

Thoughts filled her head as she tried to remember any detail she could use to track down the Ghost. She was in front of the door to her apartment before she noticed it was slightly ajar.

"What the hell?" she said, sensing a strangely familiar sensation. "Couldn't be..."

She pushed the door all the way open and stepped into her apartment, and saw a familiar figure sitting comfortably on her couch.

"Good afternoon, Agent Sommers," Ambrosius said. "I hope you don't mind, but I let myself in."

—Chapter 28

She did her best to try and save face.

"What is it with you Ambrosius? Do you have your own key or something?"

"In a manner of speaking," he said, standing politely as she stepped further into the living room.

"Oh no, please go right ahead and make yourself at home," she said sarcastically. "I mean, with a little thing like home invasion between us, I don't think we need to stand on ceremony."

With the ice now broken and her initial shock diminishing, she turned and shut her door. She ignored the British agent, who remained standing as she hung her coat up and moved into the kitchen. Wisely, Ambrosius did not follow.

Once she was alone, she leaned against the counter to collect her thoughts. Her anger was mounting and if she was unable to get a handle on it she knew she would lash out. She'd had it with surprises. Over the last few days she'd had her fill of the unexpected to last a lifetime.

The window above the sink offered a decent view of the small park across the street from her building, where a group of five or six kids ran around playing what appeared to be a game of tag. She envied their carefree playfulness. What she wouldn't give to be able to turn back the clocks to a time of innocence.

She did not know what to do about Ambrosius. She had half a mind to charge back into the living room and throw the pompous jerk out on his butt. He had abandoned her, after all. But the more rational side of her brain wanted an explanation, not just for his disappearance but for Ambrosius' seemingly magical abilities. She deserved at least that much from the man. And, to be honest, after what they had been through she owed him a chance to give her that explanation.

It had only been a few been a few days since she had last been home, but it felt like years. She looked around her kitchen, a little distressed at how alien the place felt to her. Reggie had helped her find this place when she had relocated to Washington from Los Angeles. Now that he was dead it was like a part of the essence which had made the apartment feel like home had been severed. Then again, everything felt like that right now.

She moved over to the refrigerator. Remembering her guest in the next room, she called out, "You want something to drink?"

"Yes, I think that would be a good idea, Agent Sommers. Especially in light of what I have to tell you."

He spoke from the doorway between the kitchen and living room. They stared at each other for several long moments. The only sounds were the hum of the refrigerator's motor while she stood unmoving with its door hanging open, and the faint sounds of the children still at play in the park outside.

"I know how partial you Brits are to tea in the afternoon, but I get the feeling this is going to be more of an adult beverage kind of conversation," she said, shutting the refrigerator and reaching up to the cabinet above the appliance where she kept her private stock.

She removed two whiskey snifters and a bottle of Johnnie Walker Black Label. She filled both glasses half full before handing one over to Ambrosius and keeping the other for herself. She sipped the Scotch, reveling in the burning sensation. When she felt the potent liquor take effect and begin spreading its warmth throughout her body, she motioned for Ambrosius to head back into the living room.

"Why don't we go have a seat where I can get comfortable? I have a pretty good idea this is going to be a whopper of a story."

"As you wish," Ambrosius said, sipping at his own glass before following her instructions.

Once they were both settled, him sitting rather nervously in her loveseat and her directly across from him Indian style on the couch, she stared daggers at him as she waited.

"I'm not sure where to begin," Ambrosius said, taking another drink in an effort to stall.

"How about you start by telling me why in the hell you bailed out on us? Why you left us there to die?"

"That's a fair question, and my initial answer is that I had no choice." He held up his hand to cut off the protest she was getting ready to voice. "Please, let me finish."

"Look, I'm going to have to bury my best friend because of this case, so you will have to excuse me if my patience is running on empty," she said. "Now please, Ambrosius tell me everything. I think I deserve it."

She watched as he finished off the whiskey in a loud gulp before massaging his brow with his hand.

"I left because if I had stayed I would now be dead. In all the confusion, Mr. Grant fired his weapon at me and his aim was true. The bullet hit my chest, puncturing a lung." At this point he leaned forward and seemed to be having trouble finding the words to help her understand. "I have ways of healing myself, but it requires some concentration. Had I stayed I would have never been able to access my power. You see, Agent Sommers I'm not exactly who you think I am."

"What do you mean?" she asked. "You're not really an agent?"

"No actually I am an agent."

"Then what? You're name's not really Ambrosius?"

"My name really is Ambrosius. I never lied about that."

"Then what is it?" she asked, frustrated.

"You know me by another name."

"Really," she said. She was getting to the point of annoyance where she had the urge to throw her glass, whiskey and all, at the man if he did not come clean. "Well, I'm all ears."

"As I told you the first time we met my name is Emrys Myrddin Ambrosius, but most people refer to me as Merlin. Merlin the Magician."

The pounding in her head from the concussion, which up to now had been lessening, returned in full force.

"Huh...uhm...what?" was all she could manage to utter.

"It's true, Agent Sommers," he said.

"You're *the* Merlin the Magician?"

"Yes, though magician is somewhat misleading. I'm not a magician or a wizard as some tales would have you believe. In fact, what little powers I do possess are tied to the elements. What you witnessed back at the chamber is pretty much the extent of my abilities."

"Oh sure," she said, not believing she was having this conversation. "I can see how people would make the mistake."

"I know this is not easy for you to understand, Agent Sommers, but is it really that hard to believe considering the circumstances?"

At first she could not understand how he could even ask her that question. Then realization set in. When the case she had been working on up to now involved finding Excalibur, was it really so far-fetched to think one of the mythical characters associated with the sword was also real?

She stared long and hard at the man she knew as Agent Ambrosius, but who claimed to be Merlin. She thought back on all the cryptic answers and odd behaviors she had been privy to ... the strange haunted and aged look she had witnessed on more than one occasion in his eyes ... not to mention the strange knack he had for appearing and disappearing. She could not forget the abilities she herself had witnessed as well. All of these instances added up to lend credibility to his story.

"But how?" she asked. "Excalibur being real is one thing, but if what you say is true wouldn't that make you more than a little old?"

"I am closing in on 900 years old," Ambrosius said, chuckling at the look on her face.

"Please, if you tell me you discovered the Fountain of Youth too I don't think I'm going to be able to handle it," she said.

They shared a laugh before the room fell silent around them. The shadows along the living room walls lengthened as it moved from early to late afternoon. She was tempted to get up and make herself another drink, but thought twice about it, as she was going to need a clear head to reason everything through.

"Okay," she said. "Tell me the rest."

"I was given Excalibur by a spirit creature the literary world has dubbed the Lady of the Lake," Ambrosius began. "She is from a realm called Avalon. Because of my abilities, I was allowed to choose who would receive Excalibur. I of course chose Arthur. You have to understand the world was a very different place during this time. It was a place full of chaos, suffering, and war. Excalibur was a talisman that, when wielded by the chosen person, had the ability to bring peace, and it did. Once Arthur's time had passed, it was my duty to return Excalibur from whence it came. This would have happened if not for Sir Bedivere."

The mention of that name sparked a memory.

"So Professor Foshay was correct," she said. "The knight did keep the sword."

"Yes, unintentionally Sir Bedivere is the one who has set everything that has transpired since into motion," Ambrosius said. "I thought Excalibur had been returned, thus freeing me of my obligation. It was not until Bedivere's death I learned the truth. By then it was too late and the sword became lost to history. I have been doing everything in my power to track it down ever since. That is why I am an agent. I figured I could use the Agency's resources to help me in my search. When I heard about this case, I knew my vigilance had paid off. I was able to maneuver myself into a position to get assigned as your partner."

"This still doesn't explain you ..." she paused there, not sure how to express what she wanted to say.

"Being alive?" Ambrosius answered for her. "My existence is tied to Excalibur. When I have fulfilled my vow and the sword is returned my time here will be up."

No wonder as they had gotten closer to finding Excalibur Ambrosius' behavior had become so erratic. The man had been searching for centuries in an effort to keep a promise. The weight of responsibility and obligation was too much for her to even fathom.

"This is incredible," she said, not knowing what else to say.

"It is imperative I find Excalibur. Now more than ever," Ambrosius said. She thought she picked up on some kind of hint behind his words.

"You're not just here to tell me this story are you?" she asked.

"No, Agent Sommers, I'm not. My experiences over these long years have taught me one thing. I can't do this alone. I need your help."

"What can I do?" she asked. "Heck, I'm not even an active agent at the moment."

"I can't fight the Ghost alone. The IRA terrorists he was hired by are overseas. We may be able to use them to track the Ghost down. Come with me to England. There we can use the Agency in London's resources. This could be our only chance."

She could hear the desperation in his voice, and frankly could not blame the man. She smiled, thinking how weird her life had become. True, she was on extended leave and therefore had no jurisdiction or authority to help on the case, but she remembered Director Smith's words. It was up to her on how she spent her time off.

She thought of Reggie. This could be her only chance to get justice. It only took her a second to determine what he would have done had he been faced with the same circumstances.

"When do we leave?" she said, feeling better with every passing second.

"As soon as you pack," Ambrosius said, and she had to smile at the excitement she heard in his voice. "I booked us passage on a flight to London for this evening."

"Okay then," she said, her own excitement mounting. "Let's go."

CHAPTER 29

Mercifully, she was able to sleep for the majority of the flight from Washington to London. Presumptuous though it had been of Ambrosius to have already purchased their tickets, it had saved them precious time. After throwing a bag together she and the British agent left for the airport, stopping briefly only to get something to eat. From there it was straight to Logan Airport.

Shortly after take-off, the adrenaline rush she had been running on since making the decision to help Ambrosius began to wane. She'd wanted to question Ambrosius further about his past, but was overcome with fatigue before she could make any inquiries. Her last thoughts before slipping into an exhaustion induced slumber were of how strange a path her life had stumbled onto.

When she was still with the LAPD, if someone had come in claiming to be Merlin the Magician, she would have locked them up for their own protection pending a psychiatric evaluation. Now, however, she took Ambrosius' claim at face value. In essence it was simply another day at the office.

She felt at least a little refreshed by the time they landed at Heathrow. She had no idea what was in store for her in London, but with a single-minded determinedness, she resolved not to return home until the Ghost had been brought to justice.

The London Agency sent a Rolls-Royce Phantom complete with a chauffer decked out in a black suit and matching cap to pick them up

"Wow. I'm impressed," she said.

"That's right, Dorothy," Ambrosius said, smiling. "You're not in Kansas anymore."

"Wait a minute, if I'm Dorothy then what does that make you?"

"Why, I'm the Great and Powerful Oz of course."

"Really," she said, teasing. "I would have guessed more like a Flying Monkey."

She laughed as he threw a wry smile her way. It definitely felt good to be laughing again, though the banter did remind her of the conversations she and Reggie had shared. Once again she felt a hollowness deep down inside her, but it only served to harden her resolve however.

Within minutes they were on their way to the Agency's British headquarters. Sommers had never been to London before. Under different circumstances, she would have been fascinated with her surroundings, trying her best to soak in the sights. She was not here as a tourist, however, and the myriad of lights from the city were merely one continuous blur outside her window.

"Where exactly is your home office?" she asked. "Are we getting close?"

"As a matter of fact we are," Ambrosius said, pointing. "We are very close indeed."

At first all she could see in the early morning darkness was the familiar image of a large, well-lit structure. After staring for a few seconds, it dawned on her she was looking at the Palace of Westminster.

"You work there?" she asked, taken aback.

"The British Agency is located at the northeastern end."

She did not like the smug look on Ambrosius' face. Then again she could not blame him for feeling superior. The Agency back home was buried beneath an old parking garage. If the axiom concerning real estate held true and it really was all about location, then Ambrosius had every right to sound boastful.

As they approached, the structure continued to grow in its immenseness. The enormity of the history left her feeling intimidated. She had so many questions concerning the British version of the Agency she did not know where to start. She did not want to sound like the stereotypical ignorant American, so instead remained quiet as she tried to take everything in.

Their driver pulled up to the security gate and flashed some kind of ID. They continued until the driver came to a stop in front of probably the most recognizable landmark in all of Great Britain, if not the world.

"This is Big Ben isn't it?" she asked, trying to keep the sound of awe out of her voice, but failing miserably.

"That it is, Agent Sommers," Ambroisus said. "It is also our destination."

"You mean your Agency is in there?"

"Sort of," the British agent said. "Much like your home office, we need to go underground."

With that, they both exited the vehicle. She strained her neck looking up at the large clock tower. It served as a huge reminder of just how far from home she really was. This was clearly Ambrosius' turf, and she could see by his demeanor the man was more relaxed and confidant.

"Shall we?" he asked.

"You lead the way," she said. "This is your backyard, after all."

She followed Ambrosius to the brick work and stone cladding base of the tower. As they neared she could see a single door which looked like some sort of service entrance. When Ambrosius paused in front it, she saw an identical electronic keypad and ID slot to the one she used at the Agency back home.

Ambrosius performed the same ritual she herself went through countless times to gain access to the Agency. The service door slid open revealing an elevator, with a similar system including a camera waiting for instructions.

"Agent Ambrosius and Agent Sommers to Facts and Research," Ambrosius said.

She grabbed hold of the handrail. The elevator moved in reverse several feet before pausing and then beginning its rapid descent. She was reminded of the Psycho Mouse roller coaster she had once ridden while visiting California Great America back in

Santa Clara. It had not been a pleasant experience then, and this ride was not any better. She was all too happy when the elevator slowed to a stop after roughly 30 seconds of what felt like free fall, and the doors slid open.

Up to this point, the set up of the British Agency was reminiscent of the one back in Washington. That all changed when she stepped off the elevator. What Ambrosius had called Facts and Research was a huge library any university would have envied, like one of the public libraries found in large cities like New York. The place was so big it was overwhelming.

"Wow," she whispered.

"If we are going to find something to lead us to the Ghost, it will be here," Ambrosius said.

Despite the late hour, several other people moved in and out of the multitude of shelves and aisles. She assumed they were other agents working cases and following up on leads of their own. Looking around the vastness of the Facts and Research department she had a sinking feeling as the phrase "needle in a haystack" came to mind.

"Where do we even begin?" she asked.

"I think our best bet is to try and find any information on the *Na Ri` Laoch*," Ambrosius answered. "We may be able to find a link that will lead us from them to the Ghost."

"Agreed," she said. "Lead on."

Amy followed along as Ambrosius made his way to an island of computers in the center of the room. Even with the two of them scouring the Agency's database looking for information on the Irish terrorist group, she knew it was going to be a long rest of the night. Time was their enemy now as much as the Ghost was. With every passing minute, the assassin would be able to hide his tracks that much more.

A woman who bore a striking resemblance to Kylie Minogue approached them, carrying an overstuffed file folder. "Excuse me," she said, in a heavily accented voice reminiscent of The Beatles. "Are you Agent Sommers?"

"Uh... yeah that's me," she said, confused.

"This was faxed over from Washington shortly before you arrived," the woman said, holding forth the file with both hands as if she was turning over one of the stone tablets containing the Ten Commandments.

Amy hesitated before reaching out to accept the material. As far as she knew, no one other than Ambrosius knew she was here. Her instincts were not sending out any warnings, but having something here waiting for her when up to a few minutes ago she herself hadn't known where she was going to be was a little on the strange side.

Seeing the woman's arms start to tremble from the weight of the folder spurred Amy to action. She took the folder surprised herself at how heavy it was.

"Thank you," she said.

"You're welcome," the pop singer look-a-like said before turning around and walking away. Amy watched until the woman disappeared down one of the many rows.

Amy walked over to an empty table next to the bank of computers, and dropped the folder. It landed with a heavy "thud" which seemed to echo in the quiet. She stared at it like it was a bomb. The seconds slipped by, and she began to feel foolish. After chastising herself for being so wary, she unwound the red string holding the folder closed. She half expected a spring-loaded novelty snake to come bouncing out at her. What she did see however was just as surprising.

Sitting on top of a thick stack of papers was a fax copy of a handwritten note. She skipped down to the bottom and was surprised to see the signature of Director Smith. She smiled in spite of her fatigue and read the letter in full.

> *Agent Sommers,*
> *I trust you are using your time off wisely. I understand you have chosen to spend some time overseas. I hope you are heeding my words and are being careful. I have faxed this material to the London office in hopes of providing you with some interesting reading. This file was found in Special Agent*

Blackburn's desk. It is every piece of information he collected over the years concerning a certain mutual acquaintance. I hope you are able to put it to good use. Take great care.

Director Smith

She closed her eyes tightly in an attempt to stem a flow of tears. Even death could not stop Reggie from reaching out and giving her a helping hand.

"Are you all right?" Ambrosius asked.

"Yeah," she said, her voice thick with emotion. "I just miss Reggie."

She waited for the British agent to attempt to offer up some solace in the way of a comforting word or phrase. She appreciated the fact that instead he sat silently, giving her time. After a few more seconds of struggling against her unbearable sense of loss she was able to prevail. Apparently Ambrosius was able to pick up on her victory as well.

"What's in the folder?"

She turned to look at Ambrosius and with a renewed gleam in her eyes. "This is Reggie's personal case file on the Ghost. Evidently Reggie had been trying to track the assassin down for years. If there is a way to find that bastard, it might be in here."

With the entire research department of the London Agency at their disposal along with the information Reggie had collected she felt certain they would find the proverbial needle in the haystack.

"I am going to continue my search for any information on the *Na Ri` Laoch*," Ambrosius said. "You dig through the case file and we'll see what we can come up with."

"Agreed."

She sat down and began poring over each document. Reggie had been meticulous in gathering data even compiled a list of the Ghost's potential aliases. She jotted down her own notes, and studied photos of the one time agent, desperately trying to find the missing piece which would solve the puzzle.

Ambrosius had been just as diligent in his own search, trudging through the Agency's database for information on the IRA terrorists who had hired the Ghost in the first place. He'd made a similar list to her own, filled with information he had picked out of the computer and thought to be important and relevant.

"What time is it?" she asked, stretching her arms up over her head.

"It's almost dawn."

"Well I have been through this whole thing," she said. "Reggie was pretty thorough, but there's nothing concrete here. I think I have a few leads we might be able to follow. What about you? You have any luck?"

"Maybe," he said.

"You care to elaborate on that?" she said, snapping at him out of frustration.

"The *Na Ri` Laoch* are a splinter cell from the IRA. Their story is pretty typical in that the leaders are made up of sons who saw their fathers imprisoned. What does set them apart, however, is that they are incredibly well funded. I was able to track some of their financial records down. Their spending is quite excessive. Their leader, Colin O'Connor, comes from an extremely wealthy family and he is the primary source behind the group."

"How are they and the Ghost connected?" she asked.

"It seems the Agency began to take notice of the *Na Ri` Laoch's* recent interest in acquiring ancient documents. Through some shady sources, they were able to get their hands on the document concerning Excalibur's location. They sent some operatives to the United States in hopes of discovering Excalibur."

"Reggie and Homeland Security intercepted those men," she said. "They were all killed while trying to be apprehended. That's how Reggie got the document in the first place."

"It would seem, in an effort to regain the document, the *Na Ri` Laoch* reached out to the Ghost," Ambrosius said.

"Now that the Ghost has Excalibur he will have to get in touch with the *Na Ri` Laoch*," she said, feeling hopeful they were on to something. "If we could somehow track the terrorist group we might find the Ghost and Excalibur at the same time."

"The British government keeps tabs on all known active IRA cells. I accessed that information. It seems around a month ago the *Na Ri` Laoch* made a withdrawal of 5 million dollars from their operating account and deposited it in an offshore Cayman Island account. The name on the account was Entertainment Incorporated. After a little more digging I was able to discern this is a dummy corporation run by someone named James Clauson. I don't know who this Clauson is, but this was right around the time the Ghost made his appearance."

She paused for a few seconds, thinking. The name James Clauson sounded eerily familiar. She began rifling through her notes until she came across the list of names Reggie had put together of possible aliases used by the Ghost. She found the name she was looking for third from the bottom of the page. What feelings of exhaustion she had been experiencing vanished as her excitement mounted.

"James Clauson is on Reggie's list," she said, her voice sounding shaky in her ears. "Clauson could be the Ghost."

Without saying a word, but with eyes as large as saucers, Ambrosius turned his attention back to the computer in front of him. He punched in the potential alias, and the man's information flashed onto the monitor.

"Could it really be that easy?" he whispered. "He's been right here under our noses the entire time?"

"What are you rambling on about?"

"James Clauson owns The End, a trendy and popular nightclub right here in London," he said, and this time she could hear his own excitement begin to rise, matching her own.

A chiming sound rang from the computer, interrupting their moment of potential triumph. Not knowing what the noise meant, she watched as Ambrosius closed out the page regarding James Clauson and opened another window. From what she could see looking over his shoulder, it appeared to be a page dedicated to information on the *Na Ri` Laoch*.

"You know, for someone close to 900 years old, you sure know your way around a computer pretty well," she said. She laughed as he turned and looked at her with upraised eyebrows.

"Honestly, Agent Sommers," he said. "I am a magician, after all."

"Riiight," she said, still chuckling.

"I don't believe it," he said, once he returned his attention back to the computer screen.

"What is it?" she asked.

"It would seem three of the top leader's of the *Na Ri` Laoch* were spotted entering London by train sometime after 2am," Ambrosius said.

"You mean the same guys who sprung for the Ghost's services are in London right now as we speak?" she asked incredulously.

"This is no mere coincidence," Ambrosius said.

"We've got to get a look at that nightclub," she said.

"Agreed," Ambrosius said. "Grab your coat, Agent Sommers, while I make arrangements to get us a car."

CHAPTER 30

The Ghost enjoyed the quiet solitude the empty club afforded him in the hours before it opened for business. He felt a strange sense of peace within these gaudy walls which allowed him to relax; a tough chore for one in his profession.

Glancing at his gold Rolex, he knew he had at least one more good hour before the club's employees began to arrive. That gave him plenty of time to prepare for his guests. The three members of the *Na Ri` Laoch* would be here around closing time. Good. Fewer potential witnesses for what he had planned.

The fools who had hired him had been all too ready to come running like lapdogs, eager for their prize. What those imbeciles did not realize however was instead of coming to claim Excalibur for their own idiotic schemes, they would be walking into the proverbial lion's den.

He had no intention of handing over such a valuable treasure to a group of small time terrorists. Excalibur was safely tucked away in his wall safe. Disposing of his employers just tied up one more loose end. There was the worry of some kind of reprisal from the *Na Ri' Laoch*, but he was unfazed. In his estimation, once the head of the serpent was removed, the body died. And the three heads of the *Na Ri` Laoch* would be here later this evening. They were the real flies about to be caught in a web of his spinning.

His thoughts kept harkening back to Blackburn's demise, which always seemed to brighten his mood, but also served as a reminder of the female agent he had left alive. Had it been a mistake? He'd been pressed for time.

He returned to his office, which overlooked the dance floor. It was deserted now, but in another couple of hours it would be crammed with writhing bodies moving in rhythm to the god-awful thumping of techno music which the club's patrons seemed to love. Ahmet, the head bartender, arrived and began preparing his work station. Soon the rest of his employees would come filtering in, and his fortress of solitude would be no more.

The Ghost, continuing to feel a nagging sensation deep within himself, knew he was being warned of some impending danger. The intricately carved jaguar on the bracelet at his wrist seemed to be staring at him with a renewed intensity. Before this night was over, he was positive he would be calling on its magic.

Something to do with the *Na Ri` Laoch*? But they were harmless for all intents and purposes. No, the danger lay elsewhere. Once again his thoughts drifted to Agent Amy Sommers. Might she be tied into how the events of this evening would play out?

Exhilaration replaced the uncomfortable nagging he was experiencing. It was moments like these he absolutely lived for, that made him feel alive. This was what those fools at the Agency could never understand. It was not so much the kill, though that was quite exquisite in its own right, but the hunt that drove him. If Agent Sommers did make an unexpected appearance, then the game would definitely be afoot.

He hoped Blackburn's protégé *would* show up. He would enjoy showing her some of his special attention before he bled her dry.

The sound of the remaining nightclub staff entering and setting up filled the quiet of his office. He glanced at his watch once again.

Only a few more hours before it was show time, and the Ghost was ready to entertain his visitors, both invited and unexpected.

CHAPTER 31

From the outside, the club did not look like anything special. It was a large two-story brick building from a by-gone era, much like the old warehouses Sommers had seen back in Los Angeles. The only thing which marked it as something other was the gold plating framed in a square arch around the entrance. The club's name, "THE END," was written above the door in shiny silver block letters.

A parking spot along the curb on the opposite side of the street, gave them a clear view of The End. Now, all they could do was wait and watch.

The hours drifted by in an exhaustion filled haze. Sommers and Ambrosius took turns napping while the other continued their vigil. The car became littered with coffee cups and food wrappers as they fueled their bodies with caffeine and sugar.

She thought about Reggie almost constantly. The last few seconds of his life, as the Ghost had poured bullet after bullet into Reggie's chest, played out in her mind over and over again.

Ambrosius remained quiet. She had so many questions she wanted to ask him, but this did not seem like the appropriate time. He was anxious though, that she could tell, and she could hardly blame him. This stakeout could inevitably lead to the end of his centuries long journey, one way or another.

The members of the *Na Ri` Laoch* had apparently gone to ground since their arrival in London. She knew they would not be coming out for anything less than the fabled sword. The Ghost had not put in an appearance either. Unsurprising. There was no way they would get lucky enough to catch the assassin strolling down the street. The Ghost would not poke his head out until it was necessary and he knew it was safe. When the Ghost finally did poke that head of his out, however, she fully intended to blow it off.

The Ghost was sitting with his feet propped on the desk's top, enjoying a very dry vodka martini, when the cell phone resting next to his expensive Italian loafers began vibrating. He frowned in annoyance. This particular phone was to be used only by the *Na Ri` Laoch*. It was their only means of contacting him.

"You're early," he said as soon as he flipped the phone open. His voice was charged with menace as his anger began to simmer.

"Does it really matter?" an Irish accented voice asked from the other end of the line.

"It does if you want this deal to go down," he said, not trying to hide the threat behind his words.

There was a pause before anyone replied. He smiled in spite of his sour mood as he pictured the fool cowering and becoming flummoxed.

"Calm down," said the Irish voice belonging to Colin O'Conner. "We may have to make different arrangements."

"And why is that?" he asked, knowing he was not going to like the answer.

"Look, we are taking on a lot of heat just being here in London," O'Conner said. "The quicker we can make the exchange, the quicker we can return home. I don't know how much longer our presence here will go unnoticed."

If the fools had any kind of sense, they would know they'd more than likely been spotted the second they entered the city. Suppose they did something stupid and got themselves arrested? He would lose his opportunity to tie up a loose end.

"Fine," the Ghost said through clenched teeth. "The club opens at 9pm. Be here by 10:00. But I swear if you are one second late the deal is off, and you will never get your hands on what it is you want. Is this understood?"

"Perfectly."

"Good," he said before hanging up.

seething, he reached out, grabbed his martini glass, and finished off the contents. He threw the glass as hard as he could across the office, where it smashed into countless shards against the far wall.

This was actually a smart move on the *Na Ri` Laoch's* part, forcing him to have to interact with them while there were plenty of witnesses around.

Well if those fools thought they were safe, they were going to be quite surprised. By his reasoning all they'd done was to shorten their lives by a few hours.

He smiled anew as he called down to the bar and ordered a new drink.

"Agent Sommers!"

She nearly wrenched her back when she shot bolt upright in response to Ambrosius' voice. She did not know how long she had been curled up on the backseat asleep, but the sun had gone down, leaving the street bathed in the white light of a streetlamp. She glanced out the windshield in the direction of the club, and saw a crowd growing in the front of The End's entrance.

"I believe a few of our pigeons have come home to roost," Ambrosius said.

He was still sitting in the driver's seat, turned to the side to face her. The light from the laptop painted his face in an eerie green glow, giving him a ghoulish appearance. The excited grimace he had only added to the effect as he motioned in the direction of the club.

"Is it the Ghost?" she asked hopefully.

"No, but I do believe a few of his business associates are paying him a visit," Ambrosius said. "The IRA terrorists?" she asked.

His only response was a nod. She followed Ambrosius' gaze as he turned to look out the windshield. A splash of red hair among the line of patrons trying to gain entrance into the nightclub caught her attention. She focused in on the man and saw him conversing with two other younger gentlemen. She watched them closely before looking back at Ambrosius.

"Are you sure it's them?"

He did not answer, but she accepted the laptop he handed over the seat to her. She studied the mug shots on the monitor and recognized the middle photo as that of the person currently entering the club. The other two she was not as sure about, but there was no question the dark-haired individual was Colin O'Connor, leader of the *Na Ri` Laoch*.

"What's our next move?" she asked.

"I think we need to get inside The End."

"Okay," she said checking her firearm before slipping it back into her shoulder holster. "I gotta warn you though; I'm not much of a dancer."

"Don't worry, Agent Sommers, I'll lead."

As soon as the office phone on his desk rang, the Ghost knew his guests had arrived. Since the *Na Ri` Laoch* had forced his hand by insisting to come earlier than he intended, he decided a change of plan was in order.

A poison he had picked up in South Africa would do nicely. He kept a special case of champagne laced with it in the club's wine cellar. He ordered one of the bottles brought to his office chilled and ready to serve.

He walked over to the windows to look down at all the clubbers who frequented his establishment. With its spring-loaded dance floor and five-way crossover sound-system, The End had quickly become a mainstay of London's club scene.

Tonight was no different. Even though it was still relatively early the place was already starting to fill up. The club's revelers seemed to be jumping in unison to the thumping beat of the techno music his DJ had cranked up to near full volume. The whole scene sickened him, and had he not needed this place as a safe house of operations, he would have happily blown it into kindling with everyone still inside.

This thought brought a malicious grin to his face. He remained lost in his private fantasy until another knock at the office door brought him back to reality.

"Enter," he said with a hint of amusement hidden in his voice.

His young and perky club manager led three men into his office. Two of the men seemed almost jubilant, but the third was a little more reserved. The Ghost knew this man was O'Connor, the leader of this trio. He noted that while O'Connor's comrades looked as if they wanted to join the party going on down on the dance floor, O'Connor looked cautious and on edge. This could be trouble.

"Gentlemen, please come in and make yourselves at home. Then we can attend to our business," he said, motioning for the three members of the *Na Ri` Laoch* to have a seat in the office's plush furniture before turning to his manager. "Thank you, Gretchen. That will be all."

"Yes sir," his pretty employee said, before leaving the office and closing the door behind her. O'Connor and his cronies stared after Gretchen luridly.

"I hope your trip was satisfactory," he said, trying to play the proper host.

"We have no complaints," O'Connor said.

"Good…good," he said. "Perhaps you gentlemen would care to partake in some of London's nightlife."

"We're just here for the sword," O'Connor said, to the obvious disappointment of his partners.

"Shall we get down to business then?" The Ghost asked, smiling like the Cheshire Cat.

CHAPTER 32

"Tell me we're not going to have to wait in line," Sommers said.

"I think a flash of the badge should give us a free pass," Ambrosius replied.

They'd watched as the terrorists were quickly ushered into The End by a young woman Sommers guessed to be the club's manager. Once the three men were inside, she and Ambrosius went into motion.

She heard a few grumbles and complaints from the people waiting outside as she and Ambrosius bypassed the crowded line and moved to the front door. She ignored them, however, as there were far more important dramas about to be played out.

A loud rhythmic thumping came from the club's entrance. She could see Ambrosius conversing with a large doorman, but the music was so loud she could not make out their words. When she saw the British agent show his badge and identification she had a pretty good guess as to what was going on.

The bouncer nodded, which had to be quite a chore; the man's neck looked as thick as a tree trunk. With barely a second glance the man opened the door and waved them inside.

The pulsating music was so loud she could feel the vibrations throughout her body, especially in her chest. It momentarily took her breath away. Ambroisus, an anxious look on his face, tugged on her arm and motioned for her to follow as he moved deeper into The End.

There were not as many people as she had thought there would be. Maybe fifty or sixty clubbers were milling about dancing and drinking, but from the ever growing line outside it would not take long for the place to fill up.

With the blinking colored lights, wafting smoke, thumping techno beat, and stainless steel look of the club, Amy felt like she had just stepped onto the set of a low budget 1970's Sci-Fi movie. She experienced a sense of vertigo. It took several seconds for the disorientation to pass. In the meantime she tried to survey the club's layout and see if she could catch sight of the three terrorists.

"I don't see them!" She had to shout to be heard over the music.

Ambrosius did not bother to answer. He squinted his eyes as he continued trying to spot their targets.

"May I be of service to you, officers?" the pretty blonde manager asked, approaching them. Her perfume smelled of lavender, which only added to the assault on the senses.

The fact the woman knew they were some sort of law enforcement officers was not lost on Sommers. She figured this info had come from the doorman, and further guessed this meant their presence had not gone unnoticed.

"We would like to speak to your boss," she said on a whim.

This surprised the blonde, and she paused before replying. "I am afraid he is otherwise detained. Is there something I can help you with?"

"It is very important we speak with your boss. We believe he may be in danger," Amy said, playing a hunch. "If you could point us in the direction of his office we would appreciate it."

She watched the woman closely, and was not surprised when the blonde spared a quick look at a bank of tinted windows on the second floor overlooking the dance floor, unwittingly telling her where they needed to go. Ignoring the manager's objections, she and Ambrosius began making their way across the club toward a staircase on the opposite wall. They were weaving their way through the throng of writhing bodies of clubbers on the dance floor when the all too familiar sound of gunshots came from somewhere above. One of the darkened windows shattered with a fresh round of gunfire.

It did not take long after that for The End to break out into total chaos.

The Ghost moved to his desk and the awaiting bottle of poisoned champagne which had been chilling in the bottle of ice.

"Before we make our transaction, I hope you forgive me this one indulgence," he said, grabbing the bottle. "This is the finest champagne in my private stock. Shall we toast to all of our good fortunes as we close this mutually lucrative deal?"

He popped the cork and quickly filled the four glasses before his guests had time to disagree, maintaining a friendly and hospitable smile the entire time.

The three members of the *Na Ri' Laoch* accepted their flutes of champagne without complaint. He could tell O'Connor was not happy about the delay, and the man's overly cautious nature was starting to grate on his nerves.

In a show of confidence the Ghost brought his own glass to his mouth and feigned taking a sip. He was careful not to allow any of the sparkling liquid to come into contact with his lips as it would have meant his own certain death. To the casual observer, it would have appeared he had imbibed.

He watched with satisfaction as two of the *Na Ri' Laoch* drank greedily; downing their glasses in long gulps. O'Connor, however, set his glass down on the black lacquer end-table without so much as a sip. The Ghost knew the man was going to be trouble. He was going to have to end this charade as quickly as possible.

"The sword if you please," O'Connor said.

The Ghost thought he picked up on a threat hidden in the man's heavily accented words. Any pretense of this being a friendly business meeting was now gone.

"Of course," he answered. He set his glass down and moved behind his desk, removing a print of Van Gogh's *Starry Night* and inputting the numerical code to open his wall-safe.

As he was lifting the polished chrome handle, the two *Na Ri' Laoch* who had drunk the poisoned champagne begin coughing. A knowing smile worked its way across his face.

With his back still to the terrorists, he opened the safe, reached his left hand in, and removed Excalibur. The famed blade caught the light and glinted magnificently like a precious gem. He heard a sharp intake of breath from O'Connor, and a rustling of fabric as the man stood up. The next thing he heard was the satisfactory sound of choking and wheezing as two of the terrorists fell victim to the poison.

"Colin," one choked out, before collapsing to the floor.

"What have you done!" O'Connor shouted.

Using the momentary confusion to hide his movements, the Ghost reached into the safe with his right hand and seized his Nighthawk Custom 10-8 handgun. Then he spun around to face his adversaries.

O'Connor's two cronies were facedown on the floor, white froth seeping out of their mouths. But the terrorist leader was better prepared than the Ghost had given the man credit for.

Though shocked at the sudden deaths of his compatriots, O'Connor had pulled out a handgun of his own "What have you done?" he asked again, this time in a hushed whisper.

"I've evened the odds a bit," the Ghost replied, bringing his own gun to bear.

O'Connor never wavered, and though he hated to admit it, he had a grudging respect for the man. Of course, it would not stay his hand from blowing the terrorist's brains all over the office walls.

"Easy," O'Connor said. "All I want is the sword. We both can still walk away from this with what we want."

"Really? Because what I want is to put a bullet between your eyes."

Like a gunfight at high noon, they faced each other down. If a tumbleweed had blown between them, the scene would have been complete.

"I see." O'Connor's shoulders sagged in what appeared to be an acceptance of his fate.

Instead, for the first time in his illustrious career, the Ghost was caught off guard as O'Connor looked up and fired.

A sharp and searing pain ripped through his left shoulder, causing him to release his grip on Excalibur. The sword landed silently on the carpet. The impact of the bullet knocked him backwards, off balance. He returned fire, but his shot went wide and he fell to the floor.

O'Connor dove for the only cover available, behind the leather sofa. The Ghost fired a couple of shots in that direction to keep O'Connor pinned down so he could move into a better position for a kill.

The pain in his shoulder was like fire burning all the way down his arm. He could not believe O'Connor had gotten the drop on him. This fact only served to infuriate him further, and in a blind rage he stood up and slowly moved around his desk until he stood in front of the tinted windows.

"Come out, coward," he said.

Surprisingly, O'Connor took the bait, and jumped up from behind the couch. The man looked like one of those ridiculous targets found at a shooting gallery.

They fired simultaneously. The Ghost's shot was truer, and he saw blood spatter hit the wall behind the terrorist. He thought he hit O'Connor in the midsection, which meant it might not be a killing shot.

O'Connor's blast whizzed by the Ghost's head, shattering the window. Glass landed among the dancers below. That had been too close for comfort and he decided discretion was the better part of valor. Activating the magic of his bracelet, he vanished.

He watched O'Connor stagger over to the broken window. He wanted to shoot the man and end this whole disaster, but the loss of blood was taking its toll. He could not maintain the necessary level of concentration to keep the magic camouflage in place and still aim.

Instead, he slipped the pistol into his pocket, then reached into his jacket and grasped the ivory handled straight razor he kept for the more personal touch.

He was getting light headed. If he did not act soon, he might pass out, which would seal his own fate.

With that in mind, despite the room starting to spin, he moved in for the kill.

The frightened clubbers, once they had figured out the bullets and broken glass were not part of the evening's festivities, stampeded like a herd of cattle. Sommers found herself in danger of being knocked down and trampled by the frenzied mob as they all fled as one in a panic to the nearest exit.

She pulled out her own weapon, and when the clubbers saw this they gave her a wide berth, flowing around her like a strong current around a protruding rock. In seconds, she and Ambrosius were alone on the dance floor, bathed in the swirling disco lights. The music had stopped and the club was now eerily silent.

She looked up at the shattered window again, and saw Colin O'Connor staring back at her, clinging to a nasty looking automatic handgun like a lifeline. She went into full on police mode, dropping to one knee and raising her firearm to line up a shot.

The move was unnecessary, however. As she watched in horrified shock, O'Connor straightened up stiffly and leaned back at an odd angle. The brightly lit room gave her a good view, but she did not see O'Connor's attacker. It took only a second for that fact to register, and she knew without a doubt who else was in there with the terrorist leader.

"Ambrosius!" she yelled, not looking at the British agent, afraid to take her eyes off the grisly scene above her.

"I see it," Ambrosius replied, and she heard his voice shake.

O'Connor jerked in some kind of spasm. A crimson arc shot from where the man's throat had been. O'Connor went rigid, then either fell or was pushed through what was left of the tinted window.

His body landed with a sickening crash on the raised DJ booth, causing a shower of sparks to fountain up from the destroyed electronic equipment. Amy knew O'Connor had been dead before taking his plunge but she still winced and had to fight back a wave of nausea.

She fired blindly into the area O'Connor had just fallen from. She knew the Ghost was up there somewhere and hoped she might get lucky.

"Agent Sommers, let's go!" Ambrosius called.

They both sprinted in the direction of the stairs.

The Ghost sat with his back against his desk. He knew he had only seconds before Sommers and her British lackey made their way upstairs.

The pain in his shoulder was now matched by a similar burning in his right thigh. He could not believe how his normally good fortune had turned against him. One of Agent Sommers' shots had clipped the upper part of his leg. This night, which had started so promisingly, had turned into an utter disaster. He knew he should not be surprised by Blackburn's protégé's appearance. Leaving the damned woman alive was a mistake he was going to have to rectify.

The tingling sensation around his body told him he was still under the spell of his bracelet. It took every ounce of his strength and concentration to keep the effects in place.

He tossed the razor away, knowing it would be useless. His only chance now was his Nighthawk Custom 10-8, and getting into a position where he could shoot as the two bothersome agents came through the office door.

With that in mind he reached for the gun, then began the arduous task of crawling to one of the leather chairs facing the door. From there, he would have a clear shot.

CHAPTER 33

Ambrosius hit the stairs first and sprinted up without slowing, Sommers hot on his heels. For all she knew, they were rushing into certain death, but there was no way she was going to let Reggie's murderer escape. If the Ghost was somehow able to slip away, he might simply disappear for good, and she would lose any chance at avenging her friend and mentor.

The stairs emptied into a short hall with one door at the end. She nodded at Ambrosius, letting him know she was ready. She saw desperation mirrored in his eyes. This might be his last chance at redemption as well.

Ambrosius swung the door open. She heard the gunshot, heard Ambrosius grunt in pain, saw him slump with a growing stain of red spreading across his white shirtfront.

Without thinking, she crouched and threw herself through the door. She heard another gunshot, and felt the bullet fly past her head, barely missing her as she landed behind a desk. She hit the floor and rolled to her side with her firearm ready. Motionless, she strained her ears in an effort to hear any sound which might give her assailant's location away.

"Agent Sommers, we meet again," the Ghost said. It sounded like he was somewhere near the far wall. "Agent Blackburn would be so proud. It's a shame he couldn't be here to see you in all your glory."

The taunt was meant to antagonize her into doing something stupid, but she knew if she was going to get through this alive she would have to keep her wits about her. In an effort to get a better view, she shifted her weight and tried to look under the desk.

When she did, her leg bumped into something hard. She spared a glance, then stared in amazement at Excalibur lying next to her.

She grabbed the hilt of Arthur's sword. Immediately she felt a strange sensation overtake her body. She nearly let go, like she would have let go of a scalding hot coffee mug. Deep down, however, on some innate level, she knew that was the wrong thing to do and held on.

She heard the brushing of fabric across leather and knew the Ghost had just risen from wherever he had been perched. She peered out from behind the antique desk. The smell of its varnish was thick in her nose and made her want to gag. With Excalibur in one hand and her gun in the other, she surveyed the room.

The two bodies on the floor were the men she had seen with O'Connor earlier. She also saw the bottoms of several pieces of expensive looking leather furniture and, remembering, the sound she had heard seconds before knew where the Ghost had been.

"What's wrong, Agent Sommers? Don't you have any last words? You should be happy. In a few minutes I'm going to send you to see your fat friend."

His voice seemed to be coming from the opposite side of the leather furniture. She knew she was running out of options as well as time. She considered strafing the office with gunfire in hopes of getting in a lucky shot, a horrible plan that would more than likely get her killed. Still, it was better than lying here waiting to die.

She was on the verge of jumping to her feet when the faintest trace of movement slipped into her line of vision. At first she was not sure if stress was causing her eyes to play tricks on her, but then she caught the flicker of movement again, and stared at the spot. She felt some sort of internal pull deep down inside. A euphoric feeling encapsulated her, starting with her left hand and then sweeping across the rest of her body.

She had no idea what was happening, but realized she could see the Ghost.

He appeared almost translucent, surrounded by a glowing yellow outline. Excalibur vibrated softly in her hand, and the

Ghost became even clearer. She realized with awe Excalibur was coming to life, giving her the ability to see past the Ghost's own magic, making him visible.

The assassin crept along the windowed wall, stalking ever closer to her hiding spot. From the way he seemed to be leaning against the windows for support, she thought he might be wounded.

Glass crackled as the Ghost moved past the shattered window. He was almost on top of her, struggling to maintain his balance and having a hard time holding his weapon steady. But, in a few more steps, he would have a clear shot.

Sommers did not waste any time. She rolled, aimed and fired two shots into the assassin's midsection.

The Ghost was thrown backwards off his feet. His gun went flying from his grasp.

Whatever magic gave him the ability to be invisible dissipated, the glowing outline fading as the assassin's physical form came into view. He was on his back with his head propped up against one of the tinted windows. His rasping breath was filled with a gurgle of blood and she knew he was still alive. It sounded like he was trying to speak, but could not form the words.

She slowly climbed to her feet, and felt a touch on her shoulder. It was Ambrosius, looking none the worse for wear, appearing to be completely healed from his wound.

Without saying a word she handed over Excalibur. Ambrosius took the sword and she measured the look of awe in his face. His part of their mission was over. Now it was time to fulfill her own vow.

She walked over to the Ghost and watched without pity as the assassin struggled for every precious breath of air. She looked directly into his eyes and was disgusted to see him smile.

"For Reggie," she said, before emptying her remaining bullets into his chest.

She continued pulling the trigger long after the gun was empty, until Ambrosius put a comforting hand on her arm.

The Ghost was dead. She turned and looked up at Ambroisus. He clutched Excalibur like it was his child. She looked at the gun in her hand and flung it across the room.

Then, as her strength began to ebb and her emotions overwhelmed her, her knees buckled and she slid down to the floor and wept. She stayed like that for a long time.

CHAPTER 34

London's Metropolitan Police Counter-Terrorist division arrived on the scene a short time later. With the recent terrorist activity of the past couple of years, they were taking no chances and had shown up in full force.

Ambrosius explained the situation, though what cover story he used to explain Excalibur Sommers did not know. She was too busy fighting off a mini-breakdown to really care.

After obtaining a brief statement, the Counter-Terrorist division agreed to take over the investigation and clean up the scene.

Ambrosius escorted her back to their vehicle and subsequently drove her to a hotel. She heard him talking to her in a soft and soothing voice, but she was oblivious.

When she saw the bed waiting in her room, she collapsed on top of it. She was asleep in seconds.

Somewhere in the thick fog of unconsciousness, a familiar yet incessant ringing pulled her out of the blackness. The journey back to a state of wakefulness was not a short or an easy one. The ringing continued throughout.

When Amy finally opened her eyes, the hotel room was bathed in shadow. She had a vague memory of where she was, but could not remember how or when she had gotten here. Her head hurt and her body ached, but she felt more rested than she had in a long time.

She sat up and swung her legs around so she could sit on the edge of the bed and answer the phone's annoying ring.

"Hello," she said, her voice cracking from lack of use.

"Ah, Agent Sommers, I'm glad to see you are finally awake," a familiar British accent said from the other end of the line. "I was hoping you might join me in the restaurant for breakfast."

"Sure. Just give some time to get cleaned up."

"I will meet you in the lobby in an hour."

"Works for me," she said.

She caught a glimpse of herself in a mirror above the dresser, and was not surprised to see she looked as disheveled as she felt. She was still wearing the same clothes she'd had on during the confrontation with the Ghost at The End.

After a much deserved hot shower and a clean outfit, was refreshed and felt human once again. The death of the Ghost and the retrieval of Excalibur were now fresh in her memory. With a renewed resolve she walked out of her room and caught the elevator to the lobby to meet her partner.

Ambrosius was sitting on a nearby sofa perusing a newspaper. What appeared to be a long rectangular looking guitar case was on the sofa next to him. When he saw her, he stood up, grabbed the case by the handle, and flashed the biggest grin she had ever seen. His mood seemed infectious and it was not long before she found herself smiling as well. It felt good after the stress of the last few days.

"Are you ready to eat?" Ambrosius asked.

"I could eat," she said. "I would also pay top dollar for a cup of coffee."

"Then let us away." He led her to the restaurant, where a hostess seated them and a waitress brought fresh coffee. They ordered and were left staring at each other in an awkward silence as the waitress walked away.

When the silence became too much for her, she asked, "So how long was I out?"

"About 36 hours."

"Wow," was all she could think to say. "I'm sorry I went all zombie on you."

"No need to apologize, Agent Sommers. You've been through quite an ordeal. Your body and mind needed some down time. I understand completely."

"I guess," she said. "You're a bit mistaken however."

"How's that?" Ambrosius asked.

"*We've* been through a lot. Not just me."

She took another sip of coffee and felt another smile reach her face. Ambrosius nodded his head and smiled back. She knew it was his way of showing his appreciation. This case had been tough on both of them on many different levels. The fact they had made it through together was something she knew she would never forget.

"So what happens next?" she asked, looking at the case carrying Excalibur.

"I was hoping you would accompany me on a trip to Glastonbury before heading home," Ambrosius said.

"I would be honored," she said, a lump of emotion catching in her throat.

When they finished their meal, Ambrosius paid the bill and she was proud of herself for accepting his generosity without arguing. They exited the hotel and were met by a London Agency car and driver. She turned to look at Ambrosius who merely shrugged his shoulders sheepishly.

"I figured we may as well travel in style," he said.

"Well who am I to argue with British logic?" she said, and they both shared a laugh.

The two hour drive from London to Glastonbury was a pleasant one. They spoke very little, neither one wanting to broach the subject of having to say goodbye. Instead they danced around the issue with small talk. With the passing of every mile, however, the weight of inevitability could not be ignored.

Amy did her best to take in all the local scenery and could not deny the beauty and charm of the English country side. She listened as Ambrosius talked about the rich history of Glastonbury. The eloquence and longing with which he spoke told her more about the near mythical area than the actual facts he relayed. From what she gathered Glastonbury was not just a place ripe in Arthurian legend, it was Ambrosius' home.

As they neared the small town, Amy could see a series of hills of varying sizes. The largest of which she could see had a tall stone tower which Ambrosius called Tor. According to the British agent, this was all that was left of a church dedicated to the Archangel Michael. Tor also reputedly marked the entrance to Avalon.

"Where exactly do you have to take Excalibur?" she asked.

"The Chalice Well," Ambrosius said in a whisper.

She heard a sadness in his voice, and when she looked at his face could see a similar sadness mirrored in his eyes. This had to be a bittersweet moment for him. Yes, it was the completion of a centuries' old journey and a life's quest, but it also meant his own time was coming to an end as well. She had the sudden urge to reach out and grab his hand, which she did not hesitate in doing, and was rewarded by a warm sincere smile at her gesture.

The car slowed to a stop in front of a raised area that reminded her of a park back home. Ambrosius stared out the window for a minute before grabbing the case containing Excalibur. Amy followed. There was a chill in the air, and she could see her breath.

Ambrosius waited for her in front of a set of stone steps. She approached the British agent, and they made the short climb hand in hand.

The Chalice Well was located in the center of a stone-paved circular area. An overwhelming sense of peace and serenity came over her. This was without a doubt the most beautiful and spiritual place she had set foot on; tears sprang to her eyes.

"What is this place?" she asked in a breathy whisper.

"This is the Chalice Well," Ambrosius answered reverently, pointing to a raised rock cairn. "This is where Joseph of Arimathea washed the cup of Christ, or the Holy Grail if you prefer. The waters that flow here run at a constant pace which never changes and always at the exact same temperature. Some even believe the water in this well holds the very essence of life itself."

She watched as Ambrosius set the case down on the ground and unclasped the latches. When he pulled forth Excalibur, the beauty of the sword in this place took her breath away. She knew she was in the presence of true magic.

She and Ambrosius crossed to the well. She helped him remove the intricately designed wrought iron covering. Several feet below in the dark interior, she could see the swiftly moving water.

"Thank you for helping me get to this moment," Ambrosius said.

She did not know how to respond, and so instead reached over and squeezed his hand again. Then, together they stepped to the well and Ambroisus dropped Excalibur in. She waited for the splash the heavy blade would cause, but it never came. She looked over the edge into the depths of the well but the sword was gone.

"Ambrosius...," she said her voice trailing off.

"It's all right, Agent Sommers. My time here is coming to an end. The car will take you back to London."

"Ambroisus...Merlin, I can't just leave you," she said.

"Don't worry, Agent Sommers. Old magicians never really die, we simply fade away. Please go and trust in the knowledge that all is as it should be."

"I'll never forget you," she said.

They embraced tightly. When she finally felt him pull away, tears were in her eyes, but a smile was on her face. They shared a nod of professional understanding before she turned and walked to the awaiting car.

She looked back at Ambrosius standing near the well. The sunlight seemed to intensify, causing a bright glare she had to shield her eyes from. When the light faded back to normal, Ambrosius was gone.

She wiped the tears out of her eyes as she settled in for the first leg of the trip that would eventually take her home.

Amy stood at her living room window, looking out at the park across the street. In the time she had been away, a winter storm had swept through Washington depositing several inches of snow in its wake.

She was used to seeing and hearing children at play in the park, but now it was deserted. Someone had stacked the picnic tables on their ends near the park shelter, giving them the appearance of headstones sticking up to mark the graves of summers past. The somber imagery fit her mood perfectly.

Her plane ride home from London had been uneventful, a nice change of pace from the chaotic whirlwind her life had become. Though many would consider her first case a success since she had achieved all the objectives, it still did not change the fact that Reggie was dead and she was now alone.

Upon arriving back in Washington, she had gone straight to the Agency and given her report to Director Smith. She had turned over the bracelet the Ghost had used so effectively during his reign of terror. Of course the Agency was pleased with her results, but the director had informed her that, due to the extraordinary nature of the case, she'd be remaining on administrative leave for the time being. Not even the director's words of how Reggie would be proud was enough to brighten her mood in the least.

Reggie had been laid to rest at Rock Creek Cemetery while she was in London. She'd missed the service, and would never forgive herself even if she had a pretty good idea Reggie would have understood. She'd stayed at the gravesite until she was so cold she could no longer feel her feet and could not stand the chilled air and the heavy emotional toll of the visit, then turned and drove herself home.

Now, back at her apartment, the place seemed so empty. She had lived by herself for the entirety of her adult life, but never had she felt so completely alone as she did in this moment.

She continued staring out the window, contemplating her future. *Resign from the Agency? Return to the West Coast?*

She was on the verge of making a life altering decision when her phone rang. The sound was so loud in her quiet apartment she actually winced. Not feeling up to having a conversation, she let her answering machine pick up.

The ringing stopped. She heard her own voice giving instructions to leave a message and was starting to slip back into her self-induced depression when a new yet familiar voice emanating from the machine caught her attention.

"Agent Sommers, this is Professor Jack Foshay. I am going to be in Washington D.C. all next week for a seminar. I was hoping, if you are not too busy, that we could get together for a drink or maybe even some dinner. I believe you have my number already. I really hope to hear from you, and I look forward to possibly getting to see you. I hope all is well with you, and I also hope to speak with you soon. Goodbye."

Just hearing the professor's voice made her smile. She felt a twinge of excitement deep down in her stomach. Her decision to leave Washington now forgotten, she picked up the phone and began dialing.

"Maybe it won't be so lonely here after all," she said.

About the Author

Shawn Oetzel was born and raised in Central Illinois where he still lives with his wife, three kids, and their frustratingly lovable pet pooches, Hemingway and Molly. When not working or writing his next project, Shawn can be found attending his children's many extracurricular activities, or tucked away in his favorite corner at home, losing himself in the pages of another good book.

The Agency is Shawn's second novel; his first, *Dying Moon*, was published in 2009 by LBF Books, and is scheduled for re-release by Belfire Press in 2013, shortly after his young adult novel, *The Adventures of Captain Kitchen*.

Shawn has always dreamed of being a superhero, knight, or a writer. He is ecstatic he has made good on at least one of those endeavors.